Pssst, hey!

Wanna see something fun?

Flip quickly through the pages

to watch the pig run!

COWBOY
Charming

DYLANN
CRUSH

sourcebooks
casablanca

Published by Sourcebooks Casablanca, an imprint of Sourcebooks
P.O. Box 4410, Naperville, Illinois 60567-4410
(630) 961-3900
sourcebooks.com

Printed and bound in the United States of America.
OPM 10 9 8 7 6 5 4 3 2 1

To HoneyBee, GlitterBee & BuzzleBee
who make everything worthwhile.

chapter ONE

DIXIE KING HOISTED THE TRAY OF LONGNECKS ONTO HER shoulder and sashayed through a busier-than-usual Thursday-night crowd. Spring finals week must be coming to a close for the frat boys and pseudo-cowgirls who considered the Rambling Rose their personal stomping ground. Sidestepping a clean-shaven guy in a polo shirt with grabby hands, she delivered the bottles one by one to the impatient patrons.

That right there was why her daddy never wanted her to take this job. As the resident preacher in the tiny town of Holiday, Texas, he feared for her moral safety. Funny thing was, he had absolutely nothing to worry about. Beyond the occasional ass-grabber or drunken proposition, Dixie hadn't been involved with a man in years.

She made her way back to the bar to snag another load. As she transferred the bottles and mugs onto the tray, a body slid onto the stool at the end of the bar.

Presley Walker.

She'd have known it was him by the hint of intoxicating cologne that drifted off the man in a hormone-inducing wave. If her daddy wanted to pray for someone, Presley should be at the top of the list. Although it may be too late for him. Dixie figured he might not have any morals still intact.

"Hey, Red." He took one of the bottles off the tray and tilted it in her direction before giving her a wink and lifting it to his lips. Even though something as simple as a smile from Presley Walker could make her thighs quiver for days, she ignored the urge to slip onto a barstool and make believe it was her mouth receiving the attention of his lips and not a mere bottle of beer. Fantasies involving Presley were just that—fantasies. She couldn't afford to get caught up in wishing anything more would ever happen between them. She'd play off his attention like she always did—with a mixture of disdain and sass. The combination had proven effective over the years at deterring any potential advances from Holiday's resident Romeo. Not that he'd follow through anyway. The way her daddy had treated her first long-term boyfriend had pretty much guaranteed no other eligible man in Holiday would be willing to subject himself to Pastor King's scrutiny.

"Red? Gosh, Presley, what wit. I haven't heard that one before." She rolled her eyes then grabbed the extra beer the bartender handed her. Her red hair came from her mother's side of the family, specifically her grandmother. Too bad she hadn't also inherited the free-spirited, devil-may-care attitude her grandma Eugenia was known for.

"Hell, Dixie, I'm just warmin' up." Presley's gaze drifted over her. The man could summon heat from an ice cube. Her skin burned under his attention. She felt like she was standing in the middle of the crowded honky-tonk in nothing but her birthday suit.

She groaned and whirled around, ready to run the gauntlet through the handsy crowd again. She'd rather face down a room full of cocky frat boys than get stuck face-to-face with Presley Walker. Her reluctance had absolutely nothing to do with the way his blue eyes sparkled or how his mouth tipped up in a crooked grin, making heat pool in places she didn't want to acknowledge. And everything to do with the string of X-rated dreams she'd been having over the past several months—starring who else but Holiday, Texas's most notorious bachelor.

Maybe she should do what her daddy had been encouraging her to do ever since she took this job—quit. But the tips were good, and working the late afternoon and evening shifts meant she could help out more at home. Besides, she needed the money if she wanted a place of her own someday. She had her heart set on opening a little artist studio where she could make and sell the handcrafted jewelry she'd been working on for the past few years. There were several other local artists in the area she'd love to feature as well. Another year or two and she'd be able to turn her dream into a reality.

Too bad that meant having regular run-ins with the blue-eyed demon. She shook her mass of red curls, trying to dislodge the memories of last night's dream from her head. It wasn't like Presley would stop coming around. Not only was he the local sales rep for the liquor supplier, but his sister, Charlie, and brother-in-law, Beck, owned the Rambling Rose.

Which meant she needed to keep him out of her head…and definitely out of her dreams.

As she gathered another load of empties, her phone buzzed in her back pocket. She balanced the tray with one hand and glanced at the screen. Charlie.

"Hey, Dixie, I need a favor." Charlie didn't usually call during a shift. She was supposed to be taking a rare night off.

"Sure, what's up?" Dixie liked working for Charlie. She was a fair boss and a good friend, and despite her unfortunate relations, Dixie would do anything for her, no questions asked.

"It's Beck. He was on his way to New York for that craft beer award ceremony and got sideswiped." Charlie's voice trembled.

"Oh my gosh, is he okay?" Dixie set the tray on the bar and made her way to the office where she'd have a better chance of being able to hold a conversation.

"Yeah. Just shook up a bit." Charlie regained her composure. "But the trailer's wrecked, and Baby Back got loose."

"Oh no. Did he catch her?" The Rambling Rose had a long history of pig mascots, and up until a year or so ago Baby Back had filled that role. Now she had a much more high-profile job as the poster pig for Beck's pride and joy—a bacon-infused maple syrup ale.

"Finally. But not before she caused a bit of a pileup on the highway. I've got to get out there and help him drive back. He sprained his wrist and won't be able to manage the pig and the trailer on his own. I booked a flight for first thing in the morning. My dad's going with me to help with the baby." Charlie sighed. "I hate to ask this of you, but I need you to handle things while I'm gone."

"Oh, sure. I'd be happy to help out." It was the least she could do. "But can't your dad just go on his own? Or take one of your brothers with him?"

"They've got too much going on. And family comes

first. I've got to get out there and make sure he's okay. I know it's silly, but—"

"I know." Everyone in town knew about how Charlie's high school sweetheart passed away in an accident while he was serving overseas. "But Beck will be fine."

"I know. I just need to see him." Charlie cleared her throat. "And that means I need you to run the Rose while I'm gone, not just pitch in."

Dixie's stomach twisted into a knotted mess. "What about Shep? Or Angelo? Or even Jinx?" Any one of the other regular employees seemed better equipped to take on the responsibility of running the oldest honky-tonk in Texas.

"I'm asking *you*. Shep knows the bar. Angelo knows the kitchen. Jinx won't be too much help. Sure, she'll try, but she's six months pregnant. You know more about everything than anyone. They'll all be around pitch in."

Dixie took in a deep breath and nodded to herself. Charlie needed her. And if she was an expert at anything, it was pitching in when someone she cared about called on her for help. "I'll do my best."

Charlie's relief flowed through the phone. "Thanks. I knew I could count on you."

"How long do you think y'all might be gone?" Dixie worked better with detailed schedules, established time frames, and clear expectations.

"I'm not sure. We've got to attend the award ceremony on Sunday night, and Beck wants to stop to see his dad as long as we're up that way. We'll be back by next weekend for sure though."

Next weekend? Dixie bit back the excuses trying to fight their way free. "We'll be fine. Don't you worry about a thing. I'll take care of everything here."

"Thanks so much. I've got to start packing, but I'll send you an email once I get my thoughts pulled together. You're going to be great. With the Chili Festival starting this weekend, and—"

"The Chili Festival!" Dixie slapped a hand to her forehead. She'd all but forgotten about the first annual Rambling Rose Chili Festival. They'd invited bands and vendors from around the country to perform and set up booths for the next two weekends. The festival would culminate in what they'd been billing as one of the largest chili cook-offs in Texas.

"You can do this, Dixie. I have faith in you."

Before Dixie could arrange the jumbled mess in her brain into a rational argument, a knock sounded on the office door.

"Coming." Dixie made her way to the door as Charlie continued to rattle off items to put on the to-do list. Thousands of people would be attending the festival. How could Dixie keep a handle on things at the Rose and still help as much as she needed to at home? She bit her lip and shook her head. Charlie couldn't expect her to do it all on her own. It just wasn't possible. She'd have to find someone else. Someone with more experience.

Charlie's voice cut through her thoughts. "I know what you're thinking. It's too much for one person to handle."

Dixie nodded. "Right. I'm glad you understand, I can't—"

"That's why I arranged for some help."

The door opened. A head of unruly brown hair poked

through, followed by those sinful blue eyes. "Hey, Red. Did you hear the good news? Looks like we're going to be partners."

—⚘—

Presley wanted to laugh out loud at the horror reflected on Dixie's face. Instead, he slipped into the room and closed the door behind him.

"What do you say? I think we'll make a great team." She continued to gape at him, her mouth hanging open like an endless black hole. "Okay then. I can see you need some time to get used to the idea." He crossed the room to take a seat and kick his boots up on the edge of the desk.

"You sure about this?" Dixie whispered into the phone. "Presley's not exactly the most..." Her gaze cut to him. He gave her a wink and blew her a kiss. Her cheeks flamed, coming close to matching the color of her garnet waves.

"Why don't you put her on speaker?" Presley suggested. Oh, this was going to be about as much fun as trying to piss into the wind. Presley wasn't exactly in favor of working side by side with Dixie King. The poor woman didn't know how to have fun. He'd given up flirting with her a couple of years ago. She either lacked the ability to handle some good-natured quips or her daddy had preached all the sass right out of her. But Charlie needed help, and one thing the Walker family always did was take care of their own.

Dixie slumped into the chair next to him then scooted it a few feet away, scraping the legs on the ancient wooden planks. He let his boots drop from the edge of the desk to the floor. "I'm not gonna bite you or anything, Red. Unless you ask me to, that is."

She didn't glance over at him, just set the phone on the edge of the desk and pressed the speaker button.

"Thanks so much, to both of you, for saying you'll help while I'm gone." Charlie's voice floated from the phone. Presley kept his gaze trained on Dixie. "I know putting the two of you together might not seem like a natural fit."

Presley snorted. Like champagne and beer. Wait, did Dixie even drink? More like seltzer water and a perfectly aged whiskey. With him being the whiskey, of course.

Dixie's jaw set, and she finally cast a glance his way. "I'm sure we'll be able to handle things in a professional manner."

"Dixie, you're so good with managing all the details. I know you'll be able to keep things organized and running smoothly while I'm gone. And, Pres, you're fantastic at managing people. I want you to make sure all the vendors and musicians are settled and comfortable."

He crossed his arms over his chest. "Making people comfortable is one of my special talents."

"Not *that* comfortable. I don't need any scandals coming out of our first chili cook-off. That's why I've got you working together. Dixie's going to keep you in line."

The only line Presley ever adhered to was the line for the bar. And that was only if he couldn't figure out a way to sweet-talk his way to the front. "I don't need a babysitter, Sis."

"No, but you do need someone to make sure you stay on task and don't get—*ahem*—distracted."

Dixie's mouth quirked up in a hint of a smile.

"Hey, before you go getting all *holier than thou*, she

must not trust you to work on your own either." Presley nodded, more to himself than anyone else.

Dixie shook her head. Charlie cleared her throat. "Presley, for once in your life will you grow up and act your age, not the size of your ideal Saturday night hookup's waist?"

That low blow made him hang his head. He wanted to deny the implication, but based on his history, his sister was right. Chasing skirts and having a good time had been his MO for so long, he'd never given her any reason to think deep down he might want something more.

"I'll do my part. Whatever you need. You focus on Beck and making sure my nephew is okay. Red and I will keep the place going while you're gone. Right?" He turned the full force of his gaze on Dixie.

She startled, whether from his serious tone or being put in the hot seat, he couldn't tell. Didn't matter. Working side by side with her might be about as much fun as getting a double root canal with no Novocain, but he'd do what he needed to do. For Charlie. For Beck. For the Rambling Rose.

"Stop calling me that," Dixie muttered into her chest. Then she turned her green eyes on him. Eyes the color of the tall grass that covered the Texas hillsides in spring. "Yes, we'll make it work."

"Good," Charlie said. "I'll get that email together tonight and send it to both of you. Sound good?"

Presley narrowed his eyes. "Sounds good to me."

Dixie stared right back. She might have more spunk than he'd given her credit for. "I'll be on the lookout for it."

"Alright," Charlie said. "Thanks again. I'll be in touch."

Dixie reached for the phone. "Take care and safe travels."

"Bye." Charlie ended the call.

Before he could figure out what to say, Dixie stood and moved toward the door, still holding his gaze. "Want to meet here in the morning to talk about how we can divvy up the tasks?"

"Sure. What time do you want me?"

"Registration opens at noon. How about we meet at eight?"

He checked his watch. If he left now, he might manage six hours of sleep, fairly shy of his usual seven to eight hours. "You really think we need that much time?"

She narrowed her gaze. "I can always see if Shep or Angelo can help out if you're not up for it."

He lifted a brow. So that's how it was going to go down? She didn't think he could pull his own weight. "Oh, Red. I'm always up for whatever you've got going."

She scoffed. "Charlie's right. You don't take anything seriously, do you?"

He'd show her. He'd show all of them that he could be more than a pretty face. "Eight's perfect."

Dixie clenched her jaw and spun toward the door. He waited until it clicked closed behind her before he took his seat again and dialed his sister.

Charlie answered after one ring. "Maybe this is a bad idea. You and Dixie will never be able to pull this off."

"I can do it, Char."

Her voice shifted, suddenly sounding much older than her thirty-two years. "Are you sure? Don't lie to me. Not about this. It's too important."

Presley scuffed his boots on the floor in front of him. "I swear I'll do my best while you're gone. Is it good timing? No. Sierra and I had plans to go camping out at Big Bend. She'll be pissed, but I'll figure out a way to make it up to her."

"Sierra? I thought you were dating April."

He shrugged. "April started talking about moving in together. You know as well as she does that's not my scene."

"Whatever. Just promise me you won't give Dixie a hard time. She's tougher than she looks, but she's not used to putting up with the likes of you."

The likes of him...what would his sister say if he told her the real reason he'd broken up with April wasn't that she wanted to get serious but that she wasn't the one he wanted to get serious with? Something inside of him had shifted over the past couple of years. When Charlie found her happily ever after with Beck, he'd dismissed it as something his baby sister would do. But last year when Jinx made an honest man out of Cash, Presley had got to thinking. Maybe there was more to life than one-night stands, partying, and raising hell with the boys.

Two of his buddies had taken the leap and gotten hitched last fall. His pack was dwindling, and he didn't want to be the only one left—trying to whoop it up when he was old and gray—and alone.

No, he wasn't ready to talk to anyone about the unsettled feeling that had taken up residence inside his chest. Not until he figured out what it meant and what, if anything, he was willing to do about it. For the time being, he'd do what he always did—be the fun-loving bad boy his family and the whole town of Holiday had dubbed him.

"Yeah, I'll walk on eggshells around Miss Dixie King. Scout's honor." Even though she couldn't see him through the phone, he held his hand over his heart.

"Didn't you quit Boy Scouts when they caught you kissing Missy Townsend behind the shed at the pinewood derby?"

"Semantics, Sis. I still have the heart of a Scout. Why, just last week I helped Maybelle Mitchell cross the street."

"You're incorrigible. I've got to go. I'm never going to get all of this stuff packed up if I don't get a move on."

Presley grinned as he got to his feet. "Just take care of Beck and baby Sully. I promise I'll try not to piss Dixie off." And he would too. But it wouldn't be his fault if Red got herself all worked up on her own.

chapter
TWO

DIXIE FINISHED OUT HER SHIFT DESPITE THE TIGHTNESS IN her chest. She felt like someone held her heart and lungs in their hands, squeezing to the point she could barely breathe. How could she work side by side with Presley Walker? The man couldn't be serious if he tried. And if Dixie was anything, it was serious. Serious about her job. Serious about taking care of things at home. Serious to the point of sucking every last drop of fun out of her own life. Nowadays the only fun she had was when she got to spend time with her sister's ten-month-old daughter, although most of the time she was too tired to totally enjoy it.

She closed out her tickets, helped Shep clean up behind the bar, and waved to Angelo as she passed by the kitchen. With only about six hours before she had to be back to meet with Presley, she was in a hurry to get home and get to bed.

All hopes for a decent night's sleep vanished as she pulled into the driveway of the two-story bungalow she shared with her grandmother. Every light blazed brightly. Why wasn't Gram sound asleep by now? It was almost two o'clock in the morning. She still wasn't used to the idea of living with Gram. But her parents had pretty much guilted her into giving up her cute apartment to keep an eye on her aging grandmother.

She opened the front door and bumped into Gram's best friend and next-door neighbor, Maybelle.

"Well, hi there, Dixie." Maybelle tugged a hand-knit shawl over her shoulders. "It must be late if you're home already."

"It's almost two, Mrs. Mitchell. What are you and Gram doing up at this hour?" Dixie peered past Maybelle into the kitchen. Where was Gram?

"Just having a girls' night." Gram came down the hallway with a huge roll of bills in hand. "Thursday night is girls' night, remember?"

"Right." Dixie had only been living with Gram for a month and had already lost track of the older woman's busy social schedule. If she wasn't off playing bridge, she was taking on one of her friends in pickleball or volunteering at the senior center. On more than one occasion, Dixie had felt like a dowdy wallflower compared with her extroverted grandmother.

"Here's your cut." Gram handed over a wad of cash to Maybelle. "We might have to try out that new place in San Marcos next week."

"Where did you get all that money?" Dixie shoved her hands on her hips.

Maybelle tucked the cash into her bra. "Your grandmother is quite the pool shark."

"No." Dixie's gaze bounced back and forth between the two older women. "Please tell me you weren't running the tables over at the pool hall."

"Oh, we got kicked out of there last month." Maybelle laughed.

Gram twirled Maybelle around to face the door. "Have a good night now. We'll talk tomorrow."

Maybelle twittered. "See you then, Genie. Goodnight, Dixie."

"Goodnight, Mrs. Mitchell." Dixie stepped out on the porch to make sure Maybelle didn't trip and fall while crossing the lawn. The older woman lifted a hand toward her before she disappeared into the house next door. Dixie took in a deep breath and tried to let the stillness of the night soothe her rattled nerves before she reentered the house.

Gram stood in the kitchen, rinsing out a couple of champagne glasses. "Maybelle get home okay?"

"Yes." Dixie leaned a hip against the counter. "You know Mom and Dad wouldn't like you running all over town, swindling money out of people at bars."

"Oh, let us little old ladies have our fun, hon. It's bad enough they've got you moved in with me."

"Gram, it's for your own good."

Gram whirled around. "Says who? I've been doing just fine on my own. Buried two husbands, raised three kids as a widow, held down a job, supported myself all my life. And now for some reason your mama thinks I need my granddaughter to keep an eye on me."

Dixie shrank under her grandmother's fiery gaze. "It's not just some reason. They're worried about you. And worried about the effect your hijinks are having on their business relationships too. Mrs. Martinez won't return Mom's calls, and Dad said Martinez Industries hasn't confirmed its commitment to the church's capital campaign."

"Well, I'm sorry about that. But they've got poor Laverne practically held hostage in that old folks' home. I can't stand it."

"You can go visit her anytime."

"Supervised visits. She's one of my best friends, and they won't even let me sit with her anymore without a chaperone."

"Well, maybe you shouldn't have taken her out to a strip club for her birthday lunch." Dixie's frustration caught up to her. "Maybe then her daughter and son-in-law wouldn't think you're such a bad influence on her."

Gram lifted her hands in the air. "I told your mama, and I'm telling you. I didn't know it was a strip club. They advertised free banana hammocks. I've always wanted one of those stands to keep my bananas fresh. How was I to know that's not what they meant?"

"I think you should have figured it out when you pulled up in front. Mom said you made it all the way through two platters of fajitas before they tracked you down."

"The fajitas were pretty good. Especially for $3.99."

Dixie groaned. Why had she let her mom convince her to move in? She leaned over and gave Gram a hug. "I've got an early day tomorrow and need to get to bed. Promise me no more corrupting the senior citizens of Holiday. Please?"

Gram let out a long breath. "I can't make promises I don't intend to keep, Dixie Mae."

Dixie pulled back and searched Gram's deep-green gaze. "At least until Dad's done with the capital campaign? It's important to him."

"I know, I know." Gram shrugged out of the hug. "I'll try to be on my best behavior."

"Thanks. I love you."

"I love you too. Now get on to bed. I'm headed that way myself."

Dixie trudged up the steps to her bedroom on the second floor. Keeping Gram in line was turning into more work than she'd anticipated. She needed to talk to her parents about exploring alternate solutions. They were worried about the series of ministrokes Gram had suffered over the winter, but as far as Dixie could tell, her grandmother hadn't endured any long-term effects. Not unless she counted Gram's new devil-may-care attitude. But right now Gram wasn't her focus. Ensuring the Rambling Rose remained in one piece until Charlie returned would require all of her attention over the next week, especially if she had to put up with working side by side with Presley. She'd have to trust Gram to keep her word and stay out of trouble.

Presley tossed the covers back and rubbed a hand across his eyes. Hell, what time was it? The light slanted across his bedroom floor from a slit in the curtains. Curtains his mother had made him when he moved into his own place on the family ranch about ten years ago. A quick look at the clock on his nightstand confirmed what he feared. He'd overslept. What a great way to start his partnership off with Red. As if she didn't have enough reasons to give him shit.

He yanked on the jeans he'd left on the floor the night before and shoved his feet into his boots. As he grabbed a T-shirt from the top of a pile at the foot of the bed, he sniffed his armpit. No time for a shower—he'd just slather on some extra deodorant and call it good for now.

Twenty minutes later he tried to sneak through the back door of the Rose.

"You're late." His sister-in-law Jinx stood behind

the bar, her belly looking like a basketball under her Rambling Rose shirt.

"How pissed is she?" He ambled toward the bar where Jinx filled an oversized mug with coffee.

Jinx laughed. "Pretty damn pissed." Before she slid the mug across the bar to him, she lifted it to her nose and inhaled. "God, I miss my morning pot of coffee."

"I'll drink an extra cup for you." Presley grabbed it by the handle and tipped the brim of his hat toward his sister-in-law. "Thanks."

"Good luck." She turned her attention to wiping down the bar.

Armed with caffeine, Presley trod lightly toward Charlie's office door. Maybe he could listen in to try to find out how much trouble he was in before he knocked.

The sound of a baby's cries drifted through the cracked office door. He moved closer, trying to sneak a peek. Dixie sat behind the desk, bouncing a baby on her knee. A very unhappy baby from the way things looked from the hallway. Shep sat across the desk, clearly uncomfortable being roped into a planning meeting.

"She's not usually so fussy this time of day," Dixie said. She held something out to the kid, who pushed her hand away. Cheerios scattered across the floor, and one landed right in front of the door.

Shep leaned over and waved a stuffed pink pig in front of the screaming kid. "You want to play with the piggy?"

Presley reached down to pick up the stray Cheerio, and the door squeaked open an inch.

"It's about time you got in." Shep's feet hit the ground, and he stood. "I take it the two of you can figure things out from here."

"Good morning." Presley took a seat next to the one Shep had vacated. The screaming baby paused, her face as red as the bandana hanging on the wall behind the desk. "I didn't know you had a kid, Red." Presley leaned over the desk to chuck the baby girl under the chin. She reached for his finger and held on tight.

"She's my niece. I watch her in the mornings." Dixie looked about to burst into tears. Her eyes were bloodshot like she hadn't slept a wink. Or like she'd been on the wrong side of a big bottle of some kind of cheap gin.

"Let me take a turn with her, huh?" Presley scooped the baby off Dixie's lap and held her against his chest. "What's her name?"

"Bea." Dixie brushed the cereal crumbs off her shirt and held a burp cloth out to Presley. "Want this?"

"Nah. We're fine without it. Aren't we, Bea?" The baby giggled while he slowly spun her around the office.

"Crazy, isn't it?" Shep gestured toward the baby as he edged toward the door. "They all go for him. Doesn't matter, young, old, anywhere in between. If y'all don't need me anymore, I'm just going to leave you to it."

Presley danced little Bea over to where Dixie sat behind the desk. "Don't you worry about a thing. We've got this."

Shep gave a final wave and disappeared through the door.

"Looks like it's just you and me." He turned to face Dixie. "Oh, and this little princess."

Dixie had paused flipping through the pages of her notebook. A hint of an actual smile graced her lips. She leaned back in the chair and crossed her arms under her chest. Nodding toward her niece, who had settled her head against his chest, her smile deepened. "Well, I'll be. I've never seen anyone handle her like that before."

"What can I say?" He lifted his shoulders in a slight shrug, careful not to disrupt the baby. "I've been told I have a knack for handling females. You let me know if you want to give it a go sometime."

A rash of red crept up Dixie's neck and spread over her cheeks. She scooted closer to the desk and skimmed the notebook. "Where do you want to start? The first weekend of the chili cook-off starts tomorrow. Competitors will start checking in as early as twelve o'clock this afternoon. I have forty-two teams signed up, but we'll take walk-ins as well. You're prepared to handle the bands, right?"

When he didn't respond right away, she glanced up. "Presley?"

"Yup?" He couldn't get over the sheer number of pages she'd filled with her loopy handwriting.

"The bands. You'll handle all of the musicians, right? I've got a spreadsheet right here that lists who's playing when and what kind of equipment they'll need. We've got the stage set up out back already. Their trailers and buses need to be parked in the roped-off area. Cash is running security to make sure the fans stay away." She paused and held a color-coded spreadsheet out to him.

He took it and scanned the text. Baby Bea startled and made a grab for the paper, crinkling up a corner of it in her tiny fist. "Careful there, girl. We don't want you to get a paper cut."

"You want me to take her?" Dixie stood, reaching for the baby.

"Nah, I got her. Did you make up this list?"

"Yes. Charlie gave me all the details, and I color-coded everything so you could keep them all straight."

Presley clucked his tongue. "Wow, your confidence in my ability is positively humbling."

"I'm just trying to help."

The last thing he needed was someone breathing down his neck, telling him what he needed to do. He'd helped Charlie with booking and managing the bands before. He could schmooze narcissistic musicians in his sleep. "Why don't you stick to the chili and I'll stick to the tunes, Red?"

Her hands flew to her hips. "Would you please stop calling me that? My name is Dixie. Dix-ie. It's only two syllables. I know that's one more than Red. Think you can remember that?"

"I can remember all kinds of things, Dixie Mae."

Her face flushed the color of Angelo's special fire-roasted salsa roja. She had to know he was making reference to their little run-in that had happened several years back. Although a few years younger than his sister, Dixie had been in the same 4-H club as Charlie. The girls had had an end-of-year slumber party at his folks' house and had been playing some sort of truth or dare game. He'd walked in, just wanting to stir things up with Charlie and her friends, and heard Dixie Mae King admit her most secret crush was none other than himself.

Her hands clenched into fists before she could pull herself together.

"It's okay, I was getting sick of calling you Red anyway." He passed the baby back to her then folded the spreadsheet and shoved it into his back pocket. "I'm gonna go check on the setup out back then run home and take a quick shower. Unless you want to talk some more?"

She sputtered, baby Bea started to wail again, and Presley made his way to the door.

"I'll see you later, Fireball." He ducked through the doorway before she could catch up. Fireball—where did that come from? Had a nice ring to it. It was one of his favorite libations, but it didn't quite suit her. She was too serious, too passive all the time.

Her footsteps clomped across the floor, and he heard the door handle bang against the wall. "It's Dixie, darn it, you self-serving donkey butt."

Presley let out a belly laugh as he turned the corner. Maybe Fireball wasn't too off base after all.

chapter
THREE

A FEW HOURS LATER DIXIE HAD TURNED HER NIECE OVER TO her sister, Liza, changed into her Rambling Rose T-shirt, and settled underneath a striped pop-up canopy at the competitor's check-in table. She'd lost count of the number of people who had approached her with questions or needing help figuring out where to go. Charlie had been so excited about making their first chili cook-off the biggest and best in Texas that she might have been a little ambitious when she planned all of the events that would happen over the next two consecutive weekends.

Thankfully Dixie had it all outlined on her spreadsheets. Tomorrow would be the white chicken chili contest. Sunday was for exotic meats. Based on a quick internet search, Dixie expected she might see ingredients such as rattlesnake, alligator, and maybe even grasshoppers. Thank goodness she wasn't eligible to judge. Next weekend they'd tackle the final categories: vegetarian and competitor's choice.

Some of their competitors had signed up to take part in all four competitions. That meant they'd have a couple of hundred extra people in Holiday for an entire week, not to mention the vendors and attendees who would be selling their wares and sampling chili. How would she keep it all straight?

She glanced through the schedule of events one more time while she waited for the next competitor to check in. An hour-long set by the regional favorites Boss Hawg and the Scallywags would kick off the festivities later on tonight. The first official event was scheduled for eleven o'clock tomorrow morning—a jalapeño-eating contest—followed by a full day of watching competitors work their best recipes into an attempt at winning that first-place blue ribbon.

The sound of someone clearing his throat made her look up. Her gaze lifted, landing straight on the stranger's crotch. A well-endowed crotch, she realized. Heat hit her cheeks like she'd just stuffed them full of ghost peppers.

He cleared his throat again, and she raised her head, her eyes moving past a snug, pec-hugging T-shirt, over a stranger's clean-shaven, clefted chin, pausing to appreciate the way his lips curved over brilliant white teeth, and finally coming to rest on a pair of ocean-blue eyes. Blue like the water just off the coast of South Padre Island. She wouldn't mind deep diving into those baby blues. They crinkled at the corners, and Dixie's cheeks heated another thousand degrees.

"Dixie? I must be hallucinating." He held out a hand.

Her heart catapulted into her shoes. He knew her name. This gorgeous stranger knew who she was, and she had absolutely no idea how. "I'm sorry, do we know each other?"

"Yeah, we went to middle school together before my family moved out west. Chandler Bristol. Remember me?" He thrust his hand at her again.

Chandler Bristol. The boy who sat behind her in English and sent her a note asking her if she'd be his girlfriend during the sixth-grade spelling bee. She'd read it then bombed out on an easy word in the first round, earning her the yearlong nickname of "Choker."

"I remember you." She finally took his hand. The last time she'd seen him he'd been tall and lanky, a much more awkward boy version of the man who stood before her now.

"I can't believe it's you. So you're still in Holiday?" he asked, clutching her hand in his.

She nodded. "Yep, I'm still here. Not much has changed. But you... Tell me what brought you back."

He gave her hand a final squeeze then glanced down at her lists. "The chili cook-off. Is this where I register?"

Register... "Oh, yes. I can help you with that." Dixie snagged a pen, trying to keep her hands busy so she didn't find herself reaching for him again. "Are you a competitor?"

"I haven't decided yet. Figured I'd stick around for the weekend and see how it goes. I'm an amateur."

"So you're just going to hang around this week?"

"Yeah." He shifted his weight from one foot to the other. "Maybe you could show me around a bit, point out what's changed. If you have time, I mean."

Time was one commodity she'd never have enough of. But a break from the predictable dullness of her social situation like Chandler Bristol might never land in front of her again, so she found herself agreeing. "I'd love to."

"Great." He pulled his phone out of his back pocket. "What's your number?"

Dixie rattled it off and felt her phone vibrate in her pocket. She reached for it to see she had a text. "Area code 949... Where are you living now?"

"Malibu."

"California?" Duh, what other Malibu could he be talking about? Especially when he looked like he surfed 365 days a year. "You're a long way from home then."

He shrugged. "I've always had a thing for Texas. It just about killed me when we had to move away."

"I've never lived anywhere else."

"It suits you." He graced her with another one of his pearly smiles.

Dixie grinned back.

A palm landed on the table next to her, breaking the magical moment. "Hey, Fireball, I need a hand with one of the bands. They're supposed to have a place to board their giant hog. You know anything about that?"

Figured Presley would have an impeccable sense of awful timing. "Just a minute. Let me finish up, and I'll be right with you."

Chandler tilted his phone her way. "I've got your digits. I'm going to go get settled, and I'll track you down later for that tour, okay?"

"Okay," Dixie sighed. She waited until Chandler walked away before turning her attention to Presley.

"You done making goo-goo eyes at that guy and ready to give me a hand?" He hooked his thumb through his belt loop and straightened, towering over her and casting shade onto the table with the brim of his straw Stetson.

"Hold your horses." Dixie shuffled through her paperwork.

"It's not horses I have a problem with, it's a giant ball-busting hog. They said they talked to Charlie about a place to pen their mascot. Name's Ham Bone, and he's gotta be the biggest, most ornery boar I've ever heard of."

Dixie made it to the end of her pile. "I don't see

anything about a requirement for penning a pig. And takes one big ornery boar to recognize another, doesn't it?" Going on the offensive with Presley was her best line of defense. Otherwise she'd sit around and daydream about that magic touch of his all day. He'd cleaned up nice, and she couldn't help but wonder how it might feel to nestle her cheek against his pecs like her niece had been able to do earlier.

"In order to maintain the state of our present partnership, I'm going to pretend you didn't just say that. Now, can you get real and help me out with this?"

Rolling her eyes, Dixie offered what she assumed was an acceptable suggestion. "Can't you put it in the pen next to Pork Chop?"

"Hell no. That's all the Rose needs…another litter of piglets. By the way, who was that pretty boy you were talking to?" Presley glanced in the direction Chandler had disappeared.

"Chandler Bristol. He used to live here back in middle school."

"Bristol, huh? Is he related to ol' Leroy Bristol?"

"I don't know. He came all the way from California to check out the chili cook-off. Charlie ought to be excited word has traveled all the way out West." This being the first year they'd tried a cook-off event, they hadn't been sure what to expect.

"Hmpf." Presley shook his head. "Doesn't look like someone who travels the chili cook-off circuit."

"And you're familiar with the chili cook-off circuit?" Dixie shot him a scowl. Leave it to Presley to ruin the one good moment she'd had today.

"Probably more familiar than you. Seeing as how

I don't think you ever go anywhere except work and church."

Dixie laughed so hard she snorted. "Oh, please. How would you know whether I attend church? Like your boots have ever crossed the threshold of a house of God."

Presley set his jaw. "You stick to smoothing the feathers of the pretty boys, and I'll do the hard work."

"Fine. Good luck then." Dixie stood to stretch her back as Presley stomped off toward the stage.

As she took her seat in her chair again, her phone pinged.

A text from the 949 number. Think you'll have time to take a quick break for dinner tonight?

She was tempted. Oh, how she was tempted. Everyone needed to eat, right? Liza would be home with Bea tonight, and Gram had plans at the senior center. The check-in table closed at seven. She ought to be able to spare an hour or so. Besides, hanging out with Chandler might take her mind off how closely she was going to have to work with Presley over the next week. Years ago, she might have welcomed the opportunity to work side by side with Presley Walker in the hopes he might finally see her as something more than a dorky teen who'd crushed on him hard. But these days she knew better. He'd never be anything but a playboy and a cad. She'd do best to steer clear of him no matter how much her traitorous teenage dreams wanted to work against her.

With a million reasons to decline running through her mind, Dixie Mae King did something she hadn't done in a very long time.

She accepted a man's dinner invitation.

Presley replayed the interaction with Dixie time and time again. Why should he care if she was making googly eyes at some blast from her past who'd be in and out of their neck of the woods within the space of a week? Didn't make sense. He'd always enjoyed giving Dixie a hard time even though he knew she'd always be off-limits. He drew the line at corrupting the preacher's daughter. But the way her cheeks flushed when he paid her a little extra attention had always given him a bit of a thrill. Looked like she might have moved on. That fact shouldn't bother him, and he didn't have time to think about it anyway. There was a boar waiting on him. A boar with big balls and an even bigger attitude.

He rounded the stage and found the spot where Boss Hawg and the Scallywags had circled their campers, creating a miniature compound within a sea of tents and trailers housing the other musicians and cook-off competitors. He didn't know which camper Boss Hawg had claimed as his own, so he knocked on the screen-door frame of the first trailer he came to. A tall brunette came to the door. Her hair hung in a curtain of chestnut around a heart-shaped face with big brown eyes. He recognized her as the band's fiddle player. The CD cover he had in his truck didn't do her justice.

"Can I help you?" she asked.

Presley cleared his throat. "I'm here to help with your hog."

"Excuse me?" A smile morphed her features from good-looking to dazzling.

"Yes, ma'am. I believe his name's Ham Bone."

Presley swept his hat off his head and held it at his waist. "Presley Walker, at your service."

"Well, come on in, Presley Walker." She pushed the screen door open, and he squeezed past her onto the steps leading into the trailer.

The scent of vanilla and musk tickled his nose. He stepped up into the main seating area of the trailer where other members of the band sat around, their instruments in their laps.

"Hey, y'all, Presley here has come to help us with that hog you insisted on bringing along." She sat down on the lap of a grizzly-bearded man who Presley recognized as Boss Hawg himself.

"Thank God." Boss Hawg thrust his hand at Presley. "Nice to meet you, Presley. I'm Boss Hawg, and this is the gang. Skeeter over there thought it would be a great idea to gift my lady friend a potbellied pig for the holidays so we could have a real-life mascot." Boss pointed at a lanky man who'd folded himself into the built-in bench.

"Aw, Boss, it seemed like a good idea at the time." Skeeter shrugged, his bony shoulders pointing skyward before he sank back into the bench seat.

"Little did we know that darling potbellied pig was actually a full-sized hog." The fiddle player patted Boss on the chest. "Now we need to find a place to put him while we're holed up here for the next week or so."

Presley shifted his weight from foot to foot. "The pigpen we've got here at the Rose is taken. Pork Chop, our resident mascot, gets first dibs on that. But my folks have a place not far from here, and I'm pretty sure we can make Ham Bone very happy there for the duration of your visit."

"Or longer," the fiddle player sighed.

"Leoni here isn't too fond of her Christmas gift," Boss said with a chuckle.

"He's mean." She grinned at Presley then climbed out of Boss's lap. "I'll show you where we have him if you want to take him over now."

"Sure." Presley figured he'd have a chance to warn his oldest brother, Waylon, who'd taken over managing their folks' ranch, but maybe it would be better if he just showed up with the hog. Surely they'd find a place for him, especially if they knew they'd be helping Charlie.

"Okay, let's go." Leoni led him down the steps and back out into the late-afternoon heat.

"So Ham Bone is only six months old?" Presley asked.

"Who knows?" Leoni waited for him to catch up with her before she took another step. "Skeeter swears he picked him out from a litter, but I think he won him at a poker game when we were performing in Texarkana."

They'd reached a dented horse trailer attached to a souped-up diesel dually. Grunts, snorts, and thumps came from deep inside. Sounded like they were housing a sleeping dragon.

"I've gotta tell you, I sure do appreciate your skills with the strings." Presley snagged his chance to share his admiration.

"Aw, thanks. I started off thinking I wanted to be a concert violinist."

"Really?" As far as Presley knew, there wasn't too much crossover between musicians who saw the violin as an instrument for playing classical music and

those who did their best to force a wild country tune from
the strings.

"Yep." She stepped onto the back bumper of the trailer.
"Then I met Boss and the others and figured I'd have a hell
of a lot more fun fiddling."

Now or never, Presley told himself. If he ever wanted
to explore the side of himself he'd been hiding from the
world, this was as good a chance as any. "I've done a little
bit of fiddling myself."

"Oh yeah? What do you play?"

He let out a nervous laugh. "I'm playing on one of my
granddad's old fiddles, but I'm working on making one
myself. It's probably not any good, but he used to be pretty
well known for his craftsmanship, and I've always wanted
to try my hand at carrying on the family tradition."

"Seriously? I think it's awesome you're making your
own. I'd love to check it out sometime."

Even though he'd been angling for an opportunity to
turn the conversation to fiddling and maybe get some
feedback from one of the best, Presley was still blown
away by the offer. "That would be great. I'd love to hear
what you think. Seems to play pretty smooth to me, but
then again, I haven't had any formal kind of training. Just
sitting on my granddad's lap when I was a kid and then
messing around on my own as I got older."

"It would be my pleasure. But first, what do you say we
get this pig out of here before he busts out on his own?"
She peered over the top edge of the trailer. "Hey, Ham
Bone, you want to stretch your legs a bit, bad boy?"

Something slammed against the door of the trailer,
sending Leoni sailing from the bumper and onto her ass.
Presley offered her a hand and helped her to her feet. She

brushed off her butt before she landed a kick to the trailer door.

"You sure that's just one pig in there?" Presley asked.

"Yep, one badass, bone-headed boar." She handed him a coiled piece of rope with a clip on the end. "Good luck."

Presley took the rope and stepped onto the bumper. The inside of the trailer was dark and stank like pig shit and wet hay. As his eyes adjusted to the darkness, he could just make out the outline of a giant beast hunkered down in the far corner of the trailer. He glanced back at Leoni, who offered an encouraging smile. This was his chance. If he couldn't handle their pig problem, she'd have no reason to give him the feedback she'd promised. And unless he wanted to spend the rest of his life doling out samples of vodka and trying to convince tightwad bar and liquor store owners to spend an extra dollar on a local libation, he'd better figure out a way to take the ornery boar off their hands. At least while they were playing in Holiday.

With a grin at Leoni and a swagger that held all the confidence he wished he felt, Presley lifted the latch on the trailer door. He wasn't sure if he'd burned all his bridges to heaven above, but he offered a silent prayer in that direction just in case.

Then he stepped inside the trailer and let the latch close behind him.

DIXIE TWIRLED IN FRONT OF THE FULL-LENGTH MIRROR hanging on the door of her gram's closet. She'd sneaked away from the Rose just long enough to throw on a sundress and dust a little bit of makeup across her nose. She was meeting Chandler in front of the Rose in twenty minutes, and she wanted to look more presentable than she did in her standard hot-pink Rambling Rose T-shirt and denim shorts.

They wouldn't have time to leave the honky-tonk, not with the live music lineup starting this evening, but at least she could treat him to a slab of Angelo's famous baby back ribs. Presley didn't appear to want her help on his side of things, so she'd be more than happy to take a backseat and just enjoy the evening.

With a final glance in the mirror, she realized she'd forgotten to put on some earrings. She went back to her room, searching for her favorite pair. She'd made them herself, back when she was first starting out. Hopefully by this time next year she'd expand from her little online store and have a real shop set up to sell handcrafted jewelry and items from other local artisans instead of working the chili cook-off.

She secured the sterling silver posts, letting the hammered silver chain links dangle down. She'd strung tiny flower charms on the ends, making them look like a bouquet of flowers spilling from her ear lobes. She missed making jewelry. She missed having free time. But most of all, she missed that piece of herself that she connected with deep down inside when she made something beautiful with her own hands.

The matching silver bracelet and necklace she'd made were lying around somewhere. After locating them in the bottom of her jewelry box, she slipped them on then checked the time on her phone.

"I'm heading back to work," she called out to her sister. Liza had promised to make sure Gram got back and forth to the senior center for dinner with her friends tonight.

"Whoa." Liza poked her head through the open doorway. "Something special going on at the Rose tonight?"

"First night of the chili cook-off weekend. I've got to be there to make sure Presley doesn't screw anything up." Dixie rubbed her lips together. "Do you think this is too much?"

"Not unless you're worried about every cowboy who gets a look at you spontaneously bursting into flames." Liza let out a low wolf whistle. "When's the last time you put that much effort into your appearance? You sure there's no one special waiting on you tonight?"

"Well, there is a guy in from California who wants to meet to grab a bite." Dixie chewed on her lip, probably ruining the lipstick she'd just spent five minutes trying to apply. No need to divulge all of the details about Chandler yet. He seemed somewhat

interested—although she was a little rusty when it came to
interpreting dating signals. Liza wouldn't remember him
anyway. She'd been in elementary school when Dixie was
in junior high.

Liza pulled her into a hug. "He'll be eating his heart
out, Sis."

"You think so?" Dixie asked, feeling a little overdressed.
"Maybe the mascara's a bit too much."

"Don't change a thing. Now get on out of here and be
glad Daddy can't see you. If you were still in high school,
he'd ground you for a week for trying to leave the house
in a dress like that."

Dixie laughed. Her sister's good mood and string of
compliments lightened the funk Presley had caused.

Liza tugged the top of the sundress into the optional
off-the-shoulder position. "There, that's better. Have fun."

Dixie took a deep breath then pulled on her high-
heeled strappy sandals. She hadn't worn them in years,
but tonight seemed like the night to break them out. "Tell
Gram not to wait up, okay?"

By the time she pulled into the back lot at the Rose, she
felt nothing like the free-spirited gal who'd left her gram's
house in a cloud of perfume, lipstick, and hope. Who
was she kidding? She was Dixie Mae King from Holiday,
Texas. Even though Chandler started off here, now he
lived in southern California and probably spent his after-
noons lounging on the beach with lifeguards who looked
like *Baywatch* babes.

As she got out of the car, she pulled a tissue from her
purse and rubbed it across her lips, removing every trace of

the reddish tint she'd applied multiple times at home. Before she reached the front door of the Rose, she'd tugged her straps up and over her shoulders again. It helped but didn't completely put her at ease. This dress hadn't seen the light of day in years. What made her think she could pull off the short skirt and sexy off-the-shoulder look?

Wishing for an excuse to call the whole thing off, she entered the honky-tonk. It wasn't quite eight, but the crowd inside was busting at the seams. Dixie made her way through the mass of people toward the bar. At least Charlie had the foresight to arrange for a ton of extra staff for the event. Dixie would usually be the one running around with a tray in her hands, but tonight that job belonged to the temporary employees they'd brought in from Austin and even as far away as San Antonio.

"Hey, Shep." She finally reached the edge of the bar. People lined up five and six deep, waiting to put in their order and get their hands on a Lone Star beer.

"Hiya, Dixie." His hands kept moving, popping tops of bottles and pulling drafts from the tap while his gaze danced over her. "You look real pretty tonight, hon."

She looked down at the bar, preferring to ignore the compliment. "You doing okay back here?"

He slid a handful of mugs down the bar and plopped some change down in front of the guy next to her. "So far so good. How's it going out back?"

"I'm about to go check. You let me know if you need anything, okay? I'll have my phone with me."

"Will do."

Dixie stepped away to search for Chandler in the crowd. They'd arranged to meet in the front room by the bar. If she'd known how many people would be crammed into the small space, she would have suggested they meet outside. The yells and cheers of the crowd faded into the background as her gaze lit on a head of white-blond hair on the other end of the room. Suddenly the energy in the crowded area shifted.

Chandler glanced up and smiled. Dixie grinned back. He snagged his bottle from the edge of the bar and threaded his way through the crowd to reach her.

"Hey."

"Hi." Dixie beamed up at him. He'd changed into a pair of white pants and a baby-blue collared shirt. The same color blue as his eyes.

"You look nice tonight." The compliment rolled off his tongue like he sweet-talked waitresses 24/7. Even though she was sure he was just being nice, she still warmed under his appreciative gaze.

"Thanks, so do you. You hungry?"

He rubbed his hand over his abs, drawing her attention to his midsection. A flash of her steamy dream starring Presley from last night exploded through her head. Presley had rubbed his stomach like that right before he leaned in for a kiss. She licked her lips in anticipation, wishing her late-night dream of tangling tongues with Presley was about to come true. Instead, Chandler's chuckle reoriented her in the present.

"Seems like I'm always hungry. Do you have time to go somewhere, or do you need to stick around?"

Dixie would have loved to have this man to herself, to get reacquainted and reconnect, if only long enough for

him to plow through a blue-plate special down at the
diner. But she was already pushing it, just letting him
distract her from things she should be doing at the
Rose. "It's the first night. I'd better stick around to
make sure things go okay. But how about we grab a
couple of rib platters and take them out back?"

"That sounds delicious. Can I get you a drink?"

"I'll stick to water. Come on, I'll put our order in
and give you a quick tour of the place."

"Ms. King, I'm all yours." Chandler offered her
his arm. She linked her arm through his and made
a move toward the kitchen. All hers. What would it
feel like to have someone actually say that to her and
mean it? Maybe tonight she could let herself pretend.
Pretend that she was just a girl in a pretty dress who
was enjoying the company of a boy with a cleft in his
chin and a sparkle in his eye.

Just for tonight.

Presley waited for his eyes to adjust to the darkness.
The sound of heavy breathing—heavy, slobbery
breathing—came from the back corner of the trailer.
He took a few tentative steps forward. "Hey, Ham
Bone. How's it hangin', fella?"

The trailer shifted and squeaked as Leoni hopped
onto the back bumper. "How's it going?"

Presley whipped around to see her peering over the
back door. "Shh. I think he's asleep."

"Don't let him fool you. He sleeps with one eye
open," she warned.

"I'm just going to try to get close enough to clip

the leash on him." Presley advanced another small step. The hulking mass in the corner rolled over, bumping into the wall of the trailer and rocking the whole contraption from side to side.

"He's faking." Leoni pointed at the pig. "See the way his ear is cocked? Be careful."

"Don't you worry about me, darlin'. I've been handling hogs since you were probably knee high to a grasshopper."

The hog rolled onto his belly and struggled to get to his feet. Presley put his hands out in front of him, trying to keep both Ham Bone and himself from doing anything rash. "Hey, buddy. How about we get you out of here and into a place where you can enjoy the sun?"

Ham Bone grunted.

"Yeah, that's what I'm talking about. Fresh straw, all the slop you can handle. Whadda ya say, big guy?"

The beast swung his massive head toward Presley and snorted. A thick glob of slobber, snot, and who knew what else sprayed from his nose. The silver ring of the collar was just inches away. Presley reached for it, taking one more tiny step forward. Ham Bone charged, knocking Presley into the side of the trailer. The air whooshed out of him then the doors to the trailer burst open, crashing against the side with a horrible clang.

Presley made a final swipe, trying to clip the lead onto the boar's collar. He missed and rolled out of the trailer onto the dirt, sending a cloud of dust into the air.

"You okay?" Leoni knelt on the ground beside him.

"Yeah." Presley scrubbed a hand over his eyes. His hat had disappeared, leaving him unprotected from the crowd of onlookers who'd gathered around. He did a quick inventory. The only thing that appeared to be injured beyond the inevitable bruising he'd suffer was his pride.

"You're bleeding." Leoni reached out, her hand stopping short of his side.

He lifted his shirt, revealing a gash over his rib cage. "Well, hell, you're right."

"What's going on?" Dixie called, as she moved from the enclosed beer garden to the parking lot.

Presley watched her navigate the dusty, uneven ground in strappy, heeled sandals. What was with that getup? She had on a lacy white sundress that hugged her hips while the low-cut top accentuated her ample assets. Her hair floated around her face in a cloud of crimson. Either he'd just knocked his head too hard and was seeing things that weren't there, or Dixie had morphed into some sort of a fiery siren.

"Had an incident with a runaway boar. What is it about the pigs around here?" Presley dusted off his ass as Dixie leaned toward him.

"Are you okay?" She glanced down and her eyes widened, probably at the sight of the four-inch gash in his side. "You're hurt."

"It's nothing." Presley didn't want her attention, not for something stupid like this. "Nothing a little Fireball won't fix." He gave her his best smirk and a wink, hoping that would get her off his back.

"What can I do to help?" The tall blond guy appeared next to Dixie. White pants? Who the hell wore white pants to a honky-tonk?

"Chandler, this is Presley. He's our, uh"—her gaze moved back and forth between them—"well, he's in charge of the music this weekend. Chandler

here is from California. I was just showing him around."
She glanced to her toes while a nice shade of pink flushed
her chest.

"Nice to meet you." Chandler offered his hand.

Showing him around? Sure looked like she and the
SoCal boy were on some sort of a date. Presley took one
look at Chandler's outstretched fingers then swiped the
dirt from under his nose with his hand. "Don't want to
get you all dirty there, bro."

Dixie's mouth set in a line. "You need a doctor to take
a look at that."

Presley narrowed his eyes. "I'll be fine."

"She's right. You need a couple of stitches." Chandler
pointed at the cut. "I got bit by a nurse shark when I was
surfing in Hawaii a couple of years ago in a similar spot.
You really want to get that stitched up."

Presley scowled. "You got bit by a shark?" He didn't
like the way Dixie startled at that news. Or the way she
took Chandler's arm.

"Yeah, just a baby. Still have the scar to show for it."
He lifted the edge of his shirt, exposing a twelve-pack of
bronzed abs. A jagged line stretched from one side of his
abdomen to the other.

"How big was that shark?" Dixie's eyes widened, and
her hand tightened on Chandler's arm.

"Just about five or six feet." He shrugged, releasing his
shirt.

Presley shook his head, hoping to clear away the sight
of SoCal's ridged abs. Dude got bit by a fucking shark, and
here he'd been injured by a pig with an attitude.

"Come on, Presley. I'll see if Doc Shubert is around."
Dixie released Chandler's arm and offered her hand.

⚡

"Fine." He'd say or do just about anything to get himself out of the unwanted spotlight. He waved off her hand then he and Chandler followed Dixie into the building. She stopped at the bar to exchange a few words with Dwight, the resident mechanic and pain in the ass, then continued on to Charlie's office.

"Here, you sit down and I'll go get the doc. Dwight said he's out back tossing horseshoes."

"Great." He sank into Charlie's chair and kicked his filthy boots onto the edge of the desk.

"I also asked him to grab a couple of the guys and go after that pig. We don't need him tearing down any fences or causing any trouble around here." She put her hand on SoCal's arm. "Chandler, can you go grab a couple of clean towels from the storeroom? Second door on the left." Then she wheeled toward the door. "Be back in a sec."

Chandler followed her out, and Presley was finally alone. He'd royally screwed up this time. Not only did he make a massive fool out of himself by being bested by a big-ass boar, but he'd also probably blown any chance he had of getting some feedback on his fiddle from Leoni.

But the biggest shock to his system wasn't the embarrassment he'd suffered on the tail end of Ham Bone's rampage or the lost opportunity to talk fiddles. It was the weird sensation burning through his chest. The mixture of dread and regret and some unidentified feeling that exploded at the sight of Dixie and her knight in blinding-white chinos. If he didn't know better, he'd almost think that for the first time in his life he'd been bit by the green-eyed monster. But, naw, couldn't be. This was Dixie he was thinking about. Dixie Holier-Than-Thou King.

But something about the sparkle in her eye when she'd leaned toward him had caught him off guard. It's like all of a sudden he realized she wasn't the awkward girl who'd blushed at the sight of him anymore. No, no doubt about it, Dixie was a woman…a woman who set him off-balance, sent his senses into overdrive, and made him yearn for something that seemed just out of reach.

And now she was gushing over some stranger who didn't fit into Holiday any more than Presley fit into the role of hog handler or honky-tonk manager.

Hell, that knock on the head must have been harder than it seemed. There was no way he could be jealous over the red-headed Fireball. No fucking way.

chapter
FIVE

DIXIE KICKED OFF THE RIDICULOUS SHOES BEFORE SHE RACED down the hall. What was Presley thinking? In typical Presley fashion, he'd probably lost some stupid bet and had to take the boar for a walk or something. Why in the world had Charlie thought it would be a good idea to leave him in charge of anything? She'd get him stitched up and out of her way. Her only hope of getting him off her mind was to focus on something else. Maybe even someone else. Like Chandler. But leave it to Presley to screw that up for her too.

She located the doc two games and three whiskeys into an impromptu horseshoe tournament. He promised he was still capable of stitching up a side though he made no guarantee of a straight line. Presley would probably prefer a botched job anyway. He'd say the bigger the scar, the more his potential conquests would "ooh" and "ah" over his injury. Dixie shook the thought away. Wouldn't do her any good to waste any energy on Presley Walker.

Five minutes later she returned to the office, Doc Shubert in tow. Chandler met her by the door.

"I got some towels. Think this is enough?" He held out a stack of bar towels, and she took them with a smile.

"I'm sure it will be fine. Look, I'm sorry about tonight."

Doc Shubert let out a burp. "Is the patient in there?" He nodded toward the door.

"He should be. It's where I left him. I'll be right in."

The doc pushed the door open, and Dixie caught a glimpse of Presley sitting in Charlie's chair, a bottle of amber liquid tipped to his lips.

She bit her bottom lip. "I probably ought to lend the doc a hand."

Chandler's mouth split into a lazy smile. "You sure you don't want some help?"

"Oh, I'll be all right. I've played doctor and nurse before."

His grin widened. "I'm sorry I missed that. You're likely the prettiest nurse I've ever met."

Her cheeks burned. "I just meant that I've kissed boo-boos and applied bandages and…"

Chandler bit back a laugh.

"I'm not doing myself any favors here, am I?" Her brow wrinkled.

He lifted her hand to his lips and pressed a gentle kiss against it. "You're adorable. Can we try this again tomorrow?"

Heat sparked in her gut. She pulled the stack of towels into her abdomen, trying to quench the burn. "I'd like that."

"Me too." He released her hand and pushed the door open for her. "I'll call you in the morning."

She stepped past him into the office then whirled around to let herself take one more look at the surprising blast from her past. "I'll talk to you then."

Nodding, he let the door close.

Dixie stood there for a moment, hugging the towels against her belly.

"You done flirting with SoCal?" Presley spit out.

"Excuse me?" The moment dissipated, replaced with a keen awareness of some impressive snoring. Dixie followed the noise to where Doc Shubert slumped in a chair. "What happened?"

"What are you trying to do to me here? He could've sterilized my wound just by breathing on it."

"I guess he might have had a few drinks."

"The man's drunker than a peach orchard boar."

"And evidently you know all about boars now?" Dixie slammed the towels onto the desk. They landed with a soft whoosh, a far cry from the satisfying thud she would have preferred.

"Can we not talk about boars or pigs or even peaches for that matter?"

"You're the one who brought them up."

Presley didn't acknowledge her statement. "Is there anyone else out there who can stitch me up right quick? Doc managed to clean it up a little before he passed out. I've gotta introduce the first band in twenty minutes."

Dixie glanced to the snoring doctor. "I suppose I can see if I can get Doc Martin over here."

Presley tried to rise out of the chair. "The vet?"

Shrugging, Dixie moved closer to the desk. "I'm sure sewing you up wouldn't be any different than putting a few stitches in an altered bull."

"I can't believe you even said that. Why don't you get over here and stitch me back together?"

"Excuse me?" She clamped her hands to her hips. "What makes you think I even know how to thread a needle?"

He gestured to her. "Because...hell, I don't know."

"Because I'm a woman? Were you about to say I should know how to sew because I'm a girl?"

"No." His words denied it, but the flush on his cheeks told her that's exactly what he'd been thinking.

She laughed. "To tell you the truth, it surprises me you've noticed."

"What, that you're a woman?" The smile that had haunted her dreams transformed his features from sheepish to wolfish in less time than it took for her to draw in a sharp breath. "A virile young man such as myself can't help but notice a filly in her prime."

"So now I'm a horse? You're not helping out your situation here, you know." Dixie cocked a hip. "I still don't get why you think I should know how to sew."

"Hell, I don't know. My mom sews. I guess I've just never had the need." Presley set the bottle down on the edge of the desk. "It's starting to sting. Can't we just get this over with?"

"I'm going to let it slide because the pain must be making you stupid. Or at least more stupid than usual." Dixie surveyed the desktop. Doc Shubert didn't go anywhere without his black doctor's bag. With any luck he had something she could use to stitch up Presley's side... and maybe his mouth too while she was at it.

Presley reached for her hand. She drew in a breath as his fingers grazed hers. "I'm not trying to be an ass, I swear. If you manage to sew me up, I promise I'll have my mom teach me how to sew on a button. What do you say?" He winced as he dropped his feet to the ground.

She slid her hand out from under his, ignoring the thrum of her heart as she broke contact. Her attention refocused on the task ahead, she rummaged through the well-organized bag.

"There." She lifted a makeshift sewing kit out of the

bag and pointed to a C-shaped needle. "This should do the trick."

Presley's brows knit together. "You know, maybe we ought to wait for the doc to wake up."

"You sure about that? Boss Hawg goes on in just a few minutes. You looked like you were getting pretty cozy with his girlfriend." She squirted a generous dose of hand sanitizer into her palm and rubbed her hands together.

"Leoni?"

Dixie squinted while she tried to thread the suture needle. "I didn't catch her name."

"She's the fiddle player. Trust me, I was *not* getting cozy."

"Whatever." Dixie squelched the twinge of jealousy before it had a chance to settle in her gut. With the needle ready, Dixie knelt down in front of Presley. "Can you hold up your shirt?"

He lifted the edge of his shirt. "Wait, shouldn't we sterilize it or something?"

"Why don't you just douse it in whatever's in that bottle you've been drinking?"

Presley scoffed. "And waste a single malt?"

"Suit yourself. I hear the cowgirls love a guy with a little gangrene."

"Are you sassing me, Dixie King?"

"Look, do you want me to sew you up or not? I have better things to do tonight, in case you hadn't noticed." She pulled her phone out of her back pocket and opened up a search bar.

"Just give it to me." Presley reached for the needle and dipped it into the bottle. "What are you looking at?"

"Nothing." The video began to play. Maybe she should have picked a different one. A guy on the screen showed off a six-inch gash in his leg. Then he went on to explain how he was stitching it up himself.

"Are you watching YouTube?"

"Thank goodness for the internet, huh?" It didn't look too difficult. Although the guy on the video seemed much more willing than Presley. "I just want you to remember this was your idea."

"Just do it." Presley lifted his shirt up and over his head.

Dixie wasn't prepared for the way the sight of his bare chest slammed into her like a sledgehammer to the gut. Oh my goodness. The man might irritate the heck out of her when he opened his mouth, but there was no denying God had given him the body of an archangel. She'd been around men who looked like this before—there were plenty of shirtless ranch hands working the land around Holiday, and one summer they'd received free HBO. But never so close up. The guys she typically dated were more comfortable working with a calculator than working with their hands. Even looking at him seemed like a sin.

Presley took another swallow of liquid. His Adam's apple bobbed up and down. She slid her gaze from his mouth, down his neck, over those perfect pecs, then lower still to a line of ridged abs. Her mouth went dry like it had been stuffed with cotton. Before she had a chance to think about it, she reached for the bottle. "Give me a sip of that, will you?"

He passed it to her with a wink. "Well now, Dixie Mae. Better be careful, we don't want people to think I'm corrupting you."

The burn of whiskey hit the back of her throat. Fire

slid down to her chest, flooding her system with a heat she felt to the tips of her toes. Maybe that would settle her nerves. Something had to. If her hands didn't stop shaking, she wouldn't even be able to hold onto the needle. "Let's get this over with, shall we?"

"Be gentle with me, darlin'." He leaned against the back of the chair and closed his eyes.

Just as well. She didn't need the weight of his gaze pressing down on her while she tried to concentrate. Her fingers reached out, but she couldn't bring herself to actually touch him. Why was she so nervous?

"You need me to stick it in?" He opened one eye.

She groaned. "Would you please stop making everything sound so dirty?"

His teasing grin mocked her. "Who knew the preacher's daughter had such a dirty mind? I'm just talking about the needle, sweetheart."

"Sure you were." She lifted her gaze from his abs to search his eyes. Being this close to him, inhaling his scent, feeling the heat from his skin—the combination overloaded her senses.

His eyes crinkled at the edges while his hand reached out to cup her cheek. "Anyone ever tell you your eyes are the color of a potent shot of absinthe?"

She wanted to lean into his hand, let herself enjoy his touch. But she and Presley were like ice cream and hot sauce…just not meant to be. So she pulled back and went on the defense again. "As in the illegal alcohol people used to get high on?"

His chest vibrated as he snort-laughed, causing his abs to roll underneath her hand. "It's not illegal, and by the time you drank enough of it to enjoy the hallucino-genic properties you'd be dead."

"Great. I'll keep that in mind." She tried to return her attention to the task at hand.

"You really are something, Dixie." Presley tucked a strand of hair behind her ear. His fingers lingered. Her eyes drifted closed, relishing his touch. "It's amazing how we never…"

She opened her eyes as his voice lowered to a whisper. His mouth hovered inches from hers. His hand tangled in her hair. His eyes half-closed, offered an invitation.

"How we never what?" she whispered back.

"How we never did this." His hand slipped behind her neck, gently pulling her face toward his.

Her heart hammered in her chest, pounding so loudly she was sure he could hear it. Closer and closer he came. Blood rushed to her face, and for a moment she wondered if she'd pass out. His mouth parted slightly. Her gaze flitted back and forth between his lips and his eyes. This is what she wanted; this is what she'd dreamed about. She braced herself, ready for his kiss.

It wasn't the furious, scorching kiss of her dreams. It was gentle, sweet, incredible. His tongue teased along the seam of her lips. She opened, tasting him for the first time—a hint of whiskey and something else.

He pulled away first. If the situation had been left up to her, she could probably go on kissing him until the end of time.

"Wow, that was—"

"What?" Worry creased her brow. She didn't want to be compared to the leagues of women he'd tangled tongues with in the past.

"Nothing." He ran a hand over his cheek. "Say, we'd better get back to the stitches. You don't want me to bleed out, do you?"

Nothing? Their kiss had meant nothing to him? It had been everything she'd dreamed of and more. More hurt than confused, she cocked her head. "No, we don't want you to bleed out."

He cleared his throat and summoned a smile. "Right. So come on, Fireball. Give it to me."

Dixie gritted her teeth.

"I know you want to."

Oh, she wanted to all right. With a final shake of her head, she jabbed the needle into Presley's side.

His hips bucked up. "Shit, that stings like a motherfucker."

The door squeaked open. "What the heck's going on in here?" Dwight's boots clomped across the floor.

Dwight's gaze bounced from the doc who still slumped passed out in the side chair to Presley's naked chest to Dixie's face, which most likely still suffered from some intense blushing. "I didn't mean to interrupt anything."

"You didn't." Somehow she stumbled to her feet. Her cheeks had to be redder than a jar of her mama's canned beets right now. "I've got to go. I'll have Shep introduce the band then I'll put a pot of coffee on for Doc Shubert. I think it's best that he take over from here."

"I'm sorry, Dixie." Presley started to get up.

"No, just stay there. I'll be fine. Everything will be just fine. Fine." She backed away from the desk. Before she reached the door, her foot landed on something sharp, and she stumbled backward. Presley sprung from the desk as she hit the ground. Her shoe. She'd tripped over her own high-heeled shoe. That would teach her to try to buck the norm and pretend to be someone she wasn't.

"You okay?" He reached out to help her up.

"I'll be fine." She had to get out of there. One more look at Presley's tan chest and she'd probably pass out just like Doc Shubert. She only had to do two things. Number one, find Shep and have him introduce the band. Number two, get Angelo to make a fresh pot of coffee. Two things. She could handle that.

She whirled away from Presley. Inches from the door she looked up, catching her reflection in the mirror hanging on the office wall. A stranger stared back at her. A woman with fear in her eyes and fire blazing across her cheeks.

She needed to get herself out of any situation in which Presley was half naked. And the sooner the better.

He sure knew how to screw something up. That was the one thing he'd always been good at. But that kiss had changed everything. He'd meant it as a bit of a dare... setting Dixie off her straight and narrow path had always held a little bit of a thrill for him. He hadn't expected her to kiss him back. Or to feel it straight down to his toes. His feelings about kissing usually ended up stopping around his crotch area. But Dixie's kiss had hit him everywhere at once.

Presley clenched his teeth as the doc tied off the last stitch and clipped the thread.

"Be good as new in a few days." The older man had

sobered up after his short nap and half a pot of coffee. Or at least sobered up enough to close Presley's side without any other major incidents.

"Thanks, Doc. I appreciate it." Presley watched while the doc secured a patch of gauze and bandage to his stomach. "What do I owe you?"

"It was my pleasure, son." The doc repacked his bag, methodically returning everything to its place after Dixie had spread the contents all over the giant desk. "You just make sure nothing happens to the Rose, and we'll call it even."

"What do you mean? What would happen to the Rose?" Maybe the whiskey hadn't quite left the doc's system yet.

Doc paused and peered at Presley over the top of his bifocals. "I was tossing horseshoes with some folks up from San Antonio. Said they were in town to bid out a project on the land right next door."

"The old Garcia land?"

Doc nodded. "They said some investor from California was going to build—get this—a country and western theme park in the space. At first I didn't think I heard him right. Can you imagine? Said the plans called for a honky-tonk twice the size of the Rose. Why would we need a new honky-tonk next door when we've got a perfectly good one right here? Isn't that the most asinine thing you've ever heard? "

"Yeah." Presley's thoughts immediately went to SoCal. There was no way that guy was in town for the chili cook-off. Something else had to be going on there. "What else did they say?"

"Oh, not much. In fact, they got a good

tongue-lashing from their boss over telling me that much. They said it was all confidential and bought me a couple of shots like they wanted to buy my silence." He zipped up his bag. "But here in Holiday we look after our own. You be sure and tell your sister to keep her eyes and ears open."

"I will." The last thing Charlie needed right now was to worry about some crazy-ass developer wanting to move in on her turf. It's not like Holiday was a tourist mecca. Sure, the Rose was the oldest honky-tonk in Texas and had put their little town on the map. But why in the world would someone want to build something like a huge theme park in the middle of nowhere?

"Keep an eye on that wound now. I'll want to see you in about a week to remove those stitches."

"Yes, sir." Presley walked the doc to the door. "Thanks again."

"And go easy on that rib." The doc paused in the doorway. "That means keeping your extracurricular activities to a minimum."

Presley laughed. With a tip of his hat, the doc disappeared down the hall. Presley needed to find Dixie. The two of them had been left in charge. They'd have to figure out what, if anything, needed to be done about the possible threat to their livelihood. But first, he needed a shirt. He picked up the one he'd been wearing. Too much blood. That meant he either went back out to the bar wearing nothing but his bandage or he dipped into Charlie's stash of hot-pink Rambling Rose T-shirts she kept on hand for staff. What was that saying...real mean wear pink? He'd always thought it was his color.

Fully dressed and somewhat cleaned up, Presley ambled back out to the bar. Business had picked up even more in the time he'd been out of commission. Shep held down the fort behind the ancient bar while a couple of waitresses threaded their way through the masses, trays held high. He scanned the top of the crowd, looking for the fire-red hair of his reluctant partner.

"Hey, Shep! You seen Dixie around?" Presley managed to squeeze by a few people and wedge his way in next to the counter.

Shep didn't slow down, kept slinging bottles and pulling drafts. "She blew through here a few minutes ago. I think she's out back."

"Thanks."

Before Presley could get through the back door and out to the beer garden, Dwight caught up to him. "Feelin' better there?"

"Yeah. Doc got me all stitched up. It's too bad that boar is a bit of a celebrity. I could go for a nice big BLT right about now."

Dwight chuckled. "Yeah, he got you good. Did Dixie tell you we got him over to your folks' place? Just drove the damn trailer up to the pen and backed him in."

"Well, hell. Why didn't I think of that?"

Dwight tapped his finger to his temple. "It was a flash of inspiration."

"Oh yeah?"

"Well, that and Dixie suggested it. That girl's tougher than I figured. Smarter too."

Presley nodded. That was the gospel truth. And that's why he needed to find her. Together they'd figure out what to do about Doc's news. "Do you know where she is?"

Dwight pointed toward the stage. "Saw her over there a bit ago. Do me a favor?"

"Sure." Presley scanned the crowd spread out over the grassy area in front of the stage.

"Give these back to Boss Hawg?" Dwight tossed a ring of keys his way.

"You bet. Thanks, Dwight." He clapped a hand on the shorter man's shoulder. They might be an eclectic crowd here at the Rose, but they did do one thing right. They looked out for each other. Spotting a flash of red in the sea of straw Stetsons, Presley stepped through the door. "I've got to talk to Dixie. I'll catch you later."

Dwight nodded and turned toward the bar. Presley was surprised he'd actually left his roost. The man had a stool with his name carved on it. Charlie had given it to him as a gift last Christmas.

The band wrapped up its set, and Dixie stepped onto the stage. That should be his job. He'd told Charlie he'd pitch in, and here he was, stitched, bruised, and failing to keep his promise. Dixie told the crowd there would be a short break while the next band got set up. That should give them a few minutes to chat. He wound through the crowd, making his way to the stage. She clambered down the steps, and he caught up to her.

"Hey, Fireball."

She wheeled to face him. "Would you stop calling me that?"

"Are you okay?"

"Never better. While you've been tossing back shots with Doc Shubert, I've been doing your job and mine."

He reached for her hand, but she jerked it away. "I'm sorry, Dixie. I didn't mean for things to go wrong."

"What did you think would happen? You go off trying to play hero, not thinking about the consequences."

He scoffed. "Damn, why don't you tell me how you really feel?"

She put her hand to her heart. "I'm sorry. I didn't mean it like it came out. It's been a long day, and things didn't exactly go how I expected tonight."

He wanted to take that opening and talk about the kiss. But he still hadn't had a chance to process it himself. It wouldn't do any good to botch that conversation as well.

When he didn't respond, she cleared her throat. "We've got one more band to get through tonight, and then things start up for real tomorrow. Can I count on you?"

"Of course you can." He meant it too.

"That means staying until close tonight and being back here by eight tomorrow morning. No skipping out if you get a better offer or to sweet-talk some musician."

A spark of fight ignited in his gut. "I know what it means."

"Good." She crossed her arms over her chest.

He mimicked her posture. "Good. Now, can we talk about something serious?"

"*You* want to talk about something serious? This ought to be good. What's up?" She cocked a hip, waiting for him to go on.

"Doc told me he was playing horseshoes with some guys from San Antonio. They're up for the weekend to bid out a project on the Garcia acreage that just sold."

Her brows knit together. "That parcel has been sitting there for years. I didn't even know if was for sale."

"It wasn't." Presley leaned closer. "He said somebody's trying to put in a country and western theme park and a new honky-tonk right next door."

Dixie let out a laugh. "That's crazy. Who would want to do that?"

Presley lowered his voice. "Someone from *southern California*."

She stopped laughing. "Wait. You don't mean—"

"Why not? You've got to admit, he doesn't look like he's here to jump into the 'beans or no beans' debate. Have you asked him what recipe he's planning on making?"

"No, but—"

"Well, I think you ought to find out what he's really doing in town. My gut tells me he's up to no good."

"Your gut?"

"Yeah."

"And you always listen to your gut?"

"What do you mean?"

"Isn't your gut what got you into trouble in the first place? If you'd kept your gut away from that horrible pig, I wouldn't be doing the work of two people."

"It's not my gut that got me in trouble there. I was just trying to help out Leoni."

"Oh, gosh"—Dixie put her hands over her eyes—"please don't tell me another part of your anatomy was involved."

"Would you cut it out?" He'd hoped to get Leoni's feedback about his latest creation. But he didn't want to tell Dixie about that. Nobody around here expected anything from him except to be Good-Time Presley. And he'd enjoyed it. Right up until about a year ago when he'd started to think about what kind of legacy he'd be leaving behind. He was about to give Dixie a piece of his mind, but the sound of her phone's ringtone caught her attention instead.

"Hello?" She turned away from him and pressed a hand to her ear, probably trying to cut out the sound of the crowd around them.

He waited, trying not to listen in on her end of the conversation. Finally, she ended her call.

"I've got to go."

"Now?" Wasn't she the one moaning to him about not following through on his responsibilities?

"That was my dad. He needs my help at home."

"So you're just going to run out on me?"

"It's my gram. It's important." The look in her eye begged him not to pry. "I just have to go. Can you lock up here tonight and I'll shut down tomorrow?"

"Is everything okay?" He took a step toward her, but she backed away.

"I'm sure it'll be fine. I just need to go."

Presley let his hand drop. "Okay."

She hobbled away in her strappy sandals, not even bothering to look back. He'd let her go tonight. But tomorrow they needed to talk. If something happened to the Rose while he and Dixie were in charge, his family would never take him seriously. And it was high time he started doing that himself.

chapter
SIX

DIXIE HOBBLED INTO THE EMERGENCY ROOM ON SWOLLEN ankles. If she wasn't careful, she'd need to be admitted as well. It was bad enough Gram had gotten involved in a fender bender. Her dad had assured her Gram was okay, but since he and her mom were having dinner with the head of their capital campaign, it was up to Dixie to step in and fetch her grandmother.

"Can I help you?" A gum-smacking candy striper sat at the information desk, more interested in her manicure than helping Dixie locate her errant grandmother.

"I'm looking for Eugenia Holbein. My dad said she was brought in about an hour ago."

Gram's belly laugh ricocheted down the hall.

"She's a hoot." The candy striper checked her computer screen. "Curtain number four. Do you want me to walk you back?"

"Thanks, but I'll just follow the giggles." Dixie grimaced then moved past the desk. If Gram was laughing, odds were she wasn't hurt too badly.

"Why, there you are, Dixie. I'm not surprised your mother and father sent you to pick me up." Gram sat on the edge of the bed surrounded by a handful of nurses.

Dixie's gaze bounced over her. No bandages, no stitches, no outward sign of any injury at all. "Are you okay?" The nurses parted, and Dixie rushed to Gram's side. "You're not hurt, are you?"

Gram shook her head. "Just a little shaken up, that's all. Though I wish I could say the same for Old Blue."

"Old Blue? Who's Old Blue?"

The three nurses launched into a frenzy of activity, making excuses about needing to check on other patients. Within moments Dixie was alone with Gram.

"Gram, who's Old Blue?"

Gram's mouth turned downward into a sheepish frown. "Old Blue is…well, was…Maybelle's truck. It was her husband's pride and joy before he died. But now, well—"

"Maybelle was with you? Is she okay?" Dixie's heart spiked. If something had happened to Mrs. Mitchell, she'd never hear the end of it.

"She's fine. Wasn't even in the truck." Gram patted the spot next to her. "Sit down, child. You look like you're about to pass out."

Dixie rubbed her breastbone where her heart still beat in triple time. "Tell me what happened." Her gaze drilled into Gram's as she scooted her butt onto the bed. "Liza was supposed to get you back and forth to the center tonight. How did you end up in a wreck?"

"Oh, you know your sister. One of her friends called, and she dumped me at the center and asked if I could find my own way home. I've had my eye on that Kermit, so I told her I'd figure out how to catch a ride. Just wasn't sure if it would be to his place or mine."

"Gram!" Dixie wasn't sure what part made her

the most upset—that Liza would leave Gram stranded at
the center or that Gram would be so brazen to speak so
candidly about her pursuit of Kermit.

"There may be snow on the roof"—Gram patted her
white head of hair—"but there's still a fire burnin' in the
hearth."

Rolling her eyes, Dixie tried to steer the conversation
back to the events of the evening. "So you took out the
truck? You know you're not supposed to drive."

"I was only going down the road. If it hadn't been
hotter than Hades, I would have just walked."

"Why did you need to leave the center? You could have
called me if you forgot something. I would have brought
it to you."

Gram patted Dixie's hand. "The Beer Barn isn't but a
couple hundred yards down the highway. I told Maybelle
I'd bring the hooch, but I left it at home."

A groan escaped Dixie's lips. "Oh no. Please tell me you
weren't going to spike the punch."

"It was my turn." Gram shrugged. "You think we go
to the center for the fine home cooking? I'd be better off
buying one of those TV dinners." Gram winked. "It's
the sweet tea that's a draw. We've got a schedule and
everything."

"A schedule for who spikes the tea?" With Dixie's luck,
her gram was the one who'd started it. "Please tell me this
wasn't your idea."

"The Senior Sisterhood prevents me from divulging
that information." Gram twisted a pretend key between
her lips and tossed it over her shoulder.

Dixie let out a long sigh. "Oh, Gram."

"You just wait until you get as old as me. I'm so sick of

everyone treating me like a toddler. Why, even little Bea has more freedom than her great-granny."

"That's not true. Mom and Dad just want to keep you safe. They—"

"They want to keep me confined to the four walls of my house is what they want. Your daddy cares more about that capital campaign right now than he cares about his own family."

"Gram, that's not fair. Dad needs the money to come through. He's got people counting on him."

"That's right. We can't forget about the great people of Holiday, Texas, whose only hope is Pastor King." Gram shook her head. "Your father has a good heart, honey, but he's letting politics and red tape color his vision. Has been for the past several years. And your mama, that girl just follows blindly behind him. I thought I raised her to have a mind of her own. Don't know where I went wrong with that one."

"I really don't think we should be talking about this right now." Dixie couldn't fault her gram for pointing out how focused her dad had been on the capital campaign. But Dixie didn't believe in airing her family's dirty laundry in someplace as public as Conroe County General. "What do we need to do to get you discharged so I can take you home?"

Gram pressed the nurse call button. Not two seconds later one of the nurses appeared. "Doctor says you're all ready to go, Mrs. Holbein."

"Well, that's a relief." Gram struggled to her feet. Dixie took her hand and helped her scoot off the edge of the bed.

"You take care now and no more driving. Doctor's

orders, okay?" The nurse parted the curtain so they could walk through.

Gram smiled a sugary-sweet grin. "Thanks, sweetheart. You tell the doc I'll stop driving when he pries the keys to my '57 Chevy from my gnarled, dead hands."

The nurse's eyes widened. She probably wasn't used to being told off by someone who looked as innocent as Gram.

Gram passed by, and Dixie paused in front of the nurse. "I'll hide them from her, okay?"

The nurse nodded.

"I heard that, Dixie Mae. You can try to hide them, but you'll have to find them first."

Dixie clamped her hands to her hips. Her feet hurt, her head spun with all of the information that had been dumped on her tonight, especially that unprecedented kiss from Presley, and her heart clenched as she thought about how she would explain all of this to her parents later. She took in a deep breath, fortifying her resolve for the car ride ahead. Then she half-stomped, half-limped through the sliding-glass door and into the night on the heels of a woman who clearly wouldn't be afraid of taking on a man like Presley Walker.

Maybe she could learn a thing or two from her dear old gram.

—❦—

At eight o'clock the next morning Dixie resumed her position behind the competitor registration table. With the first day of the cook-off stretching ahead of her, she didn't know what to expect. Competitors had until ten to sign in and get set up. The judges would start making the

rounds at four, and the finalists would be announced
before the evening concert kicked off at seven. She
took a sip of her coffee and eyed a crew headed for
the table. At least Presley had shown up this morning.
After their exchange last night, she wasn't sure if she'd
inspired him or pissed him off. Maybe a little bit of
both. Served him right.

"Good morning." She greeted the group sporting
pig-printed aprons with a cheery grin. "Are y'all here
to sign in?"

Yes, they were. Along with the dozens of groups
that came after them. By the time ten o'clock rolled
around, Dixie was ready to stretch her legs and check
on the rest of the items on her spreadsheet. As she
stood from her seat, she saw Chandler headed her way.

"Good morning." He looked even better than he
had the night before. A deep-blue T-shirt brought
out the color of his eyes. Coupled with the snug jeans
and well-worn ropers, he should have been a welcome
sight. But after that kiss Presley had laid on her and
the concerns he'd voiced about Chandler's real reason
for returning to Holiday, Dixie couldn't help but
view him in a more skeptical light.

"Good morning to you too."

"Everything go okay after I headed out of here last
night?"

Dixie shuffled her paperwork into a stack. "We
had a few kinks to work out, but all's well." She
thought about what Presley had said the night before.
How could Chandler be involved in any kind of plan
to hurt the Rose? He was too—she searched for the
right words. Too darn nice.

"So about that rain check." He lifted a brow. "Do you have plans for lunch?"

She nibbled on her lower lip. There were a thousand things she should be doing over lunch. Checking in with the competitors, making sure the kitchen staff was keeping up with the lunch orders… "I can't. I'm sorry. I'd really like to, but there's too much to do today."

"That's okay. Maybe later on tonight then?"

Dixie's shoulders slumped. She should be seizing the opportunity to spend more time with Chandler. It might be the only thing that would distract her from how it felt to have Presley's lips on hers for real. But it wasn't likely she'd be any less busy this evening. She should probably just tell him to find someone else to chat up. Between her family obligations and everything she needed to do at the Rose, she didn't have the time or the energy to entertain a relative stranger. She peeked up at him through her lashes. Not even a handsome, interesting, kind, caring out-of-towner who had no idea she and the local men had given up on each other years ago. It's not that she didn't want to find someone to share her life with, but besides Presley, she hadn't felt much of a spark for anyone else. At least, until now.

"Or"—his lips split into a dazzling smile—"I could help you."

She gaped up at him, stunned by the offer. "Help me?"

"Sure. I've got experience. I'm a project manager by trade. I haven't actually organized a music festival or chili cook-off, but I'm great at managing details."

Oh, that was tempting. Hanging out with Chandler all afternoon would definitely make the time go by faster, not to mention raise the level of enjoyment by about a thousand degrees. Plus maybe she could get Presley off her back if she could steer the conversation toward the potential development next door. She thrust her hand toward Chandler, eager to feel his skin on hers. "You might regret this, but I'm going to take you up on your offer."

"If I get to work with you all day, there's no chance of regret." His words rolled over her as he took her hand, warming her cheeks and filling her with an almost-forgotten sense of anticipation.

She pulled her hand back, the feel of his touch still ricocheting through her system. "Okay then, let's get started."

"What's first on the list?"

"The jalapeño-eating contest starts in an hour. I'd better go find Presley and make sure he's got his checklist so we get it all set up in time."

"Right. That's the illustrious pig fighter from last night."

Dixie giggled. A vision of Presley waving a bright-red tablecloth in front of an angry boar played through her mind. "That's the one."

"Did the doctor get him all fixed up?" Chandler put his hand at the small of her back, gently guiding her through the small crowd standing at the edge of the stage.

"As best as he could. I suppose there are some things about Presley that can't ever be fixed." Things like his lackadaisical attitude and his inability to commit to anything more than a day or two ahead. It was a wonder, with all of his faults, that he still managed to get under her skin and invade her dreams

at night. Maybe spending time with Chandler would set
her straight and flush Presley Walker out of her system
once and for all.

"Well then, the Rose is lucky to have you here to keep
things going. Someone said the owner is out of town
right now?"

"That's right. Beck had to go to New York to accept an
award for the Rose's first craft beer. He had a little trouble
on the road, and Charlie flew out to help." She leaned down
to pick up a beer bottle someone had left lying in the grass.

"They must trust you a lot to leave you in charge."

"I suppose." A tiny seed of anxiety planted itself in her
stomach. Were these casual questions? Could Presley's
suspicions be on point?

"I bet this place does a ton of business." He glanced at
her face, like he wanted to gauge her reaction to the change
of subject.

"Sure. It's been around forever."

"Do you get a lot of tourists in the summer?"

She decided to keep her answers vague, wanting to see
where he'd go with the conversation. "Sure."

"Holiday seems like it's still got tons of charm. Would
you say there's enough to do around here?"

"Like what?"

"Oh, like recreation. Looks like you have to go into
one of the bigger towns for hotels, restaurants, any kind
of entertainment."

She stopped in her tracks. "If you haven't noticed, the
Rose just happens to have a wonderful restaurant. We've
had reviewers from Austin, Houston, even Chicago come
down to try out our barbecue."

Chandler smiled, surely an attempt at distraction. "I

didn't mean anything against the Rambling Rose. But even you said it's been around forever. The project manager in me just can't help but think folks around here might be ready for something new. You know, an alternative option. I remember my granddad saying there wasn't much to do in Holiday unless you happened to like beer and country music. Thankfully he liked both."

"What are you getting at?" She couldn't help herself. Any desire to play things cool evaporated into the air, like steam rising from the pit where Angelo stood turning the spit.

He backed away, hands raised as if in surrender. "Nothing. Just curious. I can't help but wonder about stuff like that when I go somewhere new. Or, in the case of Holiday, somewhere I haven't been for a very long time."

By then they'd arrived at the stage. Dixie shot a doubtful glance at Chandler before she headed up the steps. Could Presley actually be onto something?

"You know I didn't mean anything by that last comment, right? You've got a great place here. The stories, the legends, the place the Rose holds in history can't be denied."

"Of course." So he'd asked a few questions. There wasn't anything illegal about that. But her hackles had risen. He'd have to tread carefully around her. If she got any sense he was trying to pull a fast one, she'd be buzzing all over him like a horsefly on a big pile of horse poop.

"Now, what can I do to help?" He'd followed her up the steps and stood in the center of the stage.

Dixie pointed to the side where a stack of tables and chairs had been set. "Let's get the tables set up and then we can start checking in the competitors."

"Sounds good." Chandler got to work putting the tables in place.

As she checked her list, the sound of someone whistling floated from behind the backdrop. Presley strode through the curtain with two huge jars of pickled jalapeño peppers in his arms.

"Well, look what the cat dragged in." He nodded toward Chandler. "You recruiting some new employees here?"

Dixie made her way to the edge of the table where Presley stood. "He offered to help out, so I took him up on it."

Presley set the jars down and faced Chandler. "Are you competing in the jalapeño contest then?"

"Who, me?" Chandler asked. He shot Dixie an apologetic smile. "I'm afraid my taste buds aren't used to Tex-Mex anymore."

Presley's eyes sparked. "Well, that's a shame. I suppose if you can't hack the heat…"

"Hey, I didn't say I couldn't hack it." Chandler cocked a hip forward.

"Oh, my bad. So you're up for entering the contest then?"

Dixie could practically feel the testosterone rise, like a seismic disturbance in the atmosphere. "You don't have to, Chandler."

"That's okay. I want to." He put a hand on her arm and gave her a smile probably meant to provide comfort and reassurance. Instead, he'd played right into Presley's not-so-veiled challenge.

"Good. I'll set up a chair for you." Presley flipped open a folding chair and slid it in place.

"You're competing too, aren't you?" Chandler asked.

"Technically I'm not allowed, seeing as how I'm on staff and all." Presley clucked his tongue. "Damn shame too. I sure do like my peppers."

"I don't think it would be a problem to make an exception, since you're so enthusiastic," Dixie said.

Presley lifted a brow as he turned her way. "I don't want anyone thinking it's rigged."

"Why would they think that? You actually have to eat the peppers, you know. It's not like you can cheat or anything." Dixie couldn't help but smile on the inside at the look on Presley's flustered face.

"What do you say?" Chandler held out a hand. "How about a little wager? I win and Dixie gets the night off."

Dixie nudged Chandler in the side. "That's not really fair. Tonight's the busiest night of the week." Plus she hadn't actually decided whether she still wanted to go out with the man.

"Okay, how about just long enough to go for that ride this afternoon and then tomorrow night I can take her to dinner. Deal?" Chandler's hand stretched toward Presley.

"Oh, I can't tomorrow night. We'll be wrapping up the festival."

"Monday then?" Chandler asked.

"I promised I'd take Gram and Maybelle to bingo."

"I'm sure Presley would be happy to go in your stead." Chandler's lips spread into a self-assured smile.

Before she could put a stop to the nonsense, Presley clasped Chandler's hand. "Deal. And if I win, you have to take care of Boss Hawg's boar the rest of the week."

"Sounds fair enough." Chandler shook Presley's hand.

Neither man let go. They stood there for a long, drawn-out handshake, clasping hands like whoever let go first would automatically be dubbed the loser.

"Will y'all get on with it? We have to get set up before the competitors start checking in." Dixie stomped to the side of the stage to grab a few more chairs.

"Yeah, let's get a move on." Presley let go and caught up to her. "Can you believe this guy? Thinking he can beat me in a pepper-eating contest?"

"I don't know what happened back there." Dixie picked up a few chairs. "All I saw was two tom turkeys strutting their stuff, wasting time and energy that could be better spent on making sure the chili cook-off goes off without a hitch."

"You know what? You're right. And when SoCal loses and has to check on that damn boar all the time, it'll free me up to help out even more."

Dixie paused, shook her head, then continued on toward the other end of the stage. "I guess we'll see about that."

She didn't have time for games between two grown men. She had plans, plans much bigger than winning bragging rights over a silly pepper contest. But still, it did give her a little thrill that someone thought enough about her to want to spend time with her.

Too bad it was the wrong man.

chapter
SEVEN

PRESLEY STUFFED ANOTHER JALAPEÑO IN HIS MOUTH. HEAT blazed through his entire body. Everything burned. He could feel it in his ears, behind his eyeballs, even in his joints. It was like someone had replaced all of his blood with jalapeño pepper juice.

Dixie walked the length of the table. "Holy smokes, that makes number one hundred forty-seven for Chandler Bristol from Malibu, California. We've got one minute left. You'd better pick up another peck of peppers if you're going to hang in there, Mr. Walker."

Presley's eyes watered as he glanced to his right. SoCal had slowed down a bit. They all had in the nine minutes they'd been going at it. Hell, the majority of the competitors had bailed and were sipping on ice-cold glasses of milk to settle their stomachs while he, SoCal, and two other serious contenders battled to the end.

"Aw, come on, Dwight." Dixie paused near the end of the table where Dwight pushed back in his chair.

"I can't take it anymore." He hopped from the stage, grabbed a longneck from a woman in the crowd, then chugged it.

The crowd assembled in front of the stage cheered.

"And then there were three." Dixie glanced at the stopwatch in her hand. "We're down to thirty seconds."

Presley scrambled to shove the slippery peppers in his mouth. He'd passed the point of pain. It was the roil in his stomach that had him most worried now. That and the actual threat of losing to SoCal. The man said he didn't like spicy food. How could he be besting a native Texan in a pepper-eating contest?

"Y'all, help me count it down," Dixie said. "Ten."

The crowd joined in. Frantic, Presley stuffed an entire handful of peppers in his cheeks as the countdown continued.

"Five, four, three, two, one."

Dixie pressed the button of the air horn she'd picked up. The blare, so close to his ear, made Presley jump in his seat. "Gentlemen, hands off your peppers."

He shot a glance to his right. SoCal wiped the corner of his mouth with a napkin like he'd just finished a gourmet meal. Presley snagged the bandana hanging from his back pocket and ran it over his forehead. He'd probably sweated out at least fifteen pounds in the past ten minutes.

"All right, let's get the results. How many peppers for Presley Walker?" Dixie stood by a giant white board, marker in hand.

The poor kid who'd been assigned to count his pepper stems as he tossed them in a plastic bucket stood up. "One hundred sixty-eight for Walker."

Presley grinned as the spectators whistled and cheered. For a moment he basked in the limelight and pushed his worries of the aftermath away. He hadn't thought the entire process through yet—what goes in must eventually come out—one way or another.

"And how about Bubba Sherman?" Dixie asked. "He's here all the way from Beaumont."

Bubba pounded his fists on the table then moved them to his chest. "I'm a pepper-gobbling beast."

His counter held up a finger, still working her way through the discarded stems. "One ninety for Bubba."

Applause filled the outdoor space. Presley clapped his hands together. Anyone who could eat a hundred and ninety peppers and still have the energy to speak ought to take the title. Let Bubba wear the crown. All Presley needed to do was best SoCal.

"That's impressive," Dixie said. "Can our visitor from California beat that number?"

SoCal sat back from the table, fingers crossed over his stomach. He looked pretty sure of himself. Too damn sure. Presley's gut twinged at the thought of losing to the outsider. He hadn't considered it a real possibility.

SoCal's helper got to his feet. "One hundred sixty-nine for Chandler Bristol."

No, no, no. Presley groaned. One pepper? SoCal beat him by one puny little pepper?

"Ladies and gentlemen, your winner of the first annual Rambling Rose Jalapeño-Eating Contest is Bubba Sherman with an impressive one hundred ninety peppers." Dixie lifted Bubba's arm into the air.

Bubba hooted and hollered then wrapped his arms around Dixie and swung her around the stage in an impromptu celebratory dance.

Presley pushed back from the table at the same time as Chandler. "Congrats on a job well done."

Chandler took his hand. "Thanks. You too. I hope you enjoy bingo with Dixie's grandma."

"Can I just ask one thing?" Presley asked.

"Go for it."

"I've just got to know, how does a guy who doesn't like spicy food manage to put away that many peppers?" Presley squinted at SoCal.

"Good question, Walker. See, I never said I didn't like spicy food. I just said I don't care much for jalapeños. You think jalapeños are hot? You should get some of the Kolhapuri chicken I get at this place by my apartment. I need a fire extinguisher in the kitchen with me when I have it for dinner."

"Nice." Presley shook his head.

"What's nice is that you'll be holding down the fort while I take Dixie out on a proper date."

"No argument from me on that. You won, fair and square." Presley clapped SoCal on the arm then watched as the man moved to the side of the stage and chatted with Dixie. He waited until SoCal ambled down the steps toward the Rose then made his way toward Dixie, intent on having a word with her himself. Losing the bet stung his pride. But now she'd have some one-on-one time with the man and could hopefully feel him out about his potential plans.

She stood at the side of the stage, snapping a picture of Bubba with a giant stuffed pepper and an oversized check of the five hundred bucks he'd won from their contest sponsor. Presley waited while Bubba preened for the camera, kissing the pepper then straddling it like he was going to take it for a spin around the pasture.

Finally, Bubba hopped down from the stage to celebrate with his newfound fans and Presley and Dixie were alone.

"That was a tough loss. How are you handling it?" The smile she turned on him smacked of sass.

"Hey, I came over here to say you're welcome, that's all."

Her eyes flared. "You're welcome? Why in the world would I have any reason to thank you?"

"You've got a date with SoCal, don't you? The perfect opportunity to find out why he's really back in town." Presley hooked his thumbs through his belt loops, an attempt to keep his hands busy so he didn't strangle Dixie. It was either that or dip her down for another long, sweet kiss. He still hadn't been able to make sense of all the feelings she'd conjured up inside. There would be time for that later. Right now he needed her to get with the program. Why couldn't she admit that SoCal was up to no good?

"I don't know. He asked a few questions that made me think, but I'm not sure it's enough to run the poor man out of town." She shook her head.

"So grill him some more." He shrugged. Easy enough. Especially if they got a couple of beers—or, better yet, something stronger—into him.

"How? I can't come right out and ask him."

"No. We don't want to scare him off. Doc said those contractors were being pretty secretive. You've got to get the intel without letting him know you're onto him."

"Right." Dixie nodded. How had he never noticed that light smattering of freckles across her nose? "So I'll ask again, *how?*"

"Do what all women do when they want to find something out." Her blank stare made him want to laugh out loud. "Come here and I'll tell you exactly what you need to do."

She leaned forward, close enough that the smell of something sweet tickled his nose. Strawberries. Or maybe cherries. Whatever it was, he liked it.

"Okay, what?" she practically whispered.

"It's easy, Fireball. Just use your feminine wiles."

"My feminine what?" Instead of a nod of agreement and the eager look of comprehension he expected, her nose crinkled.

"Wiles. You know, sidle up to him, maybe run your hand over his arm. Make him feel good about himself, and he'll be like putty in your capable hands." He waggled his eyebrows at her. Surely someone who looked like Dixie would know how to work what God gave her to get whatever she needed out of an unsuspecting male.

"Oh, I'm the wrong gal for that." She shook her head. The fruity smell hung in the air between them.

"No, you're not." He put a palm on either cheek, holding her head still. "You've already got an in with the guy. He likes you. I've seen the way he looks at you." Like he wanted to order her right off the menu with a side of creamed corn to gobble up alongside his chicken-fried steak.

Her hands covered his, and she removed them from her cheeks. "No. There's no way I'm using any kind of feminine anything to try to finagle information out of Chandler."

"Okay then. I guess I'll just give Charlie a call and see what she wants to do." He studied his hands, waiting for a response.

"You can't bring Charlie into this. Not until we know more."

"Bingo!" He tapped his pointer finger against her nose. "Which is why you need to try to find out what he's up to. It's probably nothing. But if Doc is right and someone's trying to buy up land around the Rose to put in some stupid theme park, a competing honky-tonk, and who knows what else, and we had an opportunity to stop it…" He let his words trail off. He couldn't tell if she knew he was totally baiting her. Based on the way she handled things at the Rose, the woman had an IQ that could probably do back flips around his. But she obviously didn't make full use of her other assets. Honestly, he found it somewhat refreshing. He usually went head-to-head with the women he made a play for. They'd trade zingers, volley some salacious banter back and forth, and finally go to her place. He didn't bring women home. That was one of his cardinal rules.

Dixie took in a deep breath. Her chest rose then fell under her hot-pink Rose T-shirt. "I want to help you out. But seriously, I'd botch this faster than you did last night with that boar."

"Well, that's where you're wrong. I may not be very good at pig handling, but there's one area where you can't argue I excel." Her lips pursed, making him want to smooth out the wrinkle on her upper lip with his thumb. Damn, wouldn't do him any good to get twisted up over someone so wrong for him.

"I don't know." Her doubt seemed to consume her. Swallow her up like a big gray cloud. She withdrew into herself right before his eyes.

"We'll start slow. I'll give you a couple of tips, and you see how it goes. If you get any info, we'll figure it out from there. Sound good?"

Those green eyes sparked. "And if we decide he doesn't have anything to do with whatever rumors Doc Shubert is spreading?"

"Then he's off the hook. I'll get my nose out of your business, and you can do whatever you please with Mr. SoCal." What if she did hook up with the beach bum from the West Coast? Wouldn't bother him at all. But then his stomach flipped at the thought of Dixie pressing those sweet, swollen lips against someone else's mouth. Maybe he'd knocked his head into that trailer door a little harder than he thought last night.

"Fine. Let's do it." A combination of resignation and spitfire flashed in her eyes.

Presley leaned in to brush his lips against that inviting pink mouth. Doing it was exactly what he had in mind.

"What the heck?" Rough hands on his shoulders pushed him backward.

His eyes flew open, registering a scowl. Damn, she looked so much prettier when she smiled. "What?" He gathered his shredded composure. "I was just giving you your first lesson."

"No. Let me give you a lesson." Her finger poked him in the shoulder.

"Ow. Hey, be careful, my cracked rib's on that side." He held his hand over his injury to protect himself.

"No kissing. No physical contact. You got it?"

He pulled himself to his full height. She tilted her head back to meet his gaze. He had to hand it to her—the woman didn't back down. "I've got it. But just for the record, when you initiate contact with me, I just want you to know that I'm all for it."

"In your dreams." As the words flew out of her mouth, her hands came up like she wanted to stop them.

He let out a laugh. Damn, that hurt. Doc Shubert should have told him not to laugh along with the other ridiculous instructions he'd given him. "Sounds like I need to start dreaming big."

"Do you ever take anything seriously?" She stared up at him.

"Not if I can help it." That was the honest truth. Life was cruel enough without forcing himself to take things seriously. "Laughing keeps you young. You should try it more often."

"Yeah, well, not all of us have something to laugh about all the time." Her tone shifted from annoyance to just shy of despair. He'd never been the touchy-feely type. He preferred to keep things light, let any worries roll right off his shoulders. The closest he came to losing his light outlook on life was when his dad had broken his hip last year. The whole family had rallied, and his dad had pulled through.

He bit back a smart-ass response and lifted a hand to tuck a strand of hair behind her ear. "Sometimes you have to look for something to make you smile."

She opened her mouth like she wanted to fire something back at him. But then she let it drift closed again. "I guess I need to start looking."

The moment dragged on, suspended between them like something heavy and heartfelt that neither of them knew how to handle.

He broke the silence first. "Right. And you can start looking by gazing deep into the eyes of Mr. SoCal himself. Did y'all make plans to meet up later?"

"Um, yeah." She startled and quickly pulled herself back together. "I was going to meet him back up by the bar, but I think I should cancel."

"Why would you cancel? This is our shot to get some information. You've got his number?"

"He gave it to me yesterday. Why?"

"So do us both a favor. Text him that you want to meet up a little later. Go home. Change into something more along the lines of that dress you had on last night. Primp. Do your hair. Put on a little lipstick. Then offer to take him on that drive around town."

She looked doubtful. "In my minivan?"

"Aw, hell. That's right." He'd forgotten Dixie was the only single female in town to drive her mom's hand-me-down grocery getter. He scrubbed a hand over his chin, thinking. "You know how to ride a bike?"

"You want us to toodle around town on a bicycle built for two?"

"What? No, not a bike, a motorcycle. Jinx has that sweet ride I bet she'd loan us."

Dixie rolled her eyes. "No. No motorcycle."

"All right. I'll come up with something. You just send the text and get yourself all dolled up. I'll be by to pick you up at, say, two o'clock, okay?"

"You really think he's up to no good?"

He met her gaze. Those green eyes studied him, like she could see deep down inside to places he hadn't ever examined himself. "I do. I really, really do."

"Fine. I'll do it." She wrapped her arms around her middle, obviously not the least bit excited about an afternoon of primping.

"Good. This is going to go well, I promise." Presley turned to walk away then immediately spun back around to face her. "Look at us working as a team. I told you we'd make great partners."

She rolled her eyes again and shook her head. "I believe the jury's still out on that."

"You wait and see, Fireball. We'll go down in Rambling Rose history...the dynamic duo who saved the Rose."

Dixie finally let a smile slip. It wasn't the huge grin he'd hoped for, but he'd take it. He'd boiled down his new plan to attacking one insurmountable task at a time. First he'd find her a vehicle that didn't make her look like a soccer mom. Then he'd worry about changing her attitude. By the looks of it, he'd have his work cut out for him.

chapter

EIGHT

BY THE TIME SHE LEFT PRESLEY AND CHECKED THE ITEMS ON her list, Dixie only had about forty-five minutes before he was due to show up on her doorstep. Why hadn't she shot down that idea as soon as it left his mouth? She didn't need Holiday's most notorious bachelor knocking on her door, not with the scandals Gram had been causing lately. Plus she didn't exactly trust herself around the man.

She dug through the makeup bag she'd borrowed from her sister and picked out a tube of lipstick. Presley wanted her to look the part, so she might as well go all out. She lined her lips then filled them in with a light shade of pink. But what to wear? That sundress she wore last night was the only thing she had that even hinted at sexy. As she dug through her closet, searching for something appropriate or something appropriately inappropriate, Gram knocked on the doorframe.

"What's going on in here? I can hear you from the front room. Sounds like a twister is ripping through your closet."

Dixie poked her head out of the closet long enough to meet Gram's gaze. "I can't find anything to wear."

Gram crossed the room to the bed and picked up a T-shirt with a mock turtleneck. "You'd roast in something like this. It's about ninety degrees out there today."

"I know." Dixie let out a groan. "What about this one?" She held out a drapey shift.

"That looks like a housecoat." Gram chuckled. "And an ugly one at that. What's the big occasion? I thought you had to wear your Rose shirts to work."

"I usually do. But I'm working on a"—Dixie cleared the giant frog from her throat—"a special project."

Gram clasped her hands together. "Oh, I love special projects. Is it a secret?" She arched a brow. "I'm good at keeping secrets."

Dixie wanted to laugh at the delighted look on Gram's face. "You're horrible at keeping secrets. That's why you keep getting in so much trouble with Mom and Dad."

"Well, some secrets are just too good to keep all to myself. You ever feel that way, sugar?" Gram winked.

No, she never did feel that way. Every time Dixie tried to keep a secret, guilt pressed down on her like a thousand-pound weight. Folks had learned long ago not to saddle her with their deep, dark secrets.

"It's not a secret, Gram. I'm helping out at the Rose tonight, but I'm not waiting tables, so I wanted to wear something more fun." She turned to her grandmother with a short-sleeve calico blouse in her hands. "What about this?"

Gram shook her head. "Looks like something you'd see in an episode of *Little House on the Prairie*. I'll be back in a sec."

That's what she got for asking Gram for an opinion. The woman had more clothes than Whitey's Western Wear down on Main Street. Her three-bedroom house had been shrunk down to two—she'd converted the smaller bedroom into her closet. Dixie shuffled hangers around, passing over a pale-pink dress she only wore to church and a mint-green skirt with tiny yellow flowers printed on it.

"Try this." Gram tossed a garment at Dixie before she dropped onto the bed. "I bought it a few years ago up in Dallas and never got around to wearing it."

Dixie held the hot-pink tank up in front of her. Fringe draped down the front. Not exactly the kind of garment a typical grandmother might wear. It was kind of cute, but way more revealing than anything Dixie had in her closet.

"Go ahead, try it on," Gram urged.

Before she could make an excuse, the doorbell rang. Dang, Presley was early. Gram sprang off the bed like someone half her age. "I'll get it."

"No, I've got it." Dixie yanked the tank over her head and thrust her arms through the armholes. The last thing she needed was for Presley to fill Gram in on their plans.

By the time Dixie made it to the landing, Gram had already pulled the door open. The sound of Presley's warm laughter hit her about halfway down the stairs. She rounded the corner into the front hall to see him clasping Gram's hand in both of his. Dixie stood in stunned silence while her grandmother invited him into the living room.

They didn't have time for small talk. Dixie stumbled down the rest of the steps. Presley looked out of place on Gram's crushed-velvet settee, though he appeared to feel right at home. One arm draped across the back of the couch, and his legs stretched out in front of him. Gram sat on the ottoman across from him, ankles crossed, the perfect picture of Texas hospitality. "Can I offer you some sweet tea, Mr. Walker?"

"That would be delicious, ma'am." Presley had removed his hat and set it on the cushion next to him.

"You're early." Dixie stated the obvious, drawing his attention to where she leaned against the doorway.

He stood and gestured to the chair next to him. "Good. That means we have time for a glass of sweet tea."

Gram swatted at Dixie's hip as she passed on her way into the kitchen. "Be nice," she muttered under her breath.

Dixie rolled her eyes heavenward and slowly crossed to the chair opposite Presley.

"You look real nice." Presley gestured to her shirt. "Pink's a good color on you."

All too aware of the skimpy top, she wrapped her arms around her middle. The compliment made her warm in places she had no business feeling anything. "Should we figure out a plan?"

"Sure."

They sat at the same time. He dwarfed Gram's delicate antique sofa. In fact, his presence in the front room made the whole house seem smaller. Dixie swallowed, forcing the bubbling apprehension back down into her gut. The only man she remembered seeing in Gram's formal living room besides her own father was Gramps, and he'd been gone for more than twenty years.

Presley cleared his throat. "So I'm thinking it'll go down something like this. You'll take SoCal on a friendly tour around Holiday and maybe stop when you get to the edge of the Garcia property."

"There's nothing out there. Why would I stop?"

"Pretend something feels weird with the car." Presley leaned forward, resting his forearms on his knees. "Then when you get out—"

"So you want me to lie?" Typical. Telling a string of untruths sure didn't keep him up at night.

He let out an unsure laugh like he couldn't tell if she was serious or not. "It's not a lie, just a reason to stop the car."

"I don't lie." Dixie tightened her arms under her chest, daring him to call her out on her statement.

"There is absolutely no doubt in my mind that you've never told a lie in your whole life, Fireball."

"Who, Dixie?" Gram bustled into the room, a tray full of tall glasses of sweet tea and a plate stacked with cookies in her hands. "Would you care for a cookie? Fresh baked this morning."

Dixie's mouth opened wide. Fresh baked? She'd been with Gram when she snagged the plastic box of chocolate-chip cookies from the grocery store shelf. Gram winked at her as she set the tray down on the ottoman.

"Don't mind if I do." Presley reached over and took two cookies and the tea Gram handed him. "I was just explaining to Dixie that there's a difference between pretending and telling a flat-out lie."

Gram nodded. "Isn't that the truth? Why, every time Charity makes her Sunday-night pot roast, I pretend it's the best thing I've had all week."

"Gram! You haven't been to Sunday-night dinner in weeks." How could Gram justify anything Presley Walker said, much less back him up on the benefits of lying?

"That's right. When your mama learns how to properly cook a hunk of meat, I'll be back. Why, she ought to try my new pressure cooker thingamajig I picked up last time I went into Austin."

Dixie closed her eyes for a moment and took in a deep breath through her nose before she spoke. "She can't try your new pressure cooker because you blew it up and almost caught your kitchen on fire."

Gram shrugged off the accusation. "I must have got a bad one. Even if she just threw it in a slow cooker, it would be more tender than that piece of rubber she tries to pass off as a meal."

"I don't think we need to have this conversation right now." Dixie bit into a cookie. Her taste buds celebrated the ooey, chocolaty goodness. Gram must have gone to the trouble of nuking the cookies in the microwave to make Presley think she'd baked them herself. Presley wouldn't need to convince Gram about the benefits of little white lies.

"I'm just trying to get to know your friends." Gram reached over to pat Dixie's knee.

Presley's grin said it all. He was enjoying this. The fact he took any kind of joy in her discomfort made her even madder.

Dixie tried to talk around a huge bite of cookie. "Prefee ith not my fend."

"What's that?" Presley smirked right before he shoved cookie number two into his mouth.

She forced the cookie down her throat and tried again. "I said, 'Presley is not my friend.'" Dixie looked from him to her Gram. "We're just—"

"Partners." Presley licked his lips. "You've got a little bit of chocolate on your mouth there." He reached over to swipe his thumb over her bottom lip.

She recoiled like he was about to burn her then violently rubbed the back of her hand over her mouth.

"Can we go? I'd like to get this over with." Dixie placed her glass back on the tray. She stood and adjusted the tank top.

Presley took his time getting to his feet. "Thank you for the refreshments, Mrs. Holbein. It was a pleasure visiting with you."

"You come back and see me anytime, young man." Gram led the way to the door.

Dixie grabbed her purse off the table in the front hall. "Have a good night, Gram. Don't forget, Liza and Bea are taking you out to dinner tonight."

"That's right. It's their turn to babysit me, right?" Gram gave her a half hug. "You two have fun tonight."

"They're not babysitting you. Liza wants to spend some time with you, and I know you love having Bea around." Dixie hugged back, wrapping her arms around Gram's frail shoulders.

"You're doing it right now, Dixie Mae." Gram pulled back, her green eyes twinkling.

"Doing what?"

"Pretending, hon. Your gentleman friend is right— sometimes it's easier to pretend than flat-out lie to someone's face."

Dixie's heart slammed into the walls of her chest, and she opened her mouth to protest.

Gram shook her head. "I know you have my best interests at heart. Now go on and have fun tonight."

Dixie leaned in to give Gram another hug. Here she thought she was the one who had to make the big sacrifice by moving in with the older woman. But, actually, Gram was the one who was tolerating *her*. What would it be like to live your whole life on your own terms and then be forced to have someone move in to keep an eye on you? Gram never would have agreed if she hadn't been a little scared of the small series of strokes she'd had. Dixie would have to circle back to that thought later. Right now she needed to focus.

Presley had put his hat back on his head and stood on the porch waiting for her. "Ready to go?"

Dixie turned back to tell Gram goodnight. Before she could speak, Gram leaned close and whispered, "I sure can appreciate a man in denim. You get the chance, you grab onto those scrumptious butt cheeks and squeeze."

"Gram!"

Gram gave her a pat on the bottom, nudging her toward the unknown. "Don't do anything I wouldn't do, Dixie Mae."

Presley let out a laugh.

Why did her heart sound like it was beating out a warning? *Thump thump thump* became *turn back now*. Dixie silenced the noises in her head and forced her feet to move toward Presley. He stood at the curb, holding the door open to his Jeep. With the weight of trying to save the Rose draped over her shoulders and the anticipation of being stuck in a small space with Presley for the next few minutes, she climbed into the testosterone-fueled vehicle and sealed her fate.

chapter
NINE

PRESLEY CLOSED THE DOOR BEHIND DIXIE AND LET OUT A sigh. What happened this afternoon would prove either that Dixie was the timid, nervous preacher's daughter he'd always thought she was or that the fiery redhead had more spunk than he'd given her credit for. Hopefully she'd come through, for the sake of the Rose.

"So, can you drive a stick?" Presley swung into the driver's seat.

"What?" Dixie looked like she was afraid to touch anything lest she be infected with lust or some airborne STD.

"I figured you could take my Jeep, but it's got a standard transmission. You ever drive a stick shift before?" He gestured toward the gear shift between them.

Dixie's frown deepened. Seemed like she did that a lot when they were together. Except for when he kissed her. His thoughts drifted to last night. He sure wouldn't mind doing that again.

"Once or twice, but it's been a long time. You know what? I'll just take the van." She put a hand on the dash and made a move to open the door.

Presley covered her hand with his. "No minivan. A chick pulls up in a minivan, and it can only mean one of two things."

She slid her hand out from under his so his palm ended up flat on the dash. "Oh yeah? Enlighten me, please."

"Fine." He lifted a finger. "One, the woman has a brood of kids at home, soccer mom style, you know?"

"Right." Dixie crossed her arms over her chest, obviously her second favorite thing to do around him after frowning.

"Two, she's got a bed in the back and she's either living in it or operating a mobile call-girl service."

"Really?" The furrowed brow should have warned him he was treading on dangerous ground, but he pressed on.

"Hey, in my experience, that's the way it goes." He lifted his shoulders in a shrug.

"So which one am I?" Her eyes narrowed to slits. "Am I hiding my gaggle of unruly children and looking for a sugar daddy, or am I a prostitute on wheels?"

"Well"—damn, let the backpedaling begin—"I didn't mean *you*."

"*Riiiiiiiiiiight.*" She drew out the word a few beats too long. "Can we get out of here before all the neighbors come out to get a good look?"

Presley glanced out the window. Mrs. Mitchell stood on her front porch, raising her hand in a tentative wave. He nodded and lifted the brim of his hat. Upon further inspection, a few more neighbors either peered through open curtains or had cracked their front doors and shot curious gazes their way.

"Afraid your neighbors will spread rumors about us?" He turned the key over in the ignition.

"Too late for that."

She was probably right. Living in a town the size of Holiday had its perks. But there were some cons too. He'd been the target of the town's rumor mill on many occasions. He didn't mind, actually got a kick out of the way the truth got twisted and torqued into something barely resembling itself by the time it made its way back around to him. But Dixie wouldn't be able to shield herself from the knowing glances, the whispers behind her back, or the brazen personal attacks if things got out of hand. He'd have to be careful about giving folks the wrong impression that there was something going on between them.

They drove through town in silence with just the faint sound of the country station from San Antonio keeping them company. As they reached the edge of town, Presley pulled into the abandoned dairy parking lot.

"Why are you stopping? We need to get back." Dixie twisted in her seat to face him. Damn if the sun filtering through the window behind her didn't make her look like a fucking angel.

He shook the image out of his head and opened his door. "Time for you to take the wheel. Let's see how rusty you are."

"No, I can't." By the time he walked around and opened her door, her face had pinked. "It's not necessary, really. I'm sure I can use Charlie's truck, or maybe Shep will let me borrow his car."

Presley leaned across her to unbuckle her seat belt. She drew in a breath and froze. As his fingers pushed on the release button, his gaze met hers. Fear, apprehension, and possibly something else made her eyes widen. His heart skipped like the stones he used to skim down at the river-bed. Could be the sweet smell of chocolate-chip cookies that clung to her. Could be the way she trapped that swollen lower lip with her teeth. Could be the sheer proximity of her chest to his. Whatever it was, he didn't have the time or the balls to go exploring that sensation. Dixie King was off-limits.

He firmed his inner resolve as he backed away and stepped off the running board. "Just give it a shot. Show me what you've got."

"Fine." She brushed past him to round the Jeep.

Dixie adjusted the seat forward while he got settled in the passenger seat. She fastened her seat belt then put both hands on the wheel.

"Aren't you going to buckle up?" she asked.

"I'll be fine. You remember which one the clutch is? Far left?" He pointed to her feet. "Just push on the clutch then ease the stick shift into first gear."

She gritted her teeth and did as he said.

"Now I'm going to release the parking brake and you give it a little gas." He let the brake go and waited for Dixie to find the release point between letting the clutch go and pressing on the gas.

The entire vehicle lurched once, twice, then stalled out. His body flew forward, his stitched-up side colliding with the dash.

"Dammit!" He splayed his fingers over his ribs.

Dixie's hands covered her face. "I told you I didn't want to do this."

He hissed a breath in through his teeth and pulled his seat belt across his middle. "You're a little rusty, that's all. Let's try it again."

"I'm sure Charlie left Sully's old truck at the Rose. I'll take that. It'll be fine, I know—"

"Sully's old truck is at the shop. You've got this. Just put your foot on the clutch or put it in neutral before you turn the engine over." He nodded toward the key.

"They don't even make stick shifts anymore, do they?" She continued to argue while she pressed on the clutch and turned the key.

"It's a life skill. Like how to make grilled cheese and how to French kiss."

She popped the clutch, and the Jeep shot forward again. He was prepared this time.

"You can't say stuff like that while I'm concentrating. Besides, I make a mean grilled cheese. Just ask my gram." Her jaw set, and fire blazed in those jade-green eyes.

"Okay, duly noted." He waited until she was ready to try again, all too aware that she hadn't addressed the comment about knowing how to French kiss.

The Jeep lurched forward, stopping and starting but not stalling out.

"Good! Just ease off the clutch. Give it a little more gas." He coached her through the start, and the vehicle eased forward a few feet.

"I'm doing it!" She laughed out loud, a smile spreading from ear to ear.

"You sure are." The engine revved. "Now, clutch in, shift into second, and press on the gas while you ease off the clutch."

She did just that, and they picked up some speed. "It's coming back to me."

"See? You're doing great." Presley offered encouragement as she navigated through figure eights across the parking lot. A look of pure joy lit her face from within. When she wasn't frowning at something he said or did, she positively glowed.

She slowed to a stop and put the engine in neutral. "I did it." Her smile hit him like a ray of sunshine, lighting up his chest until it seemed like warmth flowed through his veins.

"You sure did. Now how about you drive us back to the Rose and take SoCal on a tour of town?"

"Right." Her smiled dimmed at the reminder of their ultimate goal, and he wanted to kick himself for taking away some of her shine. But business was business. Neither one of them was in this for pleasure.

"I've got to ask you one more question." His stomach clenched, not sure if he really wanted to go through this next bit with Dixie.

She turned toward him, waiting. "What?"

"You do know how to French kiss, right?" His hands immediately went up, protecting himself from the inevitable slap that was sure to follow a question like that.

Instead, she gripped the wheel, her knuckles going white from the effort. "Of course I do. What kind of question is that?"

"If things go well, you know SoCal is going to make a move on you. Remember, he's from the land of bikinis and beaches. I just want you to be ready for it, that's all."

Her shoulders sagged as she turned to face forward. "I'm sure I can handle it."

"Okay, as long as you're good to go." He nudged his chin toward the road. "All right. Then let's get back. It's probably better if we don't lock lips. It'll be easier to keep things business related."

Her hair flew around her shoulders as she whirled

to face him. "You think a kiss from you would scramble my brain, make me lose track of the goal at hand?"

Presley gave a slight shrug. "It's been known to happen."

"Get over yourself. You're not the gift to women that you think you are."

A chuckle escaped. She seemed so serious. "Never said I was."

"I've kissed plenty of boys." Dixie's lower lip stuck out in a pout.

"I'm sure you have. But we're not talking about boys here, we're talking about *men*." At the mention of the word *men*, her head snapped up. "As far as I know, you haven't been involved with anyone in quite a while. Do you really want your first kiss back out there, your warm-up kiss, to be the one you lay on SoCal?"

Her throat rose and fell as she swallowed and peered out the driver's-side window. "You kissed me last night."

"Yeah, but that didn't really count."

"I can't believe I'm even considering this." Her eyes rolled skyward. "Fine. Let's do this."

"Great, we'll get the awkward stuff out of the way. Then when SoCal leans in, you'll be ready for it. Sound good?" He leaned his seat back a couple notches and clasped his hands behind his head. "Go for it, Dixie Mae. Give me what you've got." As he waited, anticipating the moment her sweet lips would touch his, he reminded himself this was for research, for the Rose, a boost for Dixie's self-esteem. This had nothing to do with his recent appreciation of his fiery partner.

Hand pressed flat on the seat next to him, she leaned over the stick shift. "This is crazy." Her gaze swept over his face while she flicked her tongue over that full bottom lip.

Uh-oh. Things began to stir under his waistband. She leaned closer, her breath catching, her mouth so close to his. He closed his eyes, eager with anticipation. Much more eager than he should be for a kiss based purely on research.

Then the slightest flutter brushed against his lips. He wanted to open his eyes and tell her that kiss was the kind she'd give to her sister. But before he could, her lips were back on his, tentative, testing. It was the hottest kiss he'd ever had, and they hadn't even tangled tongues yet. His hand moved to cradle her head. She tilted her face to meet his mouth with hers again and again.

The arm she'd been resting on began to shake, and he pulled her over the center console, needing to be closer, wanting to feel all of her pressed against him. She'd started it, but he took control. He deepened the kiss, wanting to taste her. She parted her lips for him, and he savored the lingering sweetness of chocolate-chip cookies on her tongue. A groan began in the back of his throat. He shifted his hips, trying to make more room for her in the bucket seat. His hands roamed over her clothes. God, he wanted to feel her skin.

A thought that maybe things were going too far knocked at the edges of his brain. But then her fingers found their way under the edge of his shirt. She shifted positions, moving to half-straddle him as she tentatively moved her hands over his abs.

He reached a hand down to the seat lever. The seat slammed backward, putting him almost horizontal. Dixie's lips stayed with his, and she stretched out on top of him, lifting his shirt to fully expose his chest. The need to have her skin on his consumed him, and he focused all of his attention on easing her shirt up, higher and higher, until she'd pulled her arms through and it hung around her neck like a scarf. With the barrier out of the way, his hands roamed freely, skimming the soft skin over her ribs then lingering at the underwire barrier of her bra. He eased a finger underneath. Her kiss deepened. Two fingers. She moaned. With a quick flick, he released the hook and cupped her bare breast with his hand.

At the same moment, a horn blared. Presley looked up as a semi roared by.

Dixie froze for a split second then dove into the driver's seat. "Oh my gosh. Someone saw us! What in the world are we doing?" She shoved her arms back through her armholes and pulled her tank down. Her bra still hung from her shoulders, making her shirt stick out in front.

"Calm down. Nobody saw anything. You okay?" Presley raised his seat back and yanked his shirt down.

"I can't believe this." Dixie tried to fasten her bra behind her, fumbling with the strap. The color of her cheeks almost matched the pink of her shirt.

"Let me help." Presley took hold of the strap, easily hooking it back together. "It was just a trucker. He probably saw something happening and wanted to be an ass. Nobody knows it was you and me."

"Well, they know it was you. Who else drives a huge Jeep like this?"

"Settle down. It's going to be fine." He took in a deep breath. Dammit, he was still hard. Shifting in his seat, he tried to catch her flailing arms in his hands.

"This is all your fault." She whirled to face him. "You and your stupid kiss critique."

"Hey, it was your idea. And if it makes you feel any better, I think you're more than ready for a peck from SoCal."

She stilled, and the glare she gave him could have burned through the metal bumper on the back of his Jeep and then some.

Without another word, she slammed the Jeep into gear. The vehicle shimmied while she tried to find the catch point between the gas and the clutch then shot onto the highway.

It was for the best. He and Dixie worked better when that thin, hostile veil sat between them as opposed to the chemistry he'd uncovered and would now need to try to avoid.

chapter
TEN

DIXIE SMOOTHED HER HANDS OVER THE HEM OF HER TOP while she skimmed the crowd, searching for Chandler. What had gotten into her back there? She'd never felt that kind of thrill before. So titillating, so forbidden, so…she searched for the right word. *Wrong.* What had happened between her and Presley was just plain wrong. Presley was the kind of man to fantasize over—the kind to inspire wicked daydreams and restless nights—not the kind of man Dixie needed in real life. She needed someone stable, someone who wanted to settle down—basically the polar opposite of a guy like Presley.

Thankfully he disappeared as soon as they got to the Rose. He was probably out back by the stage, getting ready to announce the next band. Amen for that. She hadn't spent much time before today alone with the man. Seeing him dwarf her gram's front room and the one-on-one driving lesson had thrown her off a bit. Presley had charm oozing out of his pores and knew how to turn it on at will. She should know better than to let it affect her. The poor sorority sisters that hung around him like a pack of groupies were a whole different story. She'd just keep reminding herself of that every time she had to spend more than a microsecond with him.

As she nodded to herself, solidifying her inner resolve, a

hand landed on the small of her back. Goose bumps pebbled her skin. She whirled around, a searing scolding on the tip of her tongue, ready to unleash on Presley Walker.

"Cat got your tongue?" Chandler smiled down at her, a teasing spark in his eyes.

She let out a gasp. "Sorry, you caught me off guard." Why was a teeny part of her disappointed it wasn't Presley standing behind her? She wadded that thought up like a used tissue and tossed it aside.

Chandler's hand lingered on her waist. "You ready to show me around?"

"Of course." Dixie slipped back into friendly hostess mode. She might have lost some of her enthusiasm for taking Chandler on that tour, but she wouldn't let it affect the good manners her mama had instilled. "The Jeep's parked around by the side. Let's get going."

Chandler followed her down the hall and out the side door. Presley's Jeep sat next to a mesquite tree, sparkling in the late-afternoon sun. He must have run it through the car wash before he picked her up. How had she not noticed that before?

"Let me get the door for you." Chandler's long strides let him reach the door before her. He held it open while she climbed inside and settled herself in the driver's seat.

"Thanks." Her cheeks burned at the memory of what she and Presley had done in that exact same vehicle not even twenty minutes before. A mistake, it was just a mistake. Dixie refocused, trying to remember Presley's lesson as Chandler rounded the front of the Jeep and climbed in next to her. Clutch in, brake off. Ease off the clutch and onto the gas.

"Thanks again for taking me around town. I think I've got the prettiest tour guide in Texas." Chandler pulled the door shut and buckled up.

Dixie's stomach flip-flopped. Her vision blurred. Why had she parked so close to the side of the building? What if she took out a wall or, even worse, Angelo's barbecue spit?

"You ready?" Chandler's hand landed on her thigh.

His touch surprised her. Enough that her foot slammed on the gas. Enough that she accidentally threw the gear shift into first and let go of the steering wheel. Enough that the Jeep flew forward, crashing through the split-rail fence of Pork Chop's pigpen.

It all happened so fast, she didn't have time to react. Before she had a chance to gather her wits about her, Chandler's hands brushed the hair out of her face.

"Are you okay?" His voice came from far away, like the end of a long tunnel. She saw his lips move, but they seemed out of sync with his words.

As the realization of what had just happened tiptoed into her conscious mind, she put her hands over her eyes. "Oh my gosh. What have I done?"

"You okay?" Chandler pressed.

She took a quick inventory. "Yes, I'm fine. But the Jeep...and the fence..."

Her fingers spread, giving her a first look at the damage she'd caused. The Jeep rested on top of the smashed fence rails. Pork Chop hunkered down in the far corner of the pen. She'd probably scared the oink right out of the poor pig.

"That's a hell of a way to start a tour." Chandler

grinned, obviously unharmed. "Should we see what kind of damage we need to deal with?"

"You're okay?"

"I've been through much worse. Come on, I'll help you down." He held out a hand, and she scrambled over the center console to exit through the passenger door.

Standing next to him, she evaluated the sorry state of the fence line. At least the Jeep didn't seem to be dinged up. Presley would probably never forgive her if she left a lasting impression on his babe magnet.

Chandler walked around the vehicle. "You want to get in and I'll see if I can push you back over the fence?"

"I suppose." She clambered into the driver's seat once more and slid the stick shift into neutral.

"What the hell is going on here?" Dixie cringed at the fury in Presley's voice. She looked over in time to see him closing in on the driver's-side window. "You want to tell me how my Jeep got hung up on the pigpen?"

"It was an accident." She pressed her hands on her face in an attempt to put out the flames burning over her cheekbones. "I told you I didn't feel comfortable driving your Jeep."

"Is there a problem?" Chandler leaned against the hood and faced Presley.

"Hell yeah, there's a problem. My Jeep is balancing on the rail of a pigpen."

"And as Ms. King said, it was an accident. Why was she driving your vehicle in the first place?"

"It's fine. Presley loaned me his Jeep so I could

take you on that tour around town." She didn't want to admit that she was too embarrassed to cart him around in her hand-me-down minivan.

"Sorry, Dixie." Presley shook his head. "Next time we'll practice more or find you an automatic."

"That sounds fair." Chandler nodded then turned to Presley. "Now, do you want to help me get her off?"

A naughty smirk lit up Presley's face. Dixie shook her head in warning, willing Presley not to take that lead and run with it. He cocked a brow and shot her a devilish grin. "Usually I'd say that's a one-man job, but I think you could use an extra hand in this here situation."

Dixie growled, ready to launch herself through the window to strangle him. "Presley, can you please be an adult about this?"

He tipped the brim of his hat her way. "Your wish is my command. Now why don't you hold on tight while we two strong, virile men get you off, Ms. King?"

Chandler let out an uncomfortable laugh, clearly not sure what to make of the banter. Dixie white-knuckled the steering wheel, pretending it was Presley's neck she gripped between her hands.

Presley and Chandler put their palms on the front of the hood and pushed. The Jeep rocked backward but didn't dislodge from the rail.

"Let's go again." Presley nodded toward Chandler. "On three, okay?"

Chandler glanced up, meeting Dixie's gaze through the windshield. She mouthed the words "I'm sorry," hoping he could read her lips through the now dusty, mud-splattered windshield. He grinned back at her, and her chest warmed.

"Throw it in reverse, will ya?" Presley strained, putting all of his weight against the Jeep.

Dixie fumbled with the gear shift. The engine groaned and screeched, metal grinding against metal, as the transmission slammed into reverse. She tried to find the balance between easing on the gas and letting go of the clutch.

"More gas. Give it more," Presley coached.

She did. The engine revved. The wheels spun. The Jeep gained purchase and bounced over the fence rail. Dixie let it roll clear then put her foot on the brake and shifted back into neutral, pleased with herself for doing her part. Convinced the vehicle wasn't going anywhere, she finally looked up, ready to celebrate their minor success. Two strangers stared back at her, covered in mud and muck. Dixie slapped a hand to her mouth to prevent desperate laughter from escaping.

"You have got to be kidding me." Presley swiped at his face, doing more to spread the mud around than clear it away. "Nice job there, Fireball."

She climbed out of the Jeep, letting the door close behind her. "I'm so sorry. I didn't mean to spray you with mud."

"Nothing a little water won't wash off." Chandler didn't look half as bad as Presley. "Good work." He held a hand out to Presley.

Presley shot a glance to Dixie then clasped Chandler's hand in his. "Thanks for your help." Presley turned toward Dixie. "Why don't you go turn the hose on him out back while I see if I can patch up the pigpen? Y'all still have that little tour around town you wanted to take, right?"

"I'm not sure I should try to take the Jeep again." Dixie dangled his keys from her finger.

"We can take my car," Chandler offered. "Can we stop by the bed-and-breakfast so I can take a quick shower before we go?"

"Sure. I'll stay here and help Presley. You want to come back and pick me up—"

"No." Presley practically shouted. "No need to stick around. Why don't you go back with him while he gets cleaned up and I'll take care of things here?"

Dixie glared at him. She didn't need to be seen at the B and B with Chandler. Tongues would be wagging all over town if people saw her riding shotgun with Presley earlier and then caught a glimpse of her going into the B and B with the visitor from California.

"It would save me a trip back out of town to pick you up." Chandler shrugged. "What do you say, Dixie?"

"She says yes," Presley answered for her. "Now you two kids go on and have fun."

Dixie opened her mouth to protest as Presley walked by. He tucked his chin against his chest and muttered, "While he's in the shower, see if you can find any paperwork in his room about why he's in town."

Her fists flew to her hips, and she whispered, "I will not."

"I've gotta say, you're not very good at this," he shot back.

"I don't want to be good at this. I'm so far out of my comfort zone right now I feel like I'm on another planet." Her cheeks burned. Yes, she was happy to help save the Rose. But they had absolutely no proof anything was even going on. And she wasn't ready to compromise her morals or her dignity on a hunch. At least not any more than she already had.

"Fine. Then I'll have to handle things on my own." His eyes narrowed. "Now if you'll excuse me, I have a pigpen to patch."

Dixie moved out of his way.

"We still on for that tour?" Chandler ambled over, the warm grin on his face a welcome distraction.

"Sure. Why don't we head to the B and B? I've got a few things I can take care of in town while you change into some fresh clothes."

"Sounds good." He dug his keys out of his pocket and handed them to her along with his phone. "Do you mind holding onto these for me for a minute? I think I'd better find that hose Presley mentioned. I drove my uncle's Caddy into town, and he'd kill me if I got mud all over his white leather seats."

"Sure, it's just around the corner." She pointed to the back of the building. "I'll go grab you a towel."

Chandler took off around the corner of the building, leaving Dixie standing there wondering. Could the uncle he mentioned be the investor Doc had warned them about? She shook the thought out of her head almost as soon as it appeared. No. Presley had to be wrong. And she'd prove it to him.

But how?

⎯⎯⎯⧸⧸⫶⎯⎯⎯

Presley stomped all the way to the pole barn the Rose used for storage. Then he stomped some more. He wasn't sure what had him more upset—having to patch up the pigpen Dixie had crashed through, the fact she didn't believe him about SoCal, or the realization that he'd developed a crippling case of jealousy ever since they'd locked lips.

The guy's sudden reappearance at the Rose after all these years couldn't be a coincidence. He was up to something, and it couldn't be good. There was no way he was an aspiring chili cook-off competitor. He was staying at the bed-and-breakfast, for crap's sake. Every other competitor traveled with a trailer full of gear and had either pitched a tent or set up their camper in the back field. It was only a matter of time before SoCal revealed his true intentions, and Presley planned on being there when he did.

But first, to secure the pig. They'd had enough trouble over the years with Pork Chop's predecessor escaping and terrorizing Conroe County that Presley knew he had to make that priority number one. If only Dixie were more willing to work with him on getting to the bottom of the potential investor scheme. He shook his head. Didn't matter. He'd handle it on his own. He didn't need her help.

Fifteen minutes later he made his way back to the pigpen empty-handed. How could they not have a single piece of lumber he could use to patch up the fence? Angelo had secured a lead to Pork Chop's collar and the other end to a fence post. That would work for about another ten minutes. Even as he stood at the fence, thinking about his options, Pork Chop nibbled on the nylon lead. Damn pig. He didn't have time to track down a piece of wood—they had a festival to run. That left him with only one feasible option. He'd have to get the pig to his folks' house. They had plenty of room there to pen her for a day or two until he had a chance to patch things up.

His gaze skimmed over the parking lot. Charlie's

truck was parked back at her place, and Beck had taken the trailer with him on his road trip to New York. Sure, he could probably find someone inside who could loan him a pickup for an hour. But that would require entering the building. In his present mud-covered state, he'd prefer to keep to himself.

"Come on, girl." He made his way through the pen toward Pork Chop. "You want to ride shotgun in a Jeep?"

She was surprisingly accommodating for a change, nudging her snout against his jeans, probably searching for a treat.

"I've got nothing for you. But if we can get out of here without causing a scene, I promise I'll find you something once we get you settled."

Pork Chop grunted, and he chose to take that as agreement. He untied the lead from the post and gave it a gentle tug. Pork Chop ambled along behind him toward the Jeep. Should he try to stuff her in the back, or would she be better off riding shotgun? Jinx had managed to cram her in the front seat of her vehicle last fall. But that was before Pork Chop had gotten so big. He eyed the small cargo area.

"What's your plan?" Angelo watched from the back steps of the Rose.

"What's it look like?" Presley reached the passenger side.

Angelo tucked a hand towel into his waistband. "Hell if I know. You taking a new girl out on the town?"

"Ha. That's a good one." He grinned and clucked his tongue. "Now get down here and help me shove this gal into the front seat, will ya?"

"You're joking."

Presley took in a breath and rose to his full height. "Do I look like I'm joking?"

"You're going to get your seats all dirty."

"My seat's already full of mud. What's a little more?"

Angelo rounded the Jeep and cocked a brow. "You're telling me you're going to put that pig in your Jeep?"

"That's the plan."

"Dude, you are nuttier than a squirrel turd."

"Just hoist her up there, will ya?" Presley leaned down to get his hands under Pork Chop's front end. Angelo shook his head but bent over to grab the back half. "On three, okay?"

Angelo nodded, his face cheek to cheek with the business end of Pork Chop's backside.

"One, two, three."

With a grunt, they levered the pig up. She squealed as her feet left the ground and kicked out in protest.

"Hang onto her." Presley scrambled to retain his hold.

The pig rose into the air. Once she had her front feet on the seat, Presley moved around back to help Angelo finish the job. Pork Chop fell into the Jeep snout first. Her head bumped the steering wheel, setting off the loud blare of the horn.

"Dammit, get her off the horn. Everyone's going to hear all this ruckus." Presley tried to wedge a hand in between Pork Chop and the wheel without success.

Angelo backed away. "Looks like you're all set. I just remembered I've got some biscuits in the oven. I'd better get back inside and check on 'em."

"Yeah, okay." Presley waved him on. "Go ahead." Angelo was as likely to actually have biscuits in the oven as Presley was to be on his way to church.

He tried adjusting the pig. She turned around, her rump bumping against the horn once more.

"Settle down, girl." Presley slapped his palm against the dash. "You don't have to pitch a hissy fit."

By the time he got the pig buckled in, quite a crowd of onlookers had gathered on the front porch of the Rose, exactly what he'd hoped to avoid. Pork Chop had probably summoned all of them by honking the damn horn. He backed into the parking lot and turned the Jeep around.

"What are all y'all looking at?" He gave them his best ain't-got-a-care-in-the-world grin. "Haven't you ever seen a pig riding shotgun?" Before anyone could give him hell, he let the tires spin in the gravel and fishtailed toward the road. Charlie had better appreciate what he was going through for her.

His cell rang. Speak of the devil. Charlie.

"Hey, Sis. How's it going?" He tried to sound casual. No need to tell her he'd been skin to skin with her favorite waitress an hour ago.

"Good. Beck's fine, and we got Baby Back settled."

"How's my nephew enjoying being on the road?"

Charlie groaned. "Baby Sully's just like his grandpa—he's not enjoying being far from home."

"Sounds like both of his grandpas." Presley chuckled to himself.

"How are things going there?"

Should he tell her he was on his way to Mom and Dad's with her pig in the front seat? Because her employee crashed his Jeep through the pigpen? While she was trying to out an investor who had secret plans to build a country and western theme park and competing honky-tonk in their backyard?

No. He could handle this. He *would* handle it. Anything he told Charlie would just get her all strung out. When there was nothing she could do about it from so far away, what was the point? He'd have to convince Dixie to take another shot at cracking SoCal for info.

"Everything's going great here."

"Are you and Dixie getting along?" Her voice dropped a notch at the end, leaving him no doubt she had no faith in his ability to work with Dixie Mae King unless she was there to supervise.

His gut hitched into a bowline knot, and he tried to laugh off her concern. "Of course. I can get along with anyone, you know that."

"Presley..." She sounded way too much like Ma when she did that.

"Honest. We're staying out of each other's way. It's all good."

"Okaaaaaaaay..."

Obviously she didn't believe him. Time to change the subject. "Hey, I'm about to pull into Mom and Dad's, so I'm going to let you go. Give Sully a big hug from me. And give your hubby a big wet one."

Charlie laughed. "Oh, I'm sure he'll appreciate that. Call me if you need anything, okay? I'm serious."

"I will, I will. Relax and try to enjoy yourself a little bit at the award ceremony. Dixie and I have everything under control."

"All right. Thanks again for stepping up. I'll check in again in a day or two. Love you, Pres."

"Love you too." He ended the call. Everything was

under control. That wasn't the first lie he'd told today. His mom had always warned him telling lies was like throwing a boomerang. The better you got at it, the more likely they were to come right back at you and thump you upside the head.

chapter
ELEVEN

Dixie sat with her back pressed against the high-back chair in the formal sitting room of the bed-and-breakfast. Her toes didn't touch the ground, and it made her feel like a child to have her feet swinging out in front of her, like she was sitting in one of those big, oversized Adirondack chairs she'd seen at a gift shop down in Galveston. She'd planned on walking down the main street to get a few errands done while Chandler got cleaned up, but then she got trapped by conversation. Mrs. Knotts smiled at her over her glass of tea. Dixie smiled back. If she drank any more tea today, she'd absolutely explode.

"It's so nice of you to take Chandler on a tour of town." Mrs. Knotts took a dainty draw on her straw.

Dixie crossed her ankles. "It's the least I can do now that he's back. He seems to have grown into a nice guy."

Mrs. Knotts arched a brow. "And very good-looking, I might add."

The sip of tea she'd just taken diverted down her windpipe, and Dixie coughed. Tea sprayed from between clenched lips. She was used to people giving her a hard time about her perpetual single status at the bar. But she hadn't expected the local lodging owner to get in on the action. While she reached for a napkin, Dixie summoned her composure.

"Oh, honey"—Mrs. Knotts swatted at Dixie's knee—"you know everyone around here is just pulling for you to find your own special someone."

Everyone around here. Since when did her love life, or lack thereof, become the preferred talk of the town? She took the high road—meaning she chose to completely ignore the comment. "He's interested in getting reacquainted with Holiday."

Mrs. Knotts nodded. "It's so nice he found his way back here after all these years. Why, he's been full of questions since he arrived."

"Really? What kind of questions?" She leaned forward, eager to find out if Mrs. Knotts would say anything to add to Presley's mistrust. Immediately, she righted herself and let her back rest against the chair. Presley had his suspicions. But what had Chandler done so far? Shown some interest in the town. That wasn't a crime. Besides, he was the first man in quite some time to show any kind of interest in her. She wouldn't believe the worst about him without some kind of proof.

"He's been asking about the tourists that come to the Rose. Whether it's a big draw, if we're busy year-round, if there are other lodging options around." She set her glass down on a handmade doily, like the ones Mrs. Mitchell tried to teach Gram to make once. "I didn't think much of it at first, but when he started asking about hotels and whether I thought Holiday could support another bed-and-breakfast, I had to bite my tongue. Jim and I have had the only B and B in town for so long. I suppose it's not very friendly of me, but I decided not to offer him a second helping of my huckleberry cobbler."

Dixie's head spun. If Chandler had been asking about lodging, maybe Presley was onto something after all. Although she'd never stoop so low as to ransack a stranger's room while he hopped in the shower. It was bad enough Mrs. Knotts was probably already wondering why in the world Chandler had returned with Dixie in tow. She didn't need to give her a reason to start any gossip by accompanying the man to his room. Even the thought of such a thing had her heating up like she was suffering from one of those hot flashes her mama complained about.

"Are you okay, Dixie?" Mrs. Knotts leaned forward, concern furrowing her brow.

"I'm sorry, what?" Pulled from her thoughts, Dixie wondered how long she'd zoned out on the conversation.

"I asked if you're okay."

"Oh, yes, I'm fine. What were you saying?" Dixie promised herself she'd put any thoughts of Presley being right right out of her head.

"I said my huckleberry cobbler recipe is a family heirloom. It belonged to my great-grandmother who came over from Germany. Why, my mother had a copy in my great-grandmother's own writing. Isn't that amazing?"

Dixie nodded. Usually she enjoyed relaxing over a glass of sweet tea on a sizzling summer afternoon. But she needed to get a move on. Presley could only be expected to hold down the fort for so long, and she was bound and determined to get Chandler his tour around town. Not only did she want to prove Presley wrong about Chandler's intentions, she also was eager to find out if that warmth she'd sensed between them might lead to something more. At least she wouldn't have to battle the stick shift. Chandler said his uncle had loaned him his car

to make the drive from California to Texas. Dixie
had never seen anything like it. And after hanging out
in Holiday for her whole life, that was saying a lot.
Chandler didn't know what year the vintage Cadillac
convertible was, but that didn't matter. Folks seemed
to pay more attention to the baby-blue paint job and
the three-foot longhorns mounted to the hood.

Before she got caught zoning out again, Chandler
sauntered down the front steps, hair still damp from a
fresh shower. Dixie stood, glad for an excuse to escape
the small talk with Mrs. Knotts. Chandler rubbed a
hand behind his neck.

"Sorry for keeping you waiting so long." The half
grin on his face erased the layers of anxiety that had
mounted while Dixie listened to Mrs. Knotts. "You
still have time for that tour?"

Dixie stood. "As long as we make it a quick one, I
should be fine."

"Good. Shall we?" He offered his arm.

"Let's." Dixie linked her arm with his. An appealing blend of shower gel and shaving cream drifted
past her nose. He smelled so…so…so unlike Presley.
Forcing her disappointment down, she plastered on a
smile. She'd make the most of her time with Chandler
and see if she could get a handle on his intentions.

"You two have a good time." Mrs. Knotts picked
the serving tray up off the table. "Make sure you show
him the footbridge down by the river. It's the best
place to see the rapids."

Dixie's face heated. The footbridge was a popular
destination for couples who wanted a private place
to canoodle under a canopy of weeping willows. Or

at least it had been back in high school. She'd never been invited to meet a boy on the bridge—a popular ritual for many of her classmates on a Friday night after the football game, of course.

The last place she needed to take Chandler was the footbridge, at least not until she'd figured out why he'd really come back to town. Although seeing him in a fresh pair of jeans and a chest-hugging T-shirt did give her pause.

She shook the last thought out of her head. What had gotten into her lately? First the inexcusable dalliance with Presley and now this? Vowing to enjoy the man's attention, if only for what remained of the afternoon, she gave Mrs. Knotts a tight-lipped smile and followed Chandler through the heavy door.

—#—

"What the hell do you think you're doing?"

Presley cringed as his older brother Waylon came out of the house and crossed the gravel drive. "Had a problem with the pigpen. This is only a temporary thing, okay?"

"This is a cattle ranch, dumbass. Not a pig sanctuary." Waylon scuffed his boot in the dirt.

"I know. I said temporary. It means not permanent, short-term. Right?" He stepped past his brother to reach the other side of the vehicle. Pork Chop couldn't have looked more uncomfortable if she'd tried. Her rump sat half on, half off the seat. She had her front hooves pressed against the dash, and her head leaned against the window frame. "How about we get you out of here, girl?"

"Yesterday you brought over that demon boar, and today you're saddling me with Pork Chop? I've got a problem with this, Bro. You need to find another solution."

Presley took his time turning around to face his brother. "Don't you think I tried to come up with another solution already? You're my last resort as it is."

"Well, find one that's laster." Waylon pressed a palm against the door of the Jeep, preventing Presley from opening it.

"*Laster*?" Presley squinted up at his oldest brother. "You learn big words like that when you were off getting your master's?"

Waylon shrugged. "Figured if I dumbed things down maybe you'd get the message and get this damn pig out of here."

"That was a good one." Presley clapped a hand around his brother's arm, trying to knock it away from the door. Waylon didn't budge. "Come on, I promise it's only until I can find someone to fix the pigpen. Dixie did a real number on it, and I need to reset some posts. I wouldn't ask you just for myself, but think of it as a favor for Charlie and Beck. How do you think they're going to feel if they come back from New York and the whole festival imploded because Pork Chop didn't have a place to stay?"

"Two days." Waylon's arm fell away from the Jeep.

Presley opened the door, and Pork Chop clambered down. "Two days, meaning have it done by Tuesday?"

Waylon didn't answer. His dark eyes glared out from under the brim of his work hat.

"I just figured since today is almost over, that would give me Sunday and Monday to make the repair and then get PC resettled in her pen on Tuesday."

"You've got forty-eight hours." Waylon spun

around, his boot kicking up the top layer of dirt as he stalked toward the barn.

"Well, that went better than I expected," Presley muttered to the pig. "Let's go see if we can find you a safe place to bunk down for forty-seven hours and fifty-eight minutes." He led Pork Chop to an empty stall in the barn. "I think you'll be comfortable here." He filled up a bucket with water then figured he'd better find his brother and check in on Ham Bone before he took off.

He found Waylon shoveling manure out of one of the horse stalls. Presley had never particularly enjoyed that part of ranch life. His brawny older brother was much better suited to it. Waylon actually enjoyed the ranch life so much he'd gotten an advanced degree so he'd be in a better position to expand the family compound and keep the Walker name going strong.

"I got Pork Chop settled in."

Waylon grunted.

"Hey, I've been meaning to ask you. How's Ham Bone doing?"

"Why don't you go see for yourself?" Waylon didn't pause.

"Yeah, okay, I guess I will." Presley clapped his brother on the shoulder. "Thanks again. I'll be back for Pork Chop faster than a goose can shit grass."

"You'd better."

Family. Can't live with 'em, can't live...well, Presley would leave it at that. He and Waylon had always had a contentious relationship. Being stuck in the middle hadn't been easy. With Waylon, Cash, and Statler being older and Strait and Charlie being younger, he often bounced between the groups, picking sides based on whatever suited him best. Usually he tagged along with the older ones, seeing as how their antics were more fun.

Dwight told him he'd left Ham Bone in the old pigpen. As Presley approached, the boar did a belly flop into a giant puddle of mud. Droplets splashed over the fence, splattering Presley's already mud-covered shirt. "I see you missed me, big guy."

He patted down his pockets, searching for some kind of treat to give the pig. All he came up with was a protein bar. Hell, worth a shot. He peeled away the wrapper. Ham Bone's ears perked. Presley pursed his lips together and made kissy sounds, trying to draw the boar close. Ham Bone appeared interested and tentatively inched near. In the light of day, the massive boar seemed even larger. What was Boss Hawg thinking trying to go on the road with an animal like that? Before he realized what he was doing, Presley reached a hand through the fence to scratch Ham Bone behind the ears. While the pig gobbled up the rest of the protein bar, Presley ran a hand over his coarse hair. How did he get swindled into caring for not one but two pigs this weekend? Waylon had always been better with the animals.

"See ya around, Ham Bone." Presley made his way back to his Jeep. With Dixie running reconnaissance this afternoon, he needed to get cleaned up and head back to the Rose. Wouldn't do any good to have her busting his balls if the items on her spreadsheet didn't get crossed off before she returned.

An hour later he sat at the bar, freshly showered, with a cold mug of Lone Star in his hands. Thankfully the Rose ran like a well-oiled machine. Even the temp help seemed to know what they were doing. With an hour to kill before his next emcee duties started, he leaned against the bar and took in the scene. Folks from all walks of life sat around chatting, drinking, enjoying their surroundings. Music from the outdoor band filtered in through the open screens. The ceiling fans spun around, creating a nice breeze, and Presley wanted to pat himself on the back for a job well done. Not that he'd had much to do with things, but still, he was on watch, and there hadn't been any issues. That had to count for something.

As his gaze drifted from group to group, he caught a glimpse of Leoni gliding through the crowd. What did a guy like Boss do to deserve a dame like Leoni? She must have spotted him. With a quick wave, she headed his way.

"Hi there. How are you enjoying the festival?" he asked as she reached him at the bar.

"It's been great. Did you see how many chili competitors you've got out there?"

"Impressive, right?"

"Sure is. I don't know how you'll ever pick a winner."

Presley leaned closer. "Thankfully I don't have to."

"Oh yeah?" Leoni grabbed a handful of the snack mix Charlie liked to keep on the bar. "Who's the lucky judge?"

"It's a group. As far as I know, Dixie set it up. We've got Blanche Mayfield, the mayor of Holiday and two-time winner of the butter-churning competition at the Conroe County Fair."

Leoni giggled. "Really?"

"Aw, you bet. She's joined by her husband, Buster, whose fifteen minutes of fame came from the time he appeared on an episode of *Dallas* in the eighties doing duck calls."

"Real duck calls?"

Presley nodded. "As real as it gets. And finally, the last judge they got is Grady Groveland, the cook at the diner downtown. You wouldn't expect it, but his chili has won worldwide awards."

Leoni wrapped a hand around his arm. "I had no idea I was surrounded by so many celebrities."

"Yes, ma'am. Holiday may not be a big mark on the map, but we definitely leave our mark on the state of Texas."

She took a loud slurp through her straw, signaling the end of her drink.

"You need a refill there?" Presley motioned Shep over.

"That would be great. Margarita on the rocks, please."

Shep nodded then moved away to fix her drink.

"So when are you going to show me this mysterious fiddle you've created?" she asked.

Wow, she remembered. Presley's heart surged. "Oh, anytime. I'd love for you to check it out."

"How about tonight?" She took a sip from the fresh drink Shep set in front of her.

"Tonight?" Presley gritted his teeth. He'd promised Dixie he'd stick around the Rose and keep an eye on things until she got back. But having an acclaimed fiddle player try her hand at his hand-hewn creation would be a dream come true. "Don't you have a set scheduled later?"

"Sure do. But I can meet you here after if you want me to take a look."

"That would be...wow, that would be great if you don't mind."

"I'm looking forward to it already." She set her half-full glass on the bar. "Meet you here after my set wraps up?"

Presley nodded. Dixie would be back by then. She'd owe him an hour or two off since he'd been keeping things in check during the day. A little fiddlin' would definitely improve his day, and having the chance to get Leoni's opinion would let him know if he was onto something with his wish for a career change or if he'd be better off sticking to liquor sales.

He'd been getting restless. Seeing his siblings make lifelong commitments and start families of their own had made him realize he wasn't necessarily destined to be a Peter Pan playboy who never wanted to grow up. When he'd found his granddad's woodworking equipment and started messing around with it, he'd discovered a part of himself that wanted more than to work all week and party all weekend. Once upon a time, his granddad's fiddles had been used worldwide. But without someone to carry on the name, the company had died alongside him. If Presley had his way, he'd resurrect it and rebuild the reputation his granddad had worked so hard to attain.

But all of that hinged on whether what he'd created was any good. Hopefully Leoni could shed some light on that question. And hopefully Dixie would be back in time with some answers of her own about SoCal's plans. Convinced that the evening would provide all kinds of enlightenment, Presley took another swig of his beer. Charlie had nothing to worry about. He had things well under control.

chapter
TWELVE

Dixie pointed out the sights to Chandler as they passed through town. "Whitey's Western Wear is over there, and the Armadillo Antique store is on your right. I used to live in the apartment upstairs until I had to move in with my gram." The words shot out of her mouth before she could stop herself. Great, that made her sound like a real vixen. Every femme fatale she knew lived with her grandmother...not.

Thankfully Chandler either didn't notice or chose not to acknowledge her revelation. "How about dining options? Where do the fine folks in Holiday go if they're in the mood for a nice night out?"

"Oh, there's the diner. It serves incredible pancakes. And the barbecue place next door does an okay job on its brisket. Although the best meal in town is definitely at the Rose. Angelo's received awards for his ribs."

Chandler eased the car to a stop in front of the diner. "What if a guy wants to impress a gal with a fancy dinner out?"

Dixie's heart skittered around in her chest like a pat of butter on a hot skillet. "You mean a place with chairs instead of benches?"

He grinned. "That's the idea. Maybe a little candlelight."

She folded her hands together, trying to keep herself still. "And cloth tablecloths?"

"An extensive wine list."

If she was reading the signs right, he fully intended on asking her to dinner. "Gosh, the closest place around Holiday would have to be in Farley. They've got the Farley Inn right downtown. Of course, San Antonio and Austin aren't that far away either."

"The Farley Inn." Chandler nodded. "Sounds like the place to take a beautiful woman I'd like to impress."

A flush crept up her neck. She tried to will it away, but the burn swept over her cheeks and up to her hairline.

"So what else is there to do around Holiday?" He eased the car back onto the road. "I haven't noticed a bowling alley, any kind of entertainment venues, or clubs. Where do the kids hang out?"

"There's a teen center not too far away. We also have a bowling alley right next door to the Suds Club. There are only a couple of lanes, but most people don't mind waiting since it's attached to the bingo parlor too."

Chandler laughed. "Sounds like fun."

Was he mocking her? She couldn't tell, but she felt the need to defend her little town. "We have a ton of festivals all year-round. The Jingle Bell Jamboree, the Father's Day Fajita Festival, the Founder's Day Parade. There's always something going on in Holiday."

"That's how I remember it. Seems like it could use some additional entertainment venues though. So where to next?"

What did he mean about needing more entertainment venues? Dixie wanted to believe Chandler only had the best of intentions. But Presley's suspicions crowded between them like a third wheel on the big bench seat, and she vowed to get to the bottom of them. "Let's head out of town, and we can drive by some of the bigger ranches.

Have you been back by your old place since you've been in town?"

"Not yet"—he navigated the big boat of a car onto the two-lane road out of town—"but it's still in the family. My grandfather passed, but my dad owns a share along with my great-uncle."

"The uncle who owns this car?"

Chandler nodded. "He loved it here. Then he joined a country and western band and moved to Nashville. Now he's retired and lives out in California. But he's been talking about moving back."

"Then we should drive by and take a look at his place." Dixie twisted her torso to face him.

His hands gripped the steering wheel hard. "That's okay. I'm not sure I remember exactly where it is."

In a move she didn't think she had the guts for, she reached out to pat his shoulder. "We've got time. If you're here all week, maybe we can go later on."

The tight-lipped smile he gave her belied the level of enthusiasm he attempted with words. "That would be great."

"Oh, to your right we've got part of the Walker ranch. They've got one of the largest cattle operations in the Hill Country."

"Walker…" Chandler's brow furrowed.

"Yep. Charlie Walker owns the Rose. Although she married Beck Holiday a few years ago, so she's technically a Holiday now. And then there's the rest."

"The rest?" Chandler cast a quick glance her way.

"Poor Charlie has five brothers: Waylon, Cash, Statler, Strait, and Presley." As Presley's name rolled off her lips, her chest tightened.

"Presley Walker, the local pig wrangler and pepper eater, right?"

Dixie's skin prickled. Why did she suddenly feel the need to defend the man she'd locked lips with earlier? She didn't owe Presley anything, much less a loyal word, but it still chafed her that Chandler would mock one of Holiday's own.

"He's much better at his real job."

"Which is?"

"Liquor rep. He's the right guy to know if you're wondering what the most popular flavored vodka is."

"I'll keep that in mind." He covered her hand with his on the seat between them. She waited for the same sort of tingles she felt at Presley's touch, but the only sensation she had was the weight of his hand on hers. "What's that over there?"

She tore her gaze away from their hands. "Oh, that's Kermit's place. He's got a Christmas tree farm on most of his land and runs a tiny conservation effort on the rest."

"Oh yeah. I think I remember cutting down a tree there a time or two. As I recall, a little sliver of his property runs right by the Rose."

"That's right. Folks have been after him for years to sell." Should she share her dreams with Chandler, or would he think they were silly? He said he had development experience. Wouldn't hurt to get his professional opinion. Dixie swallowed her apprehension. This weekend was about taking chances. "I think it would be the perfect spot for a little retail place."

"Oh yeah? What do you have in mind?" His smile of encouragement opened the floodgates.

"A place where local artists can work and sell their wares. Kind of a combination of studio and retail. I've seen that done in other towns and have always thought it would be a hit in Holiday."

"Are you an artist?"

She shrugged. "Kind of. I make jewelry. Earrings, necklaces, bracelets." She dangled her wrist in front of him. Her silver chain bracelet slid down her arm.

"Nice. I just wonder if Holiday has the kind of traffic to support an effort like that."

"I've sold some online. But I'd love to go full time and find a way to showcase other local artists." Dixie's lips screwed into a frown. "Maybe it would work out, maybe not. I suppose it doesn't matter anyway since Kermit's not planning on selling. He runs a conservation effort on the rest of his property and is pretty committed to it."

Chandler's patronizing smile faded into a slight frown. "What kind of conservation effort?"

"You probably wouldn't believe me if I told you." She could hardly believe it herself. But a few of Gram's friends had decided that due to the lack of eligible elder bachelors, Kermit had become target numero uno for the desperate set of older women in town. They'd been taking turns pestering him for the past six months by bringing him home-cooked meals twice a week. Gram had even joined in on the effort, and last time she went out there she spent a couple of hours hearing all about Kermit's commitment to save the local horned toad population.

"Try me." He slowed the car to a crawl.

"You asked for it." Dixie twisted to face him. "Kermit is committed to saving Holiday's population of horned toads."

"Seriously?"

She nodded.

"What exactly is a horned toad?" He didn't look like he believed her.

"They're actually not a toad at all. The Texas horned lizard is the state reptile, and populations have been declining for the past several years. Kermit's doing his best to turn that around. He's got a good heart. I just don't know how much longer he'll be able to keep going."

"Really? Why do you say that?"

"Well, he's had some health concerns. Nothing major, but being out on that land all by himself...traipsing through the weeds and marshes and working with those lizards can't be easy on him."

Chandler tapped a finger against his lips. "Has he thought about moving into town?"

"Kermit?" Dixie tried to picture the reclusive older man living near other people. "You'd have to drag him out of there by what's left of his hair. Gram said Kermit will probably leave his land to the toads along with a trust to make sure they can keep up on the taxes for years to come."

"Oh"—Chandler shot her a glance full of concern—"we can't have that."

"We can't?" Where was this *we* coming from? And why the concern over what Kermit would do with his property?

"No. Poor guy. Sounds to me like he really needs to be closer to town if his health is deteriorating."

"Maybe." The skepticism she'd been tamping down bloomed in her chest.

"How much do you think his land is worth? Maybe he could sell it, buy a nice place in town with a pond for his toads, and then you wouldn't have to waste any more of your energy worrying about him."

She bit back the response that almost flew out of her mouth.

"Oh, I'm sorry. I didn't mean that the way it came out." His hand covered hers again.

She fought the urge to give him a piece of her mind. In a voice dripping with more syrupy sweetness than her mama's bourbon brown sugar maple brown betty, she asked, "Then how exactly did you mean it?"

"Just that I can tell Kermit is a special member of the community. I'd hate to think concern for his welfare was causing you any kind of distress, especially since you have so many other things to keep track of…like the Rose."

"Mm-hmm." Not completely sold on his flimsy explanation, Dixie tried to steer the conversation to more stable ground. "Hey, there's something you probably don't see in California. Up ahead on your right, we've got Sage's rattlesnake farm."

"I don't remember that from when I was a kid. She actually farms rattlesnakes?"

"She breeds them. Some people like a little rattlesnake every once in a while. Plus there's a big market for snakeskin boots." A shiver flowed through him, all the way to where his hand still covered hers.

"Does she ever lose track of a snake or two?"

"You mean do any of them ever escape?" He nodded. "Rarely. But if they do, she's usually pretty quick to track them down. You know what? We should stop in."

"Oh, no, that's okay. Don't you need to get back to the Rose?"

"I'm sure Presley has things well under control. Besides, I wouldn't want you to miss out on the opportunity to hold a real live rattlesnake during your visit to Texas."

"I don't think that's necessary."

Dixie decided to push it. If Chandler wanted info on Kermit's land so badly, this would be one way to find out. "She and Kermit go way back. I know she's helped him with his horned toad efforts. She might have a better idea of whether he's ever talked about moving into town."

"Well…" His foot eased off the gas. "For your peace of mind, it might be worth a conversation, right?"

"Absolutely." Dixie squeezed his hand, enjoying the almost-palpable shift in power. If Presley was onto something, this would be her chance to either prove him wrong or jump on the crazy train right behind him.

Chandler pulled into the gravel drive leading to Sage's place. With any luck, the next half hour would either confirm everything Presley had been spouting off about or prove she should try to enjoy Chandler's attention without fearing any ulterior motives. Even though she'd never been much for gambling, she hedged her bets. As far as she was concerned, all signs pointed to Chandler being just an interested tourist with a tie to the town. She envisioned how it would feel to tell Presley once and for all to lay off. Relief and a little something that felt like disappointment flitted through her gut. She shook them off. Putting Presley in his place would be oh so satisfying. She hoped that for once in her life, the stars would align in her favor.

Presley nursed another beer. Where the hell was Dixie Mae King? He'd tried her cell with no answer. She wasn't responding to text messages. Boss Hawg and the Scallywags had been onstage for almost an hour. Any minute now, they'd wrap up their set and he and Leoni would meet up at the bar for their little fiddlin' rendezvous. His pulse ratcheted up as he tried to picture her reaction to his homemade instrument. He'd gone home to grab it and had it sitting in his truck. If any of the guys around the Rose found out about his secret obsession, he'd never hear the end of it. How would it look for Holiday's resident playboy to admit all he wanted in life was the feel of hand-hewn wood under his chin and catgut strings under his fingers? Carrying on his granddad's vision of creating the best fiddles for the best country artists had become his dream.

Strains from the last song faded away, replaced by the cheers of the crowd. Presley ambled onto the stage as the band filed past him.

Leoni gave him a wink then whacked him on the ass with her bow. "I'm going to go hop in the shower. Meet you up at the bar in a few?"

He smiled. "You bet."

She skipped away while he grabbed for the mic. "Thanks, everyone, for coming out. We've got one more band tonight. I hope you'll all stick around for the Texas Twister Sisters. We'll take a short break and be back with you in a few."

Presley stepped out of the way as the crew swapped out the set. If Dixie didn't show up soon, he might have to postpone his meeting with Leoni. He was ready to make a move and figure out his future. With the opportunity to get some feedback from one of the best fiddle players he'd seen in his own lifetime, he couldn't toss that away.

Maybe Shep wanted to make his debut as the closing emcee for the festival tonight. The Texas Twister Sisters were the last act for the night. A smile played across Presley's lips as he recalled the last time they'd been in town. Not only were they sisters, they were twins. That had been a once-in-a-lifetime opportunity. With a purpose in his step, he scrambled down the stairs and headed to the bar.

A few minutes later, he'd worked his way through the crowd and stood at the end of the long wooden counter. Shep lifted his chin, acknowledging his presence. Things had picked up inside while Presley had been down by the stage. Hopefully the fire chief didn't stop in tonight. He'd be likely to shut them down for being over capacity. Charlie would be thrilled at the turnout. He put his foot on the footrest of the stool next to him and rose up to snap a picture of the crowd to text it to her.

As he pressed Send, an incoming text popped up on his screen. Dixie…finally.

> **Dixie:** Sorry for the delay. I'll be back soon. We need to talk. I think you're right about Chandler.
> **Presley:** Where have you been? I've got plans tonight.
> **Dixie:** Cancel. This is important.

A growl rumbled through his chest. Cancel? What right did she have to make him call off what promised to be an important night?

Presley: Not an option. Get back here and we'll talk tomorrow.

He tucked his phone in his back pocket, satisfied he'd told her. His phone dinged again. He chose to ignore it. Tomorrow would be soon enough to respond.

"Hey, what's up?" Shep finally made his way down the bar. "How are things out by the stage?"

"Good, real good. In fact"—Presley leaned over the bar—"I was wondering if you wanted to close down the stage for me after the last set?"

Shep barked out a laugh. "You're joking."

Presley shook his head back and forth.

"I'm not much for speaking in public, you know. You got the gift of the gab, and seems I got stuck with the gift of running up people's tabs." He shrugged.

"Wow, the rhyming bartender. Seems unfair to deprive the crowd of someone with so much talent."

"Nice try." Shep swatted at him with the bar towel he pulled off his shoulder. "But still…no. Now if you'll excuse me, I've got about five thousand more beers to pull before I get to go home tonight."

Presley's butt dinged. Damn, Dixie. He was about to reach for his phone when he spotted Leoni. She lifted an arm and waved to him over the crowd. Maybe he could have the best of both worlds. A quick check at his watch showed he had about forty-five minutes to kill before he'd have to wrap up the stage. Plenty of time to show her his fiddle. He pushed off the bar and cut through the throng.

As he reached Leoni, she lifted to her tiptoes and pressed a kiss against his cheek. She smelled earthy, like musk and something subtly sweet and seductive. Usually that would have him more interested in fiddlin' around than showing an attractive woman his fiddle. But she was taken, and this was business.

"My fiddle's out in the parking lot. You ready to go take a look?" he asked.

He felt her agreement in the nod against his chest. With his hand at the small of her back, he guided her toward the door. The air seemed to drop a dozen degrees as they pushed through the front door onto the porch.

Cash looked up from where he was bent over an ID. "You takin' off?"

Presley twitched under his older brother's gaze. "Nope. Not until Dixie gets back. Unless"—he sidled up next to Cash—"you want to close down the stage and lock up tonight?"

Cash's stare could have burned holes through a Kevlar vest. "I've got a pregnant wife and a daughter at home. I promised Charlie I'd stick around until eleven, but then I'm outta here, so don't go getting any big ideas, okay?"

"Just trying to give you an opportunity to connect with people in a positive way for a change." Presley clapped his brother on the back.

"If I decide I need your help with my public persona, you'll be the first to know. Now get out of the way—you're holding things up." People were still lined up, waiting to get in. Tonight would be one for the record books.

"Everything okay?" Leoni asked.

"Yeah, just fine. Seems I have an obligation that will cut our time together short."

She smiled up at him. "That's all right. Shouldn't take me but a few minutes to give you an opinion."

"Is that right?"

"Yep."

"Well, that's the best news I've heard all day. What do you say we head to my Jeep and check out the fiddle then?"

"Sounds good to me."

They reached the Jeep, and Presley pulled his case out of the back. A ripple of apprehension snaked through him. What if she told him his fiddle was crap? What if he got so nervous he fumbled the bow? What if she laughed at his dream of quitting his job and working with the strings for a living?

Only one way to find out. He set the case on the front seat and unclasped the hinge. As he took in a deep breath, he squeezed his eyes shut and slowly lifted the lid.

Leoni laughed.

She hated it. Could tell it sucked just by looking at it. Presley's eyes flew open. What the hell? His case didn't hold a fiddle at all. Nestled inside, tucked in among the red velvet interior, sat a rubber chicken.

"Dammit." Presley grabbed the fake chicken by the neck and flung it to the ground.

Her mouth quirked into a grin. "I take it that's not what you wanted to show me."

He hung his head. "I'm sorry. Someone must have played a joke on me."

"If you find your real fiddle, I'll be happy to take a look. Right now I think there's a barstool with my name on it." She pointed toward the porch of the Rose.

"Yeah, sorry to waste your time."

She nodded as she gave his arm a squeeze then turned on her heel and stalked back toward the Rose.

"Aw, hell." Presley scuffed his boot, kicking up a cloud of dust in the gravel. His phone rang. What now? Wondering how the evening could get any worse, he answered.

chapter

THIRTEEN

"WHY IN THE WORLD HAVEN'T YOU GOTTEN BACK TO ME yet?" Dixie snapped through the phone. Thank goodness she was still a few miles away. If she'd been able to get her hands on Presley in that moment, she might be tempted to do something absolutely unladylike.

"I've been busy handling things at the Rose. Where are you? You were supposed to be back hours ago."

She clamped a hand to her hip in an effort to keep her tone civil. "We're stranded out at Sage's. Chandler ran over a stake, and his tire went flat. I need you to come get us."

Presley's tone turned patronizing. "I'm so sorry, Fireball. Doesn't SoCal know how to change a tire? Or is he afraid he'll get his khakis dirty?"

"The spare's flat too. If you could just pick us up and run Chandler back to town—"

He interrupted her. "Excuse me, but what exactly makes you think that's my responsibility? Call Dwight—he's the one with the tow truck."

Oh, the man irritated her something fierce. "I did call Dwight. He's about ten sheets to the wind." She gave Chandler a reassuring smile and turned away to mutter under her breath. "And it's your fault we're out here anyway."

"My fault?" Presley asked.

"We can talk about that later." Dixie let out a little laugh, trying to assure Chandler all was well. "Right now we just need a ride." Did he think she wanted to call and ask him for anything? But who else could she call this late? Not her parents. Her sister was probably sound asleep next to Bea. Gram wasn't supposed to drive anymore, and Charlie was out of town. Besides, it *was* Presley's fault she was in this predicament.

"Unbelievable. I've got to shut down the stage first. Give me twenty minutes."

"Thank you so much. We'll see you then." Dixie shoved her phone back into her purse as she turned to Chandler. "Presley will be here in just a bit."

"That's great. Sorry again about the tire. I never thought to check the spare."

"Oh, it's fine. Good thing you didn't break down on your way to Holiday though." Maybe if he had she wouldn't have gotten her hopes up that her knight in shining armor—or her knight in a powder-blue Caddy with horns—had finally arrived to sweep her off her feet. From what she could tell, Presley was definitely onto something. Chandler hadn't come right out and admitted anything directly, but the questions he'd been asking and the comments he'd made left no doubt his interest in Holiday went well beyond the chili.

Sage had locked up and retired an hour ago. She'd offered to drive them into town, but Chandler had balked at the sight of her rickety truck. She'd been driving it for years, and Dixie figured by now it had to be held together with duct tape and string.

"I'm sorry the evening turned into a bit of a bust." Chandler sat in the driver's seat. When they figured they'd be waiting a while, he'd mentioned he'd feel safer in the car. Dixie didn't blame him. After walking through Sage's place, she felt like creepy-crawly things were lurking around and under everything.

"Oh, it's okay." She tried to keep her tone light. Inside, her anxiety threatened to boil over. She couldn't wait to fill Presley in on everything.

Chandler turned toward her and put his arm on the seat behind her. "I don't suppose you'd be willing to give me another chance?"

"Another chance at what?" As far as she was concerned, she didn't need to spend any more time with him. Over the course of the evening, it had become clear his interest lay in the town, not the people in it. And, unfortunately for her romantic heart, that meant her too.

His fingers played with the hair at the nape of her neck. She wrapped her arms across her middle.

"Are you cold?" He dropped his arm to her shoulders and gently pulled her close.

Cold? It had to still be eighty-five degrees out. Of course she wasn't cold. But what had Presley advised? To use her feminine wiles?

"So what do you say? Another chance at sharing a nice evening together?" His eyes peered out at her, his skin bathed in a silver haze from the light of the full moon.

A thousand reasons to say no ran through her mind. She didn't want to be anyone's patsy. But what if…what if she could get to the bottom of what might be going on with the potential investors? "I think that would be nice."

"Good. Are we still on for dinner Monday night? I thought it might be fun to try out the Farley Inn." With one arm wrapped around her, he scooted closer and ran his fingers up and down her arm.

"Um, I don't know about that, Chandler." She'd be busy making sure things were good to go for the continuation of the Chili Festival next weekend. Plus she had commitments. She'd been telling the truth earlier about her promise to take Gram and Mrs. Mitchell to bingo, and she wasn't sure whether she could trust Presley to come through for her instead.

"So I ate all those peppers for nothing?" He leaned close, his breath brushing against her cheek.

He had to play the pepper card. Guilt bloomed in her stomach. Technically she did owe him a date, even though she no longer had much hope that he'd be the perfect distraction to end her late-night dreams about Presley Walker.

"I suppose I do owe you a dinner." Her toes curled in her sandals. If she was reading the signals right, it seemed like Chandler was about to kiss her.

"Good. Monday night then." He moved even closer. "I figured with Presley coming to the rescue, I won't get an opportunity to walk you to the door tonight."

Dixie let out a breath and tried to gulp in some air. With her back pressed against the car door, she didn't have anywhere to go. She didn't want Chandler to kiss her. Her next kiss should be with someone she really liked. Someone who could set her soul on fire and make her wish for things she never thought possible. Someone like Presley. Before she could stop herself from thinking it, her brain conjured up memories of her and Presley locking lips.

Lights swept over them, illuminating the front seat of

the Caddy. Presley. Her heart surged in her chest, and relief flooded her system.

"Damn." Chandler pressed a quick kiss to her temple. "Looks like our ride is here."

She'd never been so grateful to see Presley Walker in her life.

Presley laid on the horn, causing Chandler to jerk away and her to jump several inches off the leather seat. "I don't have all night." He leaned out the window.

Chandler hopped out of the car and walked around to open her door. Dixie smoothed her skirt as she climbed out. "I'm going to put the top up and make sure I get it locked. I'll just be a minute if you want to go ahead and wait in the car."

"Do you need help?" Dixie asked.

"No. I'll be right behind you." Chandler offered a reassuring grin as he began to pull the convertible top up.

Dixie nodded and picked her way across the gravel parking lot to Presley. She opened the passenger door to find him messing around on his phone.

"Thanks for the ride," she mumbled.

"Yeah, you're welcome. How'd the big date go? Get any intel?" He twisted to face her as she climbed into the backseat.

She settled in as best she could. "We need to talk. He didn't come right out and say anything, but he sure did ask a lot of questions."

"Oh yeah? Like what?"

"Like what there is to do for fun around here, what kind of restaurants we have, that kind of thing."

"Hmm"—Presley's brows lifted—"what did he say about the Garcia acreage?"

"We didn't make it that far."

"Damn, Fireball. I told you to take him out that way. That would have been the perfect spot to stop and see what gives."

"Look, I'm a waitress. I make jewelry on the side. Nowhere in either of those professions does it say anything about spying." She clenched her jaw. "If you want to find out what he's up to, why not just ask him?"

Presley lifted his eyes heavenward like she was the most naive person on the face of God's green earth. "I can't ask him. Then he'd be onto us."

"Shh, here he comes." Dixie pulled the seat belt across her midsection as Chandler opened the door to the Jeep.

"Thanks for coming to get us." He offered a hand to Presley, who gave it a firm shake.

Without even waiting for Chandler to shut the door behind him, Presley gunned the gas and spun the tires on the gravel. "My pleasure. Now let's get you both back to town before Dixie Mae turns into a pumpkin."

Chandler glanced back toward Dixie and let out an unsure laugh. "I, uh, hear you have someone in town who can take a look at the tires tomorrow?"

Dixie leaned forward. "I'll give you Dwight's number. He can tow it in to his shop and get you patched up in no time."

His pearly white smile twinkled at her in the darkness. "Thank you."

Presley jerked the wheel, and the Jeep bounced over a deep pothole, sending Dixie flying backward.

"Sorry, didn't see that one until it was too late." His gaze met Dixie's in the rearview mirror.

As she sat and stewed in the backseat, he had the audacity to give her a wink. That man might be the death of her. Summoning every iota of self-control, she returned his gaze and stuck out her tongue.

His lips quirked up in a lopsided grin. Even at his worst, he still did something to her insides. Something that made her feel like she'd never been so out of her element.

H

"Enjoy the rest of your night now." Presley drummed his fingers against the steering wheel while Chandler scrambled out of the Jeep.

"Thanks again for the ride." SoCal held the seat so Dixie could climb out behind him.

They stood face-to-face on the sidewalk of the B and B. What kind of move would Chandler try to make? Presley ran through some potential options in his head. Based on the way the poor guy made moony eyes over Dixie, he was probably hoping for a goodnight kiss.

"You gonna walk your date to the door, Dix?" He smirked at the look on her face—a mixture of horror and panic.

"That's not necessary." Chandler pulled her in for a hug and muttered something against her ear.

Presley strained to catch a hint of the conversation. Dixie said something back, then they broke apart. She climbed into the front seat of the Jeep, and Chandler shut the door behind her.

"We'll talk soon." He patted the doorframe.

She nodded.

"That's it?" Presley asked.

Dixie whispered through the smile pasted on her lips. "Can you please drive away now?"

"You got it." Presley raised his hand in a wave and pulled away from the curb. "What the hell was that all about?"

Dixie turned on him. "I'm about ready to kill you, Presley. Do you have any idea what you got me into?"

"I take it Prince Charming ain't as charming as you'd hoped?" He watched her out of the corner of his eye, ready to defend himself if necessary. At this point Dixie could go one of two ways. She'd either get pissed and start swatting at him or get emotional and be reduced to a puddle of tears.

In an unexpected turn, she did neither.

A burst of laughter bubbled up, and she began to laugh. "I'm sorry."

Concern creased his brow. What was this? Had she completely lost her marbles?

"It's just—just—" She doubled over in laughter, arms wrapped around her middle.

"What's going on?" He hadn't been prepared for this.

"I can't help it. When I get overwhelmed, I laugh." She sat up again then erupted into another fit of giggles.

"Do I need to be worried here? Should I drop you off at urgent care? Maybe for a psych eval?"

Dixie drew herself up against the seat back. "No." Her chest heaved as she took deep breaths in and out.

"You want to tell me what just happened there?" He eased the Jeep to a stop on the side of the road. His nana talked about people being overcome by the spirit. Maybe Dixie had been momentarily possessed.

"I'm okay." She put her hands on the dash. "It's been a weird night. I just needed to let some steam out."

"You sure about that?" He eyed her with a degree of skepticism her outburst deserved. "You're not going to bust out speaking in tongues?"

Dixie shook her head.

"Head's not going to spin around before you puke pea-green soup on me, is it?"

"No." She turned to face him, fully composed. "I'm sorry you had to see that. Now, if we could just head to the Rose, I think we need to talk."

"You sure you don't want me to take you home?" Doubt lingered. What if she had a relapse?

"Was Doc still there when you left?"

"Yeah. He was spinning tall tales at the bar."

Dixie nodded. "Then we need to get to the Rose. I want to ask him myself about what those boys up from San Antonio said to him."

"All right then. To the Rose we go." Presley pulled back onto the road, eager to get his unpredictable passenger delivered to their destination before something else happened.

Fifteen minutes later they entered the Rose. Cash had left long ago, before Presley had a chance to ask him about the chicken in the fiddle case. It had to be him. Despite their attempt to call a truce on the Walker brothers pranks, the hijinks were still happening—some of them more dangerous than others. Cash was still trying to get even for the rubber snake Presley had put in his Christmas tree last year. If it had been him who put the chicken in the fiddle case—and it had to be, Presley just knew it—then he'd upped the ante. Cash was the only one who had an inkling about Presley's dreams. He'd caught Presley in their granddad's old woodshop one afternoon. After Presley and Dixie found Doc and figured out what to do about the SoCal threat, he'd have to spend some serious time mulling over options for retaliation.

"You want to go see if Doc's out back?" Dixie grabbed onto his arm to rise up on her tiptoes. She craned her neck and scoped out the crowd. How cute. Even raised above her full height, she still didn't reach his eye level.

"Is it safe to leave you alone?"

"Of course." She put her hands on his shoulders and tried to turn him around. "You check out back, and I'll make sure he's not in here."

He didn't budge. "When I left, he was sitting on Dwight's stool at the bar." Presley nodded toward where Dwight held an audience of cook-off competitors captive. No telling what kind of nonsense he was spouting.

"Well, then I'll just ask Dwight where he went." Dixie nodded then took off toward the bar. She bent close to Dwight, who wrapped an arm around her backside. Presley tensed. The sight of Dwight's grease-stained hand pressing against Dixie's shirt didn't sit well with him. Before he had a chance to decide what, if anything, he wanted to do about it, she was back. "Dwight says Doc went home about a half hour ago. Darn it."

Presley bit his lip.

"What now?" Her hands went to her hips.

"Darn it?" The smile escaped. "Hell, Fireball, have you ever said a four-letter word in your life?"

Her eyes narrowed. "What in the world does that have to do with anything?"

"Nothing. It's just—sometimes it feels good to let one loose."

"Sure, as long as it feels good, that's your MO, right?" Green eyes blazed. "Some of us choose to alleviate our frustration in other ways."

"Oh, don't you worry, I do my alleviating in plenty of other ways too."

Her gaze shot toward the sky. "Can we talk about the Rose so I can get home before it's light outside?"

He gestured toward the hall. "After you. You've already ruined all my other plans tonight."

She stepped ahead of him, making her way to the office. "What other plans? Don't tell me you'd almost charmed some poor girl out of her knickers and that's why you were so mad when I called."

"What?" He feigned mock innocence. "Just trying to work on my alleviating." She didn't need to know about his foiled attempt to get an opinion on his fiddle. The idea of him wanting something beyond a one-night stand and a lifetime supply of free Lone Star would probably be as foreign to her as him suddenly starting to speak Greek.

Dixie groaned. "Can you be serious for five minutes?" She held up her hand, fingers splayed, as if he needed a visual on what the number five might look like.

"Five minutes." Presley slumped into the chair behind Charlie's desk. "Go. Why don't you tell me all about your date with the hotshot from California?"

She perched on the edge of the chair in front of the desk. "Well, he said a few things that made me a little suspicious."

"Such as?"

Her brow furrowed, creating a wrinkle on her forehead. "Nothing specific. It was just a feeling I got. The questions he asked about other entertainment venues and dining options made me wonder."

Presley clucked his tongue. "Told ya so."

She slumped back against the chair. "I don't know. Maybe I was reading too much into it. You made me overanalyze everything he said."

"Overanalyzing isn't something I've had much practice at. You did that all to yourself. The question now is"—he paused for dramatic effect—"what are you going to do about it?"

"Me?" The chair skittered backward as she launched herself out of it. "What do you mean 'me'?" Her face flushed, making her green eyes burn even brighter.

Presley leaned forward. "I mean, he seems to like you. So how are you going to play it?"

Her arms cinched around her waist. "I told you, I'm not playing anything. I'm no good at these kind of games."

He stood, meeting her eye to eye on his way out of the chair. "Lucky for you, I am. Now that we've got enough info to be suspicious, I think we need to launch a full-blown investigation."

Dixie huffed out a breath. "And what might a full-blown investigation entail?"

"Well, first I think you need to get him drunk. Yeah." Presley rounded the desk. "Then steer the conversation toward his business. See if he lets anything slip."

"And when is this supposed to happen?"

"You've got a date Monday night, right? He's obviously into you."

"How do you know that?"

The smug grin he always seemed to wear around Dixie made another appearance. "Body language, Fireball. That poor sucker has it bad for you."

"Why?" She looked like she'd just swallowed a jar full of pickle juice.

"Sweetheart, I don't know where you've been getting your self-esteem, but you, darlin', are what a guy like me would call the full package."

"Oh my gosh, stop. It's obviously way past my bedtime, and I must be hearing things. Can you please take me home?" Her spine ramrod straight, she smoothed out her skirt and shifted from foot to foot.

"You bet. Just answer me this."

"What?"

"Your place or mine?"

Dixie rode the entire way back to Gram's in silence, mulling over everything Presley had said. If Chandler was up to something, like it or not, she did seem like the most obvious person to try to weasel it out of him. But how? She couldn't get him drunk. That didn't feel right. She wasn't even sure she wanted to spend another evening together. There didn't appear to be much of a chance of a future with him, so what was the point?

"Door-to-door service, Miss Dixie King." The Jeep came to a stop in Gram's drive. "Think about what I said, will you?"

"About getting Chandler drunk and trying to force information out of him?"

"Well, if that's how you want to put it."

"Look, I'm no femme fatale."

"I told you I'd help you with that part."

He seemed sincere. But her judgment wasn't at its best. Not after a long day at the Rose and spending the evening doing her best to pry information out of a stranger. "Let's talk about it tomorrow, okay?"

"It's a deal." Presley stuck out his hand to shake on it.

Dixie reached for it, relishing the burn that simmered in her gut as her hand slid into his. What was it about Presley that set her hormones into overdrive? Before she let herself get carried away, she broke contact and climbed out of the Jeep. "Thanks for the ride tonight."

"My pleasure. See you tomorrow. Sweet dreams."

She stepped back from the drive and watched as he backed out. He flashed his brights at her then sped off down the street. Maybe toward home. Maybe toward some hookup. Maybe toward somewhere she didn't even have the imagination to imagine. She and Presley lived in different worlds. It would be best if she kept reminding herself of that.

chapter

FOURTEEN

THE NEXT MORNING DIXIE woke to the sound of GRAM strangling a chicken. At least that's what she thought was happening based on the high-pitched shrieking coming from downstairs. She grabbed her robe off the foot of the bed and raced down the steps. Gram stood in the mudroom in full waders, holding something in both hands.

"Are you okay?" Dixie barely had time to wrap her robe around her and cinch it closed.

"Dixie, thank goodness. Grab that bowl from the cabinet, will you?"

"What's going on? What was that noise?"

"I just got a fright. Don't worry, everything's fine."

Dixie held out the bowl. "But what are you doing?"

Gram opened her hands so Dixie could see what she'd captured. "It's a young one. Maybe only a few weeks old."

The thing in her hands looked like some prehistoric baby dinosaur. "But what is it?"

"Why, Dixie, it's one of those horny toads Kermit's trying to save. He told me all about it last time I took him some dinner. They're fascinating. Now hold the bowl, and I'll slide it in. Kermit's going to be so excited when he sees."

Dixie held out the bowl with one hand, wishing she could just set it down and walk away instead. Since when had Gram been concerned about the fate of the horned toad? Dixie didn't wish the entire species ill, she just didn't want to deal with it on such a personal level. "Now what are you going to do?"

"Get dressed. We've got to run it over to Kermit's." Gram put the lid on the bowl then raced through the kitchen toward her bedroom.

"Your boots!" Dixie called after her. Why she even needed waders was a mystery. The only water they had within walking distance of the house was a mucky pond a few blocks down. The state health department had banned anyone from venturing in on the suspicion it contained some sort of weird bacteria. Oh, Gram. If she'd been splashing around in that water, no telling what she might have picked up.

"Come on, we've got to get to Kermit so he can catalog it."

"I've got to get to the Rose. Today's the final day of competition for the weekend. Besides, I haven't even had my coffee yet. Can you slow down a sec?" Dixie stood still while Gram raced around her.

"Running out to Kermit's will just take a bit. You'll have plenty of time to get to the Rose." Gram continued to spin circles around her. Just watching her made Dixie feel nauseated. "I made a whole pot of coffee this morning. There's probably a cup or two left. I'll pour you one in a to-go cup while you run up and put some clothes on."

Not willing to spend the energy it would take to try to dissuade Gram from her wild plan, Dixie spun to face the stairs. Going along would be easier. It would take less energy in the long run. She never won when she tried to hold her ground with Gram anyway.

By the time she returned to the kitchen, Gram had called

Maybelle over. The two of them sat at the kitchen table oohing and aahing over the weird creature in the bowl, their legs covered in toe-to-hip waders.

"What are you going to name it, Genie?" Maybelle asked.

"Oh, I don't know. Maybe Fernando. I've always wanted to have a Fernando in my life."

Maybelle giggled. "I've always been a sucker for a Fred, like Fred Astaire. How about you, Dixie?"

Dixie held her coffee cup to her lips, mulling over the most appealing name when she spotted a Jeep pull into the drive. "Presley."

"Presley? I never figured the two of you as a fit, but stars, that man does know how to fill out a pair of jeans. Good choice, hon." Gram lifted her mug in a gesture of approval.

Maybelle snorted. "Oh, you can't mean Presley Walker. Why, everyone knows that boy's just a—" Maybelle stopped talking when the man in question appeared at the back screen door.

"Morning, Mrs. Holbein, Mrs. Mitchell. Hi there, Dixie."

Dixie stood, dumbfounded, the travel mug of coffee halfway to her lips.

"Y'all mind if I come in?"

Gram recovered her manners first. "Of course. Can I get you some coffee?"

"That would be much appreciated, ma'am." As he stepped through the doorway, he removed his hat.

Gram snagged the travel mug out of Dixie's hand. "Here you go. I hope you don't mind a little cream and sugar."

"No, ma'am, that's just how I like it. Something sweet to balance out the strength." He brought the cup to his lips, winking at Dixie as he took a sip.

"Gram, that was my coffee." She clamped her hands to her hips. It was too early in the morning to deal with Presley Walker.

"Oh, honey, we'll get you some more." She twirled Dixie around by the shoulders and gave her a gentle nudge toward the stairs. "Now, why don't you go get dressed?"

"What's wrong with this? We're just going to Kermit's, aren't we?" She glanced down at her favorite jeans. The kind of jeans she could live in. Frayed around the edges, they were about worn in just right.

Gram leaned close. "You've got a gentleman caller. That's two days in a row. Please, go do something with your hair before you scare him away."

Dixie sighed. Since when was Gram so concerned about her love life…or lack thereof? Committed to keeping the peace, she retreated upstairs. She had no intention of changing, but it wouldn't hurt to try to contain her hair in an elastic.

When she came back to the kitchen, Gram and Mrs. Mitchell were sitting at the table, sipping on their coffee while they gazed appreciatively at Presley's backside. As he reached up to put a bowl on the shelf of the tallest cabinet, his shirt lifted, exposing a sliver of skin. "Is that where you wanted it?"

"Oh, on second thought, maybe you should move it back over there." Gram pointed to the cabinet on the other wall.

Presley grinned and moved over to the other side. "This better?"

Mrs. Mitchell must have noticed Dixie come into the room. She cleared her throat and swatted at Gram.

At least Mrs. Mitchell had the decency to flush, but Gram just shrugged her shoulders. "He said he'd help out with some honey-do chores while he waited for you." She sighed. "And goodness knows, we have plenty of tasks around here that could keep him busy for a nice long while."

"Presley, can we talk?" Dixie grabbed him by the arm and pulled him toward the door as she cast a glance back at Gram. "I'll be back in a sec."

He snagged his coffee on the way out. "Simmer down. You're going to make me spill my coffee."

She shoved him through the door to the screened-in porch. "That's my coffee by the way."

"We can always share."

Dixie chose to ignore the spark that flickered at the notion of sharing anything with Presley beyond a harsh word. "What are you doing here? It's barely after seven."

"Couldn't sleep last night, so I came up with a plan." He sat down on one of Gram's white wicker chairs with a frilly floral cushion. "Here's what we're going to do."

Dixie stared at him like he'd lost his mind. "That will never work."

"Why not?" He'd been up half the night brainstorming their options. At three in the morning, this had seemed like the best plan. But now, in the light of day, sitting on Eugenia Holbein's ruffled chair with her prissy granddaughter, maybe he'd overestimated Dixie's abilities.

"Because I can't play the vixen. There's not one ounce of sexy in my entire body."

Presley reached out and grabbed her hand with his. "Listen here, Fireball. You've got great potential. You're already cute. We'll just up the effort a bit and get you into vamp territory."

She yanked her hand away. "Oh my gosh, that's the most pigheaded thing you've ever said to me."

"What?" He backed away as she stood and started pacing the porch. "I just paid you a compliment." A compliment that hit a tad too close to home. In the past few days, he'd started to see Dixie as much more than the high-strung waitress who worked for his sister at the Rose. How was saying she was cute not a compliment?

"That wasn't a compliment. Anything followed by a *but* doesn't count as a flattering remark." She stopped at the front of the porch, her back to him.

"Hell, Dixie. I didn't mean to insult you. You are cute. Cute as a baby possum."

Her whole head rolled. "Stop. Please, just stop."

"Cute as a bug's ear." He took slow steps toward her in case she went on the offense. "Darlin' as a duck's ruffle-feathered bum."

"I'm sure your posse loves it when you compare them to insects and woodland animals, but that's not exactly my style. Now, can we talk seriously about what we need to do?"

"Yep. That's why I'm here. We need to call Charlie." Before she could object, he pulled out his phone, and Charlie's number appeared on the screen.

"Wait. We don't want to bother her. I'm sure she's

busy with Beck and the baby. Surely we can figure something out."

He pressed the button for the speakerphone. "Who died?" Charlie's voice filtered through.

"Nobody."

"Presley, why else would you be calling me on a Sunday morning unless there's bad news to share?"

He set the phone down on the table and resumed his place on the chair. "Well, there is bad news of a sort. There's a guy sniffing around town about the Rose and entertainment and dining options. Plus Doc said some guys up from San Antonio were here to do some estimates on a big project. Sounds like some investor may have bought the Garcia acreage."

"What?" Sounded like she would have jumped through the phone if she'd had the chance. "That's right next to the Rose. It's a free country, and I don't expect to always be the hot spot in town, but why right next to us?"

"Yeah, Dixie and I are trying to figure out a plan to get some intel. There's a guy here from southern California who's been making some noise."

"Oh my gosh, do I need to come back there? How are you going to figure out what's going on?"

"Well, if you don't mind me making a suggestion, we could come right out and ask him." Dixie leveled a smoldering gaze at Presley. It hit him square in the gut. The woman could turn it off and on at will. She just needed to learn how to control it.

"If we ask him, we run the risk of scaring him off. I'm suggesting a more subtle approach." Presley stared back, waggling his eyebrows.

"Such as?" Charlie's voice went all muffled for a minute. "Oh, hold on a sec. Sully's crying in the backseat because he dropped his pacifier."

"Asking outright is better than your plan." Dixie held her ground.

"No, it's not. We don't want him to run back to California before we have a chance to figure out his ultimate goal."

"This isn't some sort of game." A flush crept up her neck, spreading across her chin and up her cheeks.

"I never said it was. But being direct isn't going to work."

"Are y'all still there?" Charlie interrupted the layered gaze.

"Yes." They both answered at the same time, not breaking eye contact.

"Sorry, this trip is going to be the death of me. We got a flat last night, and it took Beck and Dad forever to get the spare on. Then Sully had a blowout diaper as soon as we got on the road again. Even Baby Back isn't happy. She puked up whatever she got into on the side of the road when I let her out for a bit yesterday."

Dixie's demeanor shifted. "Oh, I'm so sorry you're having a tough time of it. We got a flat last night too."

"You and Presley?" Charlie asked.

"No, Dixie had a hot date last night." Presley narrowed his eyes. "You should ask her who she went out with, Sis."

"Dixie? What's going on down there? Who was in charge at the Rose?"

Dixie glared at him. "I left your incapable brother in charge. I promise not to do it again. Don't worry, everything was fine. The flat was with the guy from California who Presley thinks is out to ruin the Rose."

"Wait. Why are you dating the guy we think is going to try to take us down?" Charlie asked.

"I'm not dating anyone. He asked if I'd take him on a tour around town."

"SoCal has a sweet spot for our Dixie," Presley added. "I'm trying to convince her to exploit his interest and see if she can get some information on what his plans might be."

"Oh, I like it." Charlie cleared her throat. "So what's the plan?"

Presley shot a triumphant smile at Dixie. "I say she accepts his invite to go out again and tries to get him a little tipsy so he might share some details."

"How do you feel about that, Dixie?"

"Honestly? Not great. Running shady recon for your brother isn't exactly my style. Especially not when he wants to vamp me up."

"But would you be willing to go out with him again? Just to see if he'll open up a little bit more?"

The silence grew into a pregnant pause. Then a pregnant pause that seemed to be about two weeks overdue.

"Dixie?" Charlie asked.

Presley shrugged his shoulders, waiting for her to respond. "For Charlie," he whispered.

She let out a deep sigh. "Oh, all right. But just one more date."

He clapped his hands together. "That's what I'm talking about. We'll get things squared away here, Sis.

You and Beck just enjoy the award ceremony and take plenty of pictures."

"If we ever get there. Thanks, Dixie. I appreciate you."

Dixie shook her head while she rolled her eyes. "I know I'm going to regret this."

"Hell, Fireball. I know all about regrets, and believe me, this one won't even register." He ended the call then rubbed his hands together. "Now, let's get started."

"I can't. Gram and Mrs. Mitchell need me to run them over to Kermit's right now. Can we talk at the Rose later?"

He checked his watch. "Competition starts up again at ten. One of us ought to be there."

"Oh, I'll be back long before that. We just have to deliver a baby horned toad."

"Then I'll go with you." He stepped toward the door. The porch creaked, and the plank felt like it might give way underneath his foot. "Y'all got some wood rot?"

"I don't know."

"Let me check." He knelt down to pull back the outdoor carpet covering the floorboards. The dark, stained boards underneath were a dead giveaway. "Yeah, these boards need to be replaced before your grandma falls right through. You got any spare wood around here?"

"I don't know. I'll call my dad to have someone come over and take care of it."

"I can help you out. I've got wood."

"What?"

He chuckled. She probably didn't even catch the accidental innuendo. "I've got a whole bunch of boards over at my place. I'd be happy to fix up the floor so no one gets hurt."

"Thanks. That's a very generous offer, but I don't want

your wood." She toed the carpet he'd flipped up so it fell back in place.

"You might not want it, but I'm telling you, you need it." She still hadn't caught on. What would it be like to live a day in the life of Dixie Mae King? So much missed opportunity for humor.

"Look, Presley. I don't want your wood, and I definitely don't need it."

"Your call. But if you change your mind, my wood is always available to you." He reached for the door handle. As he pushed it open, Dixie's grandmother jumped back. "Have y'all been listening in on us?"

"No." Mrs. Holbein shook her head with a little too much enthusiasm. "I just wanted to check the weather to see if I needed to bring my umbrella."

Presley glanced outside where the sun shone bright, guaranteeing another gorgeous Texas summer day. "I don't think you'll need it today, Mrs. Holbein."

"Please call me Genie. Mrs. Holbein is so formal."

He chuckled. "Genie it is. How would you ladies like to catch a ride over to Kermit's in style? I can run us all over in the Jeep if you want."

Mrs. Mitchell clapped her hands together and looked to Genie for approval.

"Shotgun!" Genie cried. Then she marched out of the house, a plastic bowl clutched against her chest.

"What's in the bowl?" Presley held the door while Mrs. Mitchell followed.

Dixie stomped down the steps behind them. "You'll see."

chapter
FIFTEEN

DIXIE SCOOTED CLOSER TO THE CORNER OF THE BACKSEAT. With Gram calling the front and Mrs. Mitchell taking up more than her fair share of the back with those ridiculous waders, Dixie could barely draw in a breath. She caught tidbits of conversation from the front seat. The general gist was that Presley had turned on the charm and was flat-out flirting with her dear old gram.

Finally, they reached the gate to Kermit's property.

"Hold onto something, it's liable to get a little bumpy here." Presley turned onto the long gravel driveway. The Jeep bounced and shimmied through ruts the size of drainage ditches before coming to a stop in front of a modest cabin.

"Well, that was exciting." Gram passed the bowl to Dixie while she climbed down. "I don't think I've had that big of a thrill since that one time we took the Women's Guild to the appliance store to test out all the spin cycles."

Dixie let her head fall back against the seat. "Gram!"

Mrs. Mitchell touched her arm. "Your grandmother's just playing with you. If you don't react, she won't bother."

"I wish that were the case," Dixie muttered to herself. Gram was Gram, it was as simple as that.

"Oh, I can't wait to show Kermit what we've got." Gram took the bowl back and scurried toward the door.

"I never did see what's in the bowl." Presley flipped the seat forward and held out a hand to Mrs. Mitchell.

She held tight and, with his help, made her way to solid ground. "Such a gentleman," she said, casting a knowing glance back at Dixie.

"Need a hand?" Presley offered to help her out as well.

"I've got it." Dixie pushed past him and met Gram and Mrs. Mitchell on the small stoop.

Gram raised a hand to knock. The bowl tipped in her arm. Mrs. Mitchell made a grab for it, but instead of saving it from tipping, she accidentally knocked it over.

"Oh no!" Gram tried to right it, but it was too late. The tiny lizard free-fell into a tight-knit patch of ground cover three feet below.

Mrs. Mitchell scrambled off the stoop to try to locate the lizard among the leaves and flowers. Gram followed. Presley shrugged then joined in the hunt, leaving Dixie standing in front of the door all by herself. As she vacillated between waiting to greet Kermit and helping them find Fernando, the door opened. Kermit's brow creased as he took in the scene, and Dixie tried to imagine seeing things through his eyes. Gram and Mrs. Mitchell crawled around in the brush next to the stoop. Presley had taken off his boots and tiptoed around the yard.

Kermit brought his gaze back to Dixie, no hint of surprise evident in the kind gray eyes. "So nice of you to come calling this morning, Miss Dixie. What can I do for you?"

"I'm so sorry. Gram found a baby horned toad and

insisted we run it over here. Now she's dropped it, and they can't seem to find it."

"Fernando! Oh, Fernando, where can you be?" Gram peered over the top of her glasses, separating blades of grass like she was inching around a field of explosives.

"I see." Kermit reached behind him for something inside. "Let me see if I can give y'all some assistance." He emerged onto the stoop with an oversized magnifying glass in hand. "The young'uns are tiny little buggers. See if this gives you an advantage."

Dixie took the magnifying glass he offered then joined her gram in the foundation plantings. It took a moment to get used to the mega-magnification, but before long she was peering into the bushes along with the rest of them. Movement caught her eye near a small clump of dirt. A tail flicked.

"I see him!" Dixie almost fell over with excitement. "He's there, see?" She pointed, expecting someone else, someone who didn't have an aversion to things with scales, to step in and nab the little guy.

"Get him!" Gram tried to tiptoe closer. "Before we scare him away, grab him."

"I don't know." Dixie waffled. The lizard peered up at her, his beady little eyes seeming to dare her to make a move.

"Go for it, Dix." Presley watched from a few feet away.

"Feels like sandpaper." Kermit nudged her a wee bit closer. "He's more scared of you than you are of him."

"Doubtful." Dixie glanced at Kermit. His calm, unflustered demeanor settled her nerves. She handed off the magnifying glass then reached out with both hands and scooped up the lizard. His claws scrabbled on her palms. "Okay, I got him. Where do I put him?"

"Let's take him back with the others." Kermit led the way around the back of the house to a huge wooden structure nestled under the trees. He opened the large barn-style door to reveal what looked like the back of the bait shop out on County Road 182.

"What the hell is this?" Presley caught up to them. Rows and rows of shallow bins lined the interior. Many of them held bigger horned toads.

"Welcome to the conservation effort." Kermit spread his arms out. "This is headquarters of the Save the Horned Toad project."

"I had no idea you had such a large operation going back here." Gram stepped to Kermit's side. "What a kind heart you have."

He glanced down at her, a hint of a smile appearing in his eyes. "It's the least I can do. They're endangered."

"I know." Gram started down one of the aisles. "Tell me more."

"Can you show me where to put this guy first?" Dixie asked.

"Let's put him over here for now." Kermit held out a clear shoebox-sized bin. "I'll want to keep him quarantined until I know he can mix in safely with the others."

"Yeah, we wouldn't want the regulars to gang up on the newbie." Presley hitched his thumbs in his front pockets.

Kermit turned to him with a serious look. "We have no idea what he might be carrying. I can't afford to let him get the others sick, so we'll keep him off by himself until I make sure he's clean."

Dixie rubbed her palms over her jeans. What he

might be carrying? Great, could she have been exposed to some horrible contagious horned-toad ailment?

Kermit must have read her mind. "There's a bottle of hand sanitizer over on my workbench. When you get where you're going, I suggest you wash your hands with soap and hot water, just in case."

Dixie nodded then retreated to where the giant bottle of germ-proofing goodness sat on the edge of a huge wooden bench. "All right, we've delivered the critter."

"Fernando," Gram corrected.

"Fine, Fernando. Now, can we go? I have to get ready to go to work."

"I'd love to learn more about your efforts here, Kermit." Gram ignored Dixie and turned to Kermit with a curious eye. "It's fascinating how much time and effort you devote to the cause."

"It's something I believe in." Kermit crossed his arms over his chest. The faded denim shirt stretched tight over his shoulders. "When those folks from California came sniffin' around about buying me out, why, I gave them a fair piece of my mind."

Dixie's ears perked. "What folks?" How could they have missed out on this piece of news?

"Some hoity-toity good-for-nothing kid in a giant blue Caddy rolled in the other day. Said he was prepared to make me a cash offer on my land."

Oh my gosh. Her heart sunk into her shoes, bouncing over every nerve ending she had along the way. Chandler.

"You don't say?" Presley's casual interest didn't fool Dixie. "What did he want to do with the place?"

Kermit turned to face him. "Wouldn't say. But he told me if I accepted his offer I'd have to sign a nondisclosure and wouldn't be able to talk about it for six months until they took possession. He sure as hell was pissed when I turned him down flat." He let out a bit of a laugh. "It's not every day I get a visitor with a huge checkbook. Heck, not every day I get a visitor at all."

Presley shot her that smug look she'd been getting accustomed to. So he'd been right. Chandler was up to no good. "Anything more you can tell us about what happened?"

"Nope. Although he did give me a card. Told me when I changed my mind to give him a call. I told him if he ever came onto my private property again he'd meet the business end of my twelve-gauge. He sure skedaddled out of here in a hurry."

"I bet he did." Presley raised his eyebrows in her direction. "What do you make of this?"

"I don't know. I need coffee. I need to wash my hands. I need to get to the Rose, for crying out loud. We have a competition starting in"—she grabbed for Presley's wrist and flipped it over to check his watch—"less than two hours."

"Okay, I'll run you back home. Anyone else need a ride?" Presley turned to Gram and Mrs. Mitchell.

"I'd love to stick around and learn more about your good deeds." Gram sidled up to Kermit. "Would you be able to give us a ride back to town a little later on?"

Kermit flushed, a nice shade of pink showed through his snowy-white beard. "I'd love to, Eugenia."

"Please call me Genie."

Dixie couldn't stand to waste any additional time watching the romance blossom between her gram and Kermit. Her parents would really flip out if Gram ended up with a new boyfriend under her watch. But right now her obligation to the Rose took precedence. "I've got to go. Presley, you ready?"

"Yep."

"Thank you for making sure my grandmother and Mrs. Mitchell get home." Dixie nodded toward Kermit as she made her way to the large opening in the barn.

Presley jogged to catch up to her. "So that was an interesting conversation, huh?"

Focused on getting to the Jeep, she didn't bother to turn around. "I just can't believe Chandler would have been so brash with Kermit. He doesn't strike me as the type."

"Well, that's what these slick investor people are like. Are you ready to try things my way now?"

Dixie battled the wave of resistance, forcing it down enough that she could agree. "Okay. But on two conditions."

"Hit me, Fireball."

"Number one, you stop calling me Fireball."

"Aw. Seriously? Don't you find it the least bit charming?"

"No."

"Okay." He raised his hands in surrender. "What's number two?"

"It's tricky. I'm not sure I want to say it out loud."

"Hey, I'm a no-holds-barred kind of guy. Anything goes around here, you ought to know that by now."

Too embarrassed to make eye contact, she mumbled into the space between them. "I need to know how to flirt."

"What?" He cupped a hand to his ear. "Couldn't hear you there."

She sighed, shifting her shoulders around, trying to

shake off the thick coat of shame. "I said, 'I need to know how to flirt.'"

"Aw, you got it. Let's head back to your gram's, and I'll tell you all about it on the way."

Great, working with Presley on this would probably make her feel like a complete and utter loser. She should have kept her trap shut and tried to figure things out on her own. Liza could help her. Heck, even Gram seemed to know a few tricks Dixie had never been privy to.

With a sense of impending failure clouding her vision, she traced Presley's steps toward the chariot of doom. The sooner she got to the Rose, the sooner she could get this whole sordid business over with.

Presley caught an eyeful of Dixie from across the bar. He'd been trying to talk to her all day, but she was always one step ahead. Looked like she was headed back to the office. He followed her down the hall, catching up to her as she pushed the door to Charlie's office open.

"Have you been avoiding me today?" he asked her back.

"Avoiding you? I've been running around like a crazy person since I got here this morning." She settled into Charlie's chair and set her clipboard on the desk.

"We need to talk about what you asked me about on the way back to your gram's this morning." He set his palms on the desk and leaned toward her.

She let out a sigh that sounded like the weight of

the world rested on her sun-kissed shoulders. "I changed my mind."

"You can't change your mind. I canceled plans tonight to take you out." He didn't need to tell her that the plans he canceled consisted of going home and watching an Astros game on TV by himself.

"I don't think we ought to go through with this." She scribbled something on the sheet in front of her.

Presley sunk into the chair across from the desk. "So what's changed? Earlier today you asked me for help. Now all of a sudden you don't need my assistance to prepare for your big date tomorrow night?"

Dixie looked up but didn't bother to make eye contact. "I thought about it, and I think the less time we spend together, the better off we'll both be."

Presley grunted out a half laugh. "It was the kiss, wasn't it?" Her eyes widened, a dead giveaway he'd hit the mark.

She didn't respond.

"Aw, come on, Dixie. I know you won't lie about it. So you're just not going to answer me?" Presley stood and walked around the office, trying to shake the tightness that began to radiate out from his chest. "It was a damn good kiss."

He stopped in front of the desk. She continued to make notes on her clipboard. The woman had the ability to focus like a laser beam. "Will you admit it was a good kiss? Stroke my ego a tiny bit?"

The corner of her mouth quirked. "Your ego does not need stroking."

He smiled. "That's the sass I know and love. How about that kiss, Dixie? Come on, throw a dog a bone."

"You're the dog, right?" Finally, she smiled. The wait had been worth it.

"Yes, I'll be the dog."

Nodding, Dixie set the pen down and took in a deep breath. "Good."

"Wait. Good I'm the dog, or are you saying the kiss was good?"

She shook her head. "You're impossible. Good you're the dog. The kiss wasn't good, it was…" Her head tilted from side to side like she was trying to figure out the right words. "It was…gosh, you're going to make me say it, aren't you?"

He nodded, a grin spreading from one ear to the other.

"Fine. It was incredible." Her cheeks colored a shade slightly lighter than her hot-pink T-shirt as she stared at the clipboard in front of her.

"I knew it."

"It doesn't mean anything though. A kiss is just a kiss, right? All in the name of saving the Rose."

He leaned across the desk and put a finger under her chin, nudging it up until her gaze met his. He'd been thinking about things. Things that involved Dixie and his recent blooming desire for a more stable relationship. "A kiss like that could be the start of something more."

She turned her head, breaking away from his touch. "We've got work to do."

"You're right, we do. So does eight o'clock work for you?"

She glanced up. "For what?"

"If you're still planning on helping me get to the bottom of this investor thing, you've got a date with SoCal tomorrow night. I figured we'd go out, have a little fun, and practice what you might say to finagle the info out of him."

"Does it have to be tonight? It's been such a long weekend. I was hoping to go home, get my jammies on, and catch up on some of my shows."

"You want to get this done, don't you?"

"Fine. Eight will work." She slid the pen she'd been using behind her ear.

"Hey, if you want to come in your jammies, that's fine with me." What kind of pajamas would Dixie wear to bed? He could appreciate a nice set of lacy lingerie. Even those knee-length cotton nighties with the graphics on them could turn him on. His favorite thing to see on a woman, though, was nothing. Nothing turned him on like crazy. Then he didn't need to waste time removing everything standing in his way. He'd be willing to bet Dixie had never slept in nothing in her entire life.

"Are you ready to make a final round of the competitors and get the judges' tabulations?" With the pen stuck behind her ear, she reminded him of all those hot-for-teacher fantasies he'd entertained as a kid thanks to his brother's Van Halen collection.

"Yeah, let's do it." It would be nice to get back to his day job tomorrow. He didn't mind helping out at the Rose from time to time, but he wasn't cut out for this round-the-clock deal. Maybe he'd run into Leoni too. He hadn't had a chance to apologize again for last night and still hadn't been able to catch up to Cash or figure out how to get even for the chicken.

Dixie rose from the chair and left the office first. He followed her through the sparse crowd inside the Rose and out into the beer garden. Hundreds of people milled around, tasting the samples of chili that remained, sitting in the shade of the tents strung up between trees, sipping a cold one, and enjoying the tunes from the last band of the weekend. After the winners were announced, there would be a break until everything started back up the following Friday night.

He stayed with her as she worked the crowd, making sure the competitors had a good time. Charlie had an awesome employee in Dixie. She didn't miss a thing. As they turned the corner to walk down the next aisle of competitors, he caught sight of a well-executed hair flip out of the corner of his eye. Leoni.

"Will you excuse me for a minute?" He left Dixie deep in conversation with a guy from Louisiana who'd managed to work crawdads into some sort of soupy concoction he claimed was chili. He caught up to Leoni. "Hey, stranger. You still mad at me about last night?"

"Oh, I was never mad."

"You sure about that?"

"Yeah." She linked her arm through his. "Did you find your fiddle?"

"Yeah. Whoever took it left it on my front porch. Had to be my brother. I'd love for you to take a look at it though. Are you around all week?"

"Sure am. How about tonight?"

He hesitated. Breaking his plans with Dixie wasn't an option. "I can't tonight. How about tomorrow morning? I can brew a pot of coffee, and we can meet up here."

"I'm looking forward to it." She squeezed his arm then took off toward a vendor across the aisle selling pig-shaped popsicles.

Amped to finally have a chance for Leoni to hear him play, he jogged to catch up to Dixie. She stood in front of a table full of what looked like dog supplies. As Presley approached, he saw that the guy behind the table held a tiny piglet in his arms.

"Presley, come see this. It's a mini potbellied pig. It looks just like Pork Chop, don't you think?"

To him, a pig was a pig whether it was black, brown, or pink. But having gotten more familiar with Pork Chop in the past couple of days than he'd cared to, he had to admit the little pig did resemble the stubborn sow. "Yeah, the resemblance is uncanny. It's almost like they're the same species."

"I meant the coloring. People keep them like pets. Aren't these accessories adorable?" She fingered a set of pint-sized feathery angel wings. "I've seen Charlie and the others dress up the pigs like Baby Back and Pork Chop for the pageant, but I've never seen stuff like this."

Having emceed the annual Rambling Rose Sweetest Swine pageant for the past five years, Presley had to agree…there were some pretty crazy costumes and even crazier pig owners out there. "Does your landlord allow pet pigs?" he asked, half-joking.

"Who, Gram? Probably not." She reached out to scratch the little pig behind the ears.

Presley grabbed her hand. "Hey, how about I treat you to some ice cream?" He tugged her toward one of the many food truck vendors that had come in for the weekend.

"Sure, ice cream sounds good."

"How could it not? It's got to be at least a hundred and two out here." He stepped into line behind his brother Statler.

"Hey"—Statler turned to face them—"how's the weekend going?"

"Good, real good." Presley nodded. "Once we make it through this afternoon, we'll be halfway done."

"I've heard people talking about how well organized everything has been. You've done a real nice job." Statler nodded toward Dixie. "Charlie would be downright proud."

Presley grinned as Dixie soaked in the compliment. She'd been working her ass off this weekend, and she deserved the praise.

"I couldn't have done it without your brother." She nudged her chin toward Presley. "He's actually been pretty helpful."

"Really?" Statler clapped Presley on the shoulder. "Nice work."

"Thanks." Presley pointed toward the window. "Looks like you're up."

"See y'all around." Statler turned toward the window to order his ice cream, leaving Presley to question Dixie's comment.

"You really mean what you said?"

"What?" She squinted at the blazing afternoon sun behind him. "That you've been helpful?"

"Yeah. Careful, that almost sounds like a compliment."

"Hey, I don't mind doling out the compliments when someone deserves them." She gave him a half smile.

"I think I'm going to let that statement just sit there for a while. Don't want to screw it up."

Dixie laughed. "So what kind of ice cream are you

going to get? So many choices." She turned to study the huge menu of flavors written on the side of the truck.

"Oh, I always get vanilla."

"Really?" Clearly surprised at his response, she quirked her lips into a doubtful frown.

"What's wrong with vanilla?" He shrugged his shoulders. "A good vanilla is just as complex as at least half of the flavors on that list."

"Mmm." The sass in that one syllable let him know she didn't agree.

"Why? What are you going to get?"

"I can't decide between chocolate overload and very berry cheesecake. They both sound so good, but I've never had either one. What if I don't like what I pick?"

"And that's why I stick to vanilla. No matter how they make it, I know it's going to taste good."

"You're impossible."

He stepped to the window to order. "One scoop of your best vanilla for me, and the lady will have a scoop of chocolate overload and another of very berry cheesecake on the side."

"Presley! I can't eat all that."

"Hey, I'm not a member of the clean-plate club. I don't care if you eat one bite or scarf the whole thing. What matters is that you try something new."

"And if I don't like it?"

He grabbed their ice cream from the window and handed Dixie her overflowing cup. "How do you know you won't like it unless you try?"

She took it from him and dipped her spoon into the chocolate scoop first. "Delicious."

"See?"

"It's really good. Aren't you going to taste yours?"

"Yeah, hold on a sec." He glanced around, looking for the taco truck he'd seen earlier. Dixie followed him as he made his way to the condiment table. "There we go. Now it'll be perfect."

"What in the world are you putting on your ice cream?"

"Hot sauce. A little habanero chili balances out the sweetness." He lifted a spoonful of vanilla dripping with sauce and offered it to her. "Want to try?"

She narrowed her eyes. "Hot sauce and ice cream?"

His mouth closed around the spoon. He let the flavors roll over his tongue and swallowed. "So good."

"But hot sauce and ice cream go together just about as well as..." Her voice trailed off.

"Me and you, right?" He winked at her as he scooped up another bite. "Yeah, seems like a weird combo, but somehow it works. Now, we'd better keep moving. The judges should be done by now."

Dixie shook her head. "Yeah, you ready to go make the announcement and wrap this up?"

Presley had never been more ready for an event to end. He had big plans...track down Cash, get ready for his night out with Dixie, and hopefully have a chance to show Leoni his fiddle tomorrow. "Let's do it."

They made their way to the stage where the judges sat, finishing up their scorecards.

"How'd we do today?" Dixie asked.

Blanche wiped her mouth with a hot-pink napkin. "We had some interesting samples. I think my least favorite was the twist on bird-nest soup."

"For chili?" Presley asked.

"Yes. It wasn't exactly my cup of chili, if you know what I mean."

"Presley, you want to collect the cards, and we'll go score them in the back?" Dixie grabbed the trash can and cleaned up the remaining sample cups.

He swept the paperwork into a pile. Looked like it would take forever to enter it all in. They probably wouldn't be done for hours.

"Thanks so much for judging. Can you meet back here in about an hour for us to announce the winners? I'd love for the three of you to be in the pictures and hand out the trophies."

"Wouldn't miss it." Buster stood and put on his hat.

Grady nodded as he rose from his chair. "It was a tough call on the samples from today. We've got some budding chili experts out there."

"See y'all in a bit." Dixie took the papers from Presley and headed toward the back of the stage where she'd set up her laptop. "I think the easiest thing to do is have you read the entrant number and the scores to me. Then I can type them in, and we'll breeze through them lickety-split. Sound good?"

"Okay. Whatever you think." Computers weren't his thing. Statler was the numbers guy. Dixie should have asked him to come in and ten-key everything. Presley settled into the chair next to her. As he sat, that same fruity smell from before wafted in front of his nose. Had to be Dixie. Damn, she smelled good.

"Let's get started. What's the first entrant number?"

Presley looked at the top sheet. "Number sixty-nine." He snorted.

"And the scores?" She sat, fingers poised above the keyboard.

"Oh, shit. Seriously?"

"Presley, language! Just tell me the scores."

"Okay. Sixty-nine, sixty-nine, and, oh, a seventy-two." He shook his head. The judges must have had a sense of humor too.

"Next?"

"No reaction?"

"Reaction to what?" She glanced up, clearly irritated.

"Sixty-nine?" He waited for her to catch on. "You know…sixty-nine."

"Yes, I know what sixty-nine means. But if you're going to sit here and crack juvenile jokes over every score, we'll end up working all night."

Presley sheepishly ducked his head. "All right, boss." Although, now that she'd mentioned it, the thought of spending all night long with Dixie wouldn't be so hard to swallow. He scanned the rest of the scores while she got resettled on her chair. When had things shifted? Somehow in the past few days, he'd garnered a new appreciation for Dixie Mae King. Now the only question was what did he want to do about it?

chapter
SIXTEEN

DIXIE'S FINGERS FLEW ACROSS THE KEYPAD. WITHIN AN HOUR they had all the scores entered and were ready to announce the winners. She held a sheet with the winners' names written on it out to Presley. "Would you like to do the honors? You've got more stage presence and experience at this than I do." Seemed like he had more experience in everything than she did. Well, after her scheduled flirting lesson tonight and her date with Chandler tomorrow, maybe she'd be on her way to catching up. Not that she wanted to join Presley in the level of debauchery where he currently resided, but she'd been thinking it was high time she started putting herself out there again.

The interest Chandler had shown her made her realize how long it had been since anyone besides the drunk patrons of the Rose had given her any kind of intimate attention. Granted, Chandler wasn't going to be "the one" thanks to his yet-to-be-proven ulterior motive. But still…it was high time she began to entertain the idea of getting involved with a man. Presley was right—she'd dated *boys* before. Her daddy might have been able to bully seventeen-year-old Mateo Hernandez, but any *man* worth dating would be able to withstand potential negative attention from her father.

Presley had awakened something inside her. He'd made

her realize she was as much to blame for letting her dating life go to hell as her overly critical dad. She'd let her father's scare tactics prevent her from putting herself out there, a move that had probably secured her position as the oldest virgin in the state of Texas. If Presley wanted her to vamp it up for Chandler, maybe she could get something out of the deal too. Or lose something...something she'd never intended to hold onto this long.

"You with me there, Red?" Presley snatched the sheet out of her hands, disrupting her private thoughts.

"Yeah, you go ahead. I'll watch from back here." She wheeled the table containing the trophies out to the stage while Presley took the mic. Then she darted back to the safety of the wings.

"Ladies and gentlemen, can I have your attention, please?" Presley's deep baritone filled the outdoor venue.

Heads turned, and patrons started pressing toward the stage. Dixie smiled and took a few pictures with her phone to text to Charlie. The weekend had gone better than either of them could have planned.

"Howdy, thanks for coming to the first annual Rambling Rose Chili Festival." A chorus of cheers and yeehaws erupted in the crowd. "Settle down now so I can announce the winners of our first weekend of competition. First off, we'd like to thank our esteemed judges. Mayor Blanche Mayfield's love for chili began as a child when she'd stand next to her granddad while he stirred his original ranch-style chili over an open fire for days at a time."

Mayor Mayfield took the stage and dipped into a deep curtsy while the crowd applauded.

"Her husband, Buster, is a renowned local food critic"—Presley snorted—"self-proclaimed, I might add."

Buster frowned. "I've earned the title, son." His hands splayed over his rather rotund gut.

"I concede. You're right, you must eat enough to qualify as a critic. Anyway, he's been judging cook-offs since he was tall enough to reach for his own spoon."

Buster walked along the front of the stage, waving and nodding at the crowd.

"And, finally, our own Grady Groveland, whose chili recipes have received five-star reviews from as far away as Dallas and Amarillo."

Grady bowed slightly to the applause.

"Another big thanks to our judges. Any comments on how you came to your decisions?"

Mayor Mayfield took the mic. "The competition was fierce. Entrants surprised me with the quality of the ingredients, the savoriness of the sauces, and their sheer creativity. All in all, it was a struggle to pick a winner."

"Thank you, Mayor." Presley handed the mic to Buster. "How about you, Mr. Mayfield?"

He leaned over to speak into the microphone. "I just really enjoyed eating your chili, everyone. To me everyone's a winner."

"Grady, want to say a few words?"

Grady took the mic. "It's been an honor to judge this group of chefs. I could taste the sweat of your effort in the spice of your sauces." Presley cringed and reached for the mic, but Grady turned to the side to avoid him. "I could taste your blood in the quality of ingredients." The crowd groaned, but he didn't stop there. "And I could taste your tears, yes, I could taste your tears of frustration in the unique flavor combinations." He nodded, finally handing the mic back to Presley.

"Well, thank you, Grady, for making all of us never want to sample anyone's cooking again. So without further ado, let's hand out some trophies for the chicken chili category."

The crowd erupted into applause. Dixie shrank in the wings.

"First up, in third place for her White Bean and Squawker Chili, we've got Maybelle Mitchell."

Dixie craned her head to see Maybelle walk toward the stage. She hadn't even seen Maybelle's name on the list. How could she have missed it? Presley handed Maybelle a trophy and read the next name on the list. "In second place, we've got Allistair Poutine from Texarkana. Wow, thanks for making the trip, Allistair. His prize-winning chicken chili recipe is called, creatively enough, White Chicken Chili."

Allistair climbed the steps to the stage and took his award.

"And in first place"—Presley squinted at the name on the sheet in front of him—"Grace Pepper?"

Grace bobbed toward the stage. Dixie clapped along with the rest of the group, happy to support a local winner.

"Any words for the judges, Grace?"

"I'd just like to thank them all for donating their time and taste buds to judge the contest. And a special thanks goes out to Statler Walker for being the first person to taste my recipe and make me think I had a chance to make something out of it."

Dixie scanned the sea of people for Statler. He stood next to the fence line. She watched along with most everyone else in the crowd while his face turned a bright shade of red and he tipped his hat toward Grace.

"Well, there you go." Presley gestured toward the winners. "Let's give all of the winners and, heck, everyone who entered a huge round of applause."

While the clapping died down, he directed the winners and judges to pose for a quick picture. Dixie brought out the trophies for the next set of winners—the exotic meats category. She shuddered at the thought of having to judge that particular contest.

Presley ushered the winners off the stage. Dixie stopped Grace to offer personal congratulations. "I'm so happy for you on your big win."

"Thanks," Grace said, holding the trophy with both hands. "I hope Statler's not mad I called him out in front of everyone."

Dixie flicked her hand in dismissal. "Well, if he is, that's his problem, not yours. Y'all aren't still seeing each other, are you?"

"No." Grace ran a hand over the shiny gold metal of the trophy. "I keep trying to get back in his good graces but haven't seemed to figure out how yet."

Dixie couldn't understand why she'd want to get back with a Walker brother. The good ones like Waylon and Cash had been taken. Even though they'd been older than her in school, Dixie knew the single brothers who remained were nothing but trouble. Presley especially.

"Well, good luck." She gave Grace a quick hug and

turned her attention back to Bad Brother Numero Uno, who was calling the third-place winner onto the stage. Sage climbed the steps to take the trophy. Her Rattler Chili came as no surprise.

"Next up, in second place with a chili containing armadillo, let's welcome Sherman Totskill to the stage."

An elderly man who reminded Dixie of Kermit hobbled toward the stage. He gripped the railing with both hands, and Presley met him at the top of the stairs to hand him his trophy.

"Thank you much." He lifted a hand toward the crowd and waved.

"And our last award for the weekend, let's put our hands together for the first-place winner of the exotic meat chili cook-off. You've got to be kidding me." Presley's gaze sought hers. "Really?"

Dixie nodded.

"All right. First place goes to Dwight for his Roadkill Chili Creation. Seriously, dude?"

Dwight didn't use the stairs, just hopped straight onto the stage. "Thanks, y'all. Glad to be a part of this here contest."

"Tell us, Dwight. What's your secret ingredient? Surely not actual roadkill?"

Dwight shrugged. "Can't make no promises there."

Presley paused for a beat, maybe waiting for Dwight to confirm he was joking. When Dwight didn't speak, Presley shook his head and spoke into the mic. "Thanks, everyone, for coming out this weekend. Vendors will be here all week, and we'll be back with more music and competition start- ing Friday night." Presley clapped Dwight on the shoulder and nudged him toward the rest of the group, who posed for a photo.

When they were all done, Presley moved toward Dixie. "One for the record books, eh? You ready to wrap things up?"

She'd never been so ready to be done with a weekend of work than she was today. Her feet hurt, her brain still spun from the influx of new names, and her heart pounded with anxiety at the next item on her schedule—her evening with Presley.

"Sure." Dixie followed him back toward the Rose as the stage crew started breaking down the setup and the crowd dispersed. She took in a deep breath, relishing the sense of accomplishment from a job well done. If only the next two evenings could go as well as the events at the Rose had gone. For some reason, she had a feeling she was in for a wild ride instead.

chapter

SEVENTEEN

Dixie evaluated the woman in the mirror. Winged eyeliner accentuated deep-green eyes. Red lips had been outlined, plumped, and puckered. Her hair was expertly styled into finger-wave curls that cascaded over creamy shoulders exposed in the spaghetti-strap sundress.

"I don't know, Liza. I don't even look like me."

"Of course you do. All I did was take what God gave you and play it up a little."

Dixie leaned forward on the stool in front of her gram's dressing table. Thank goodness she and Mrs. Mitchell had gone to a senior singles night at the VFW with a few other lady friends. "Where did I get cleavage like this?" A deep cleft appeared between her breasts. She imagined dropping a bite of food over dinner, never to be seen again.

"You've had it all along. Are you uncomfortable? I don't want you to feel awkward at all."

Dixie had bypassed that an hour ago when she'd stuffed herself into the polka-dot sundress that clung to her ribs like a second skin. She wasn't sure why she'd decided to let Liza talk her into a makeover. Maybe she wanted to know how it would feel to look like one of Presley's regulars. Maybe she wanted to see if it would make a difference to him.

"You want to try the shoes?" Liza dangled a pair of

strappy sandals from her fingers. They matched the red of the polka-dot dress perfectly.

Dixie shrugged. "May as well. In for a penny, in for a pound."

"That's what Gram always says," Liza said.

"What time is it?" Dixie fastened the post of an earring.

"Almost eight. Now those are super cute." Liza bent down to admire the dangling floral earrings.

"Thanks." Dixie tossed her hair out of the way to fasten the other one.

"When are you going to start making jewelry again?" Liza fingered the tiny metallic flowers. "I adore them."

"I don't know. Doesn't seem like I have anywhere to sell them."

"You've got a place online. Maybe you just need to promote it more. I could help." Liza straightened and met Dixie's gaze in the mirror. "You look gorgeous."

Something in Dixie's stomach fluttered around. She pressed a hand to her gut, trying to still the flip-flops going on inside. "Thanks."

"All right. Now stand up and twirl in front of the mirror. I want to take it all in." Liza flounced onto Gram's bed.

Dixie gave a tiny twirl, trying to catch a full 360-degree view of herself in the large mirror propped against the wall.

"You're stunning. Absolutely gorgeous. He's going to be squirming in his jeans tonight."

Dixie hadn't decided yet if that would be a good thing. Yes, she wanted to see Presley's eyes light up in appreciation. But could she really pull this off? And what would she do when it was time to actually go out on a real date with Chandler?

Before she could gather her wits about her, a heavy knock sounded at the door.

"That must be Presley." Liza jumped to her feet, rubbed her hands together, and raced downstairs.

Dixie gave the stranger in the mirror one more look. She crossed her fingers behind her back and offered a silent prayer that she wasn't about to make the biggest mistake of her sheltered life. She heard Presley before she saw him. He swept into the entryway and started chatting up Liza...asking about Bea and how things were going down at the diner. Before she lost her nerve, Dixie launched herself through the doorway and down the steps.

"Let's get this over with." She tossed her purse over her shoulder and made her way to the front door.

"Whoa. What happened to you, Fireball?"

She rounded on him. "I told you not to call me that anymore. That's part of our deal."

"You're right." He swept his arm across his middle and bent over at the waist, taking a deep bow. "I am so sorry. You look absolutely stunning, Ms. King. Forgive me?"

"You two are going to have so much fun tonight!" Liza tucked a chiffon scarf into Dixie's purse. "To keep your hair under wraps while you're on the road, okay?"

Dixie nodded. A little of her spitfire had seeped out with Presley's mocking bow.

"You ready for this, Dixie? Practice date night."

She turned to Liza. Wrapping her arms around her sister's shoulders, she pulled her in for a hug. "Thanks for everything."

"You're welcome." Liza stepped back, releasing her. "Give me a call tomorrow and let me know how it went, okay?"

Dixie nodded then followed Presley outside. "Where are we going?" she asked. She was surprised she hadn't thought to ask that question before. What if her parents or Gram or anyone for that matter happened to come across her and Presley on a fake date?

"I don't think we have much of a choice except to go back to my place." He stated it so matter-of-factly that Dixie's chest blazed.

"Your place?" That's the last thing she'd expected him to say. "What in the world makes you think I'd want to spend any time at your place?" She didn't want to sit in the same chair as the rest of his conquests or wonder the whole time if she was setting her plate or anything else on a spot that had been violated by Presley and one of his many paramours.

"You got a better idea?" He reached for the door handle. "We go anywhere in town, and people will be all up in our business before we even get our drinks ordered."

"What about someplace farther away?" She climbed in as he held the door.

"We can go into Austin if you want. But something tells me you'd rather get this over with sooner than later. You really want to deal with a three-hour drive round-trip?"

He had a point. She had to get back at a decent time to check on Gram. The way she'd been talking about Kermit had Dixie worried she might sneak out some night and try to drive herself over to his place for a little moonlit romance.

"Fine."

He rounded the Jeep and climbed in on the driver's side. "Don't sound so excited about it. It's not like it's a real date. I promise not to make you suffer too much. Now, you hungry?"

Her stomach growled in response. "A little." Truth be told, she'd been so nervous earlier she hadn't bothered to eat much. Plus her stomach was still feeling a little queasy thanks to reading over all of the exotic meat chili entries.

"I figured we could grab a six-pack and something to go and then take it home. Sound good?" He tossed a glance her way.

"Wait, do you mean at your place?"

"Unless you'd rather go out?"

She shrugged. "I don't care. This was your idea." She'd do well to keep reminding herself to stop thinking of Presley as a man. She tried to picture him as an object. Something with no feelings, no emotions, no thoughts. It didn't work. Sex appeal rolled off him with no effort on his part.

She tried to sneak a glimpse out of the corner of her eye. He looked like he'd freshly showered, and his shirt held the crispness of one that had been recently ironed. Could he have put as much effort into his appearance as she did tonight?

"You look real pretty tonight, Dixie." He didn't meet her gaze, just stared straight ahead, down the double-yellow lines in the center of the highway.

She cleared her throat, uncomfortable with the compliment.

"See, now this is where you say thank you. Then say something nice back to me."

She screwed her mouth into a frown. "What is this, remedial dating?"

He shrugged. "Call it what you will, but if you're going to charm the snot out of SoCal, you need some practice."

"Now wait just a minute." She twisted her torso to better face him.

"It's true. He's slimier than a whole bucket of bait. If you want to best him, you'll need all of your wits plus mine. Now, say something nice to me."

Whatever. She didn't want to admit Presley might have a point. "Okay, um, your nails look nice."

"My nails?" He laughed. "That's the best you could come up with?"

"Just forget it." She cinched her arms across her waist and turned to face the window. Fields of cotton flew by. The breeze blew her hair out of the headband Liza had so carefully tied into her hair. "Oh gosh, I forgot the scarf." She scrambled for her purse as Presley hit a pothole. Her head flew into the dash. "Ouch."

"You okay?" His hand went to the back of her hair, smoothing down the wild strands as they whipped around her face.

"Can you shut the windows and turn the air on for once?" She lifted her head as he pressed the buttons to raise the windows.

"Better?"

"Yes."

"We're off to a great start, aren't we?"

"Seems to be the way things always go when we're together."

His mouth tugged into a grin. "How about we start over?"

"Isn't it a little late for that?"

"No." He whipped the steering wheel to the right and pulled over on the side of the road. "See that farmhouse over there?" He pointed to a white farmhouse with black shutters that sat about a hundred and fifty yards from the road.

"What about it?" Dixie squinted into the setting sun.

"We're going to pretend that's where you live, and I'm going to come pick you up for a date."

"What? Who lives there?"

"You do." Presley eased the truck forward twenty feet and turned into the long gravel drive. She grabbed onto his arm, intentionally ignoring the way his muscles tightened under her hand.

"What are you doing?"

"I'm doing a do-over." The Jeep bounced over the ruts in the drive. A ragged old dog came out from behind the barn, wagging his tail and offering a friendly bark.

"Presley, this is someone's house. You can't just pull up in the drive like this." Her heartbeat vibrated through her entire body, and her cheeks tingled.

He brought the Jeep to a stop then walked around to open her door. "Now you just go stand on the stoop and I'll wait a minute then pretend like I'm coming to pick you up for our date."

"Don't be ridiculous. Let's get out of here."

"No can do. Not until I have a chance to properly greet you."

Dixie glanced toward the house. It didn't look like anyone was home based on the way the shades were drawn tight. "This is crazy."

"Take all the time you need. I can wait all night." He leaned against the side of the Jeep and examined his nails.

"Nails, huh?"

"I'm sorry, it's the first thing I notice about a man. You have nice hands, okay?"

"Aw, darlin', just wait until you see the rest of me."

Her face flamed at the implication. She shook it off. "Has our new first date started yet?"

"Not until you get out of the Jeep."

"Fine. What do you want me to do?"

"Just go stand on the stoop. I'll be around to fetch you momentarily."

"I can't believe you." But yet she climbed out of the vehicle and crossed the drive to stand on the first step. "Okay, I'm ready. Hurry up."

Presley walked to the hedge and plucked a freshly bloomed gardenia from its stem. "Why, Dixie Mae King, look at you. You sure are a sight for these sore eyes tonight."

She couldn't help but giggle as he held out the flower.

"Shall we?" He offered her his arm, and she wrapped her hand around his strong forearm.

"Hurry up. Let's get out of here before someone sees us." She kept glancing back at the house, but nothing moved. The dog, however, stuck to her side, nosing into her as they made the short walk to the Jeep.

"I'm so glad you decided to come out with me tonight. It's going to be a good one, I can feel it." He winked as he handed her up into the passenger seat.

"Tone it down a bit there."

"Too much?" he asked in a conspiratorial whisper.

"Just a tad." She buckled in as he shut the door.

He whistled as he crossed in front of the Jeep. "I've

got special plans tonight. I'm taking you to the Farley Inn."

"Oh, I can't go there. That's where Chandler's taking me tomorrow." Her heart took a swan dive in her chest at the thought of showing up at the same place two nights in a row with two different men.

"Okay, then we'll do something else." He fired up the Jeep and sped down the long drive. "What are you in the mood for?"

Before she could answer, a pickup pulled off the main road and headed straight toward them on the drive. "Who's that?"

Presley lifted his hand in a wave as they passed. A man and woman sat in the front seat. They both craned their necks as they drove by. "Best guess is those are the folks who live here."

"Well, then go faster!" she urged.

"You got it." He pressed on the gas, and they fishtailed onto the highway into what Dixie was beginning to believe might be one of the best nights of her life.

chapter
EIGHTEEN

PRESLEY TRIED NOT TO LET ON THE TYPE OF THOUGHTS HE was having about Dixie. They definitely didn't have anything to do with a fake date. He'd planned on just taking her back to his place to hide out from the town and maybe driving through somewhere on the way. They could practice feeding each other french fries and he'd pretend to be Chandler. But now, with Dixie beside him, he didn't want to pretend anymore. Something in her had lightened, seemed to shift the tension between them over the past several days. And damn if he didn't like it.

"So the Farley Inn is out, and you don't seem so sure about going back to my place. What'll it be then, option A or B?" He tapped his thumb on the steering wheel to the beat of the radio.

"Are you going to tell me what my options are?" she asked.

"Nope. You'll have to just go with your gut." There was something different, more playful about her tonight.

"Hmm. Well, I typically like to go with my first instinct, which would be to pick option A."

"Option A it is."

"But"—Dixie held up a perfectly red–tipped pointer finger— "you probably figured I'd go with the first option, so maybe I'd better pick option B."

"Those are some fabulous deduction skills. Hurry and make a choice. I need to know which way to turn up here." She didn't need to know he had no idea where he was taking her. But the longer he could delay, the more time he'd get to spend with this fun version of Dixie.

"But then you'd probably think I wouldn't pick option B because I'd know you were onto me. So I'm back to option A."

"For sure this time?"

Dixie nodded. "For sure."

"Okay then." He took the hard right at fifty miles an hour. Dixie leaned into him.

"Presley! What was that?"

"I told you to make up your mind."

"Where are we going?"

"Option A." Five minutes later he pulled into the parking lot of Primed to Putt, the only mini-golf course in Conroe County. "How are you with a putter?"

"I've never held a putter in my life."

"Good. Then I might have a chance of beating you." He raced around the Jeep to open her door for her. She let him take her hand and help her out. That faint scent of strawberries drifted under his nose. Strawberries were quickly becoming his favorite fruit. "Right this way."

He led her toward the putt shack, where he picked up two putters. "What color ball do you want to use?"

Dixie mulled over her choices. "Doesn't matter. I probably won't be able to hit it anyway."

"How about red to match your dress then?" He held out a painted-red golf ball.

She made a move to grab it but accidentally knocked it out of his hand instead. It bounced once, then twice, and rolled into a strand of flowers. Dixie bent down to retrieve it, giving him a full-on glance at the miraculous cleavage the sundress had managed to summon. He picked up a blue ball for himself. If he was going to have to be subjected to those curves all night long, he might as well have a matching set.

He guided her to the first hole with a hand at the small of her back. "Now this here is easy peasy. You just set your ball down like so"—he dropped his ball onto the fake grass—"then figure out what angle you want to hit it at to try to sink it in the hole."

He tapped the ball with the putter, sending it bouncing off the wooden frame of the putting green past a set of horseshoes set up as a trap and landing it a few inches from the hole.

"You certainly make it look easy…" Dixie bounced her putter against the Astroturf.

"Now you try." He pointed to the ground. "Just set your ball down and give it a tap."

She bent over to place her ball on the green. Dammit, she needed to stop doing that. Maybe mini-golf was a bad idea. How could he keep her from flashing her chest every time she moved?

"Like this?" Wide green eyes peered up at him.

He tore his gaze away from where a silver pendant dangled between her breasts. "Yeah, now stand up and take a swing at it." Wrapping his hand around her elbow, he guided her to a standing position. The sooner the better too.

"So how do I hold this?" Dixie held the grip in one hand, more like a baseball bat.

"Stand to the side, just like I did." He demonstrated, keeping his distance from the strawberries and the distracting cleavage.

Dixie shifted her weight from one foot to the other. "Do I keep my feet together or apart? Sorry"—she graced him with a smile—"I wasn't paying attention when you took your turn."

"What? That was like one of the best shots I've ever had. Look how close to the hole I got it." He pointed to the ball, sitting mere inches from the cup.

"Yep, very impressive. Do you want to help me out here, or should I just whack it?"

He took in a deep breath. A cleansing breath. A breath that was meant to empower him and keep him from being affected by the sheer proximity of Dixie Mae King, especially when she kept flashing her cleavage and saying words like *ball* and offering to "whack" things. Then he stepped close, put an arm on either side of her, and nestled his front against her backside.

"What's this?" She tried to turn to face him.

He forced the slam of indecent thoughts from his brain. "Focus on the ball. Now wrap your hands around the grip."

She bent at the waist, sliding her hands under his to hold the metal of the putter.

"Not the shaft—take hold of it by the grip." It was bad enough her gorgeous ass pressed into his crotch, making him painfully aware of their closeness. Now he had to use words like *shaft* and *grip*. Good God, someone up above was punishing him for past transgressions.

Dixie's hands moved to the grip. He put his over hers and nudged her feet apart with his boot. With his arms snuggled tightly around her, the scent of strawberries washed over him. He tucked his cheek against hers, relishing the feel of her soft skin on his.

"Are we going to hit the ball?" she whispered.

Damn, how long had they been standing there, back to front, cheek to cheek?

"Yeah." He cleared his throat. "Just pull back a little and hit it square in the middle." He guided her swing, letting her lead with the follow-through.

The ball bounced over the edge of the green and landed in a man-made pond of water.

"Oh no." Dixie's shoulders sagged. "I've lost my ball. What do we do now?"

Presley reluctantly released her from his arms. "Don't worry, Red. I'll get you another one." He took his time walking back to the putt shack, taking the opportunity to breathe in some fresh air. Air not tainted by the arousing scent of Dixie Mae King. What the hell had he gotten himself into?

She waited at the hole, a hand cocked on her hip. "I think I'll try this one on my own."

"Good idea." Presley didn't think he could handle sidling up against her again.

She set up her shot, swung, and managed to keep the ball on the green. It bounced over the horseshoes and stopped a couple of feet behind his.

"See? It's not as hard as you make it sound." A smug grin covered her face.

"Oh, you think you can beat me now, huh?"

Her shoulders lifted in a shrug. "Maybe."

"You willing to wager on it?"

"What, like a bet?" Eyes narrowed, she spun her putter around in her fingers.

"Yeah, like a bet. We'll play nine holes. If I have the lowest score, I win. If you get the lowest score, you win."

She tilted her head to one side. "What do I win?"

He closed the distance between them. Lowering his voice a notch, he mumbled close to her ear, "What do you want?"

Her body stiffened next to him. "I don't know. What are you good at?"

A low rumble of laughter shook his chest. "Oh, darlin', you sure you want to know?"

She took a step back, her cheeks flushed. "I didn't mean it like that."

"Flirting 101, you should have meant it like that. When you're out with SoCal tomorrow, let the innuendos and double entendres fly, okay?"

Dixie nodded. "I'll try. What do you want if you win?"

He tapped his finger against his lip. "Hmm, that's a tough one." If he'd been betting against Sierra or April or any one of the gals he'd dated in the past, he'd insist on some time between the sheets. But he had to be careful with Dixie. He couldn't afford to go there again. That searing kiss she'd laid on him the other night had taunted him for days.

"Dinner. If I win, I want you to make me dinner. Home cooking with all the fixings. Sound fair?" He raised a brow while he waited for her response.

"Fine." She nodded.

"So what do you want?" He lined up to take his shot.

"Can I think about it?"

"You bet. Won't matter anyway. I don't intend to lose." He tapped the ball, and it rolled into the hole. If he could keep this up, he'd be well on his way to a home-cooked meal.

Dixie sunk her putt as well. Tied. Maybe this wouldn't be as easy as he thought.

By the time she completed the ninth hole, he was three shots in the lead. As long as he kept his ball on the green and didn't do something stupid, that homemade dinner would be his. He could almost taste the victory: brisket, barbecue beans, fresh-baked rolls, and something sweet for dessert.

"You ever figure out what you're playing for?" He wiggled his hips from side to side, getting ready to tee off. "What are you giving up when I get a hole in one here?"

She tiptoed close. The scent of strawberries he'd been trying to avoid tickled his nose. "It's embarrassing," she whispered against his ear.

What could she want that would be embarrassing? Did she need help applying some sort of rash cream in a delicate area? Need him to play the heavy to somebody who owed her money? Not likely. Whatever Dixie thought was embarrassing he'd be able to handle, especially since she had no chance of winning.

He refocused on the ball in front of him. As he swung the putter back, ready to hit the ball, she spoke. "Sex. If I win, I want you to take my virginity."

﹏

Dixie wrapped her arms around her waist and pressed her back against the passenger-side door. Presley hadn't said a word to her as he paid for their golf. The final score sheet sat on the console between them. He hadn't filled in his score from the last hole, but they both knew she'd won.

She hadn't decided yet if her victory would go down as sweet or tragic. That would probably depend on whether Presley came through on his end of the deal. Based on the way he white-knuckled the steering wheel and the way his dark eyes glared out at the world from under the brim of his hat, it didn't look good.

Obviously it would be up to her to break the silence. "Sorry, I didn't mean to surprise you with—"

"Surprise?" Sarcasm leeched from his voice. "Grabbing my ass would have surprised me. You do realize there's no way I can keep up my end of the bet, right?"

She chewed on her lip while she contemplated the best way to respond. "You said yourself it's best to practice. To get the warm-up out of the way so I don't make a fool out myself when it comes time for the real thing."

He slammed the gear shift into what she now recognized as fourth. "We were talking about kissing."

"Riiiiiiiiiiight…" Dixie drew out the word. "But after kissing comes the other stuff."

With one eye on the road, he twisted to glare at her. "I know plenty about the other stuff."

"I know." She toyed with the handle of her purse. "That's why I want it to be you."

"Can you imagine what your dad would do to me? What Cash and Waylon and, holy hell, even Charlie would do to me if they found out about this? I value my body parts, darlin', all of them, and I refuse to be deprived of any of them if someone were to catch wind of this."

"I won't tell anyone." She reached over to put her hand on his arm. "I'm twenty-seven years old…way past the age I thought I would be when I lost it."

He grunted. "I figured you were saving yourself."

"I might have been at one time. But since my dad pretty much guaranteed no one in Holiday would come near me, I've decided I'd rather just get it over with."

"Yeah, I heard about the Hernandez kid."

Dixie slumped lower in her seat. "Everyone's heard about that. He made sure he warned every guy within a fifty-mile radius not to dare hook up with me for fear of my father."

"Why didn't he do the same with Liza?"

"He couldn't." She blew out a laugh. "Liza tore out of here as soon as she graduated high school. Came back a few years later pregnant with Bea. How old were you when you did it for the first time?"

"It?" He shrugged off her hand. "You can't even say it." He eased the Jeep to a stop on the side of the two-lane highway. "Dixie, I'm flattered, really I am. But this is going way too far."

She bit her lip again, noticing the way he drew in a breath and stared at her mouth. This, this right here is what he'd been trying to teach her to do with Chandler. Play up her feminine wiles. If it would work on Chandler, maybe it would work on him too.

Fighting back her nerves, she twisted in her seat to face him while she tucked a strand of hair behind her ear. "Does that mean you don't find me"—she stumbled over the word, forcing it past her lips—"attractive?"

"No." His hands went to his head, lifting his hat and funneling through his hair. "Hell no, it's not about that at all."

She unclipped her seat belt. "Then what is it?" Leaning over the center console, she nudged her nose into his ear. "I promise not to tell anyone."

"Why me?" He turned his head. Their noses bumped. His gaze searched hers, looking for an answer.

Her hand worked its way past the buttons on his short-sleeve shirt. She found her way past the T-shirt he had on underneath. Pressed flat against his stomach, her hand caressed the ridges of well-toned abs. "Because you know what you're doing. And I know you'll keep it between us."

"Dixie…"

She met his lips with hers. "I trust you, Presley."

His eyes closed, and he nodded. "I'm going to regret this."

"I won't," she promised. Then she brushed his lips with hers again. While her hand explored the planes of his chest, her tongue danced over his. A thrill swept over her. She'd waited long enough. Besides, if she was going to play the femme fatale, she ought to have the experience to go along with it.

Presley broke the kiss by gently nudging her back to her seat. "You sure you want to do this?"

She nodded.

"Dammit." His hands scrubbed over his chin. "Then let's get to it before I come to my senses."

Smiling, Dixie bounced back into her seat and clipped her seat belt. "Thanks so much."

He shook his head. "This is crazy. I've got a really bad feeling about this, Red."

"That's probably the chili dog you ate around hole four that's talking. Everything's going to be fine." A giddiness she wasn't expecting bubbled up inside. Kind of like when she'd drunk the carbonated water straight out of the soda dispenser at the Rose.

Presley didn't speak again until they'd stopped in front of his place. Even though it sat on the Walker ranch, Dixie had never been there before.

"This is nice."

He opened the front door and ushered her inside. "I don't typically bring women back to my place."

Dixie set her purse down on the table by the front door. "Then don't think of me as a woman."

"This is going to be a hell of a lot awkward if I can't think of you as a woman, you know."

She giggled, apparently unable to contain her nervousness over the situation she'd chosen to put herself in. "I suppose."

He dropped his keys into a Texas-shaped ceramic bowl. "I'm sorry to keep beating a dead dog, but I need to ask one more time."

Dixie met his gaze. The cocky cowboy was gone. Presley's eyes reflected uncertainty. "I'm sure about this. I promise."

He nodded then removed his hat and set it on the table. "I've done some pretty strange stuff and found myself in some downright dangerous situations over the years, but this right here takes the cake."

"So where should we do it? Here?" She flounced down on the couch and patted the cushion next to her. "This seems comfortable enough."

Presley shook his head. "It's your first time. I'm not going to take you on the couch."

"Oh." Her tummy twinged. Maybe she should have thought this all the way through.

Presley stalked toward her, removing his boots as he came closer. "It was pretty hot out there playing golf."

"Mm-hmm," Dixie agreed.

"What do you say we take a nice shower to cool off first?"

Now that he mentioned it, she had worked up a little bit of a sheen while she swung the putter and tried to beat him in mini-golf. "If that's what you think is best."

He held out a hand to help her off the couch. "Come on, this way."

She took it, letting him lead her into his bedroom. At the sight of his king-sized bed, her heart did a somersault in her chest. A red, blue, and khaki quilt stretched over the top. He paused as they entered the bathroom to grab two giant towels from the linen closet.

"I like the quilt on your bed. Did your mom make it?"

He pinched the bridge of his nose. "If we're going to go through with this, you can't do that."

"What?"

"Bring up my mother in conversation right before we have sex."

Her gaze dropped to the floor. His white athletic socks looked out of place against the slate-colored tile on his bathroom floor. She kept her eyes trained on the little green line that designated the toe area on his left foot. "I'm sorry."

"Come here." He set the towels on the counter and pulled her close.

Her body stiffened at the initial contact, but then she relaxed into him. She wanted this. He was doing this for her. The least she could do was try to keep his mother out of it.

His hand climbed up her spine to cradle the back of her head. She tilted her face, matching her mouth to his. A shiver of anticipation tingled its way up the entire length of her body from her toes to the top of her head. She stamped out the doubt and deepened the kiss. He responded, pressing her back against the bathroom vanity.

Her backside hit the granite, and she lifted her hips to slide onto the counter. He nudged her legs apart. Her skirt bunched around her thighs as he nestled his hips between them. His kisses moved from her mouth to her neck. Tiny sparks danced across her skin everywhere he touched. Her breasts felt heavy, swollen with lust, she thought to herself. She almost giggled, but then his hands found their way under her ruffled crinoline, and her lungs seized.

"You okay?" Presley paused, barely lifting his lips from where they'd settled on her collarbone.

Rendered mute by the sensations rocking through her body, she nodded. He lowered his head, flicking his tongue along her breastbone then lower to the bodice of her haltered sundress.

Her head rolled back as he dipped his tongue in the cleft between her breasts. His hands continued to inch their way up her thighs. She wrapped her arms around his shoulders, trying to get him to lift his head. She needed his lips on hers in the worst way.

Instead, he pulled his hands away, raising them behind

her neck to untie the halter of her dress. She reached behind her and unzipped the back. He didn't say a word. He didn't have to. The heat in his eyes told her everything she needed to know. As the straps of the sundress fell to the side and the front of her dress peeled away from her chest, Presley grinned.

chapter
NINETEEN

Miles of unexplored skin waited for his touch. Presley's conscience bounced back and forth—he shouldn't be doing this. But she'd asked for it. If he didn't go through with it, would she tap SoCal for the favor? Or some other guy who might hit on her at the Rose? She deserved to be treated like the goddess she was. He wanted her first experience to be memorable—to set the bar for everything that would come after.

He trailed his tongue along her breastbone, savoring the taste of her skin. Her moans turned him on more than he expected, more than a woman's response had in quite some time. He needed to slow things down.

"Hey, Dixie?"

"Mmm?" With her eyes closed, leaning back against the mirror, she looked more like she was ready for a nap than a night of hard-core lovin'.

"How about that shower?" He reached behind him to turn on the faucet.

Before he had a chance to reach it, her eyes eased open. "I don't want to put you out."

He furrowed his brow. "You afraid my water bill will get out of control?"

She grinned. "No. But you have to work tomorrow, and I need to get home to Gram. It's already ten thirty."

"Are you going to turn into a pumpkin?"

"No." She swatted at his chest.

"Got a curfew?"

"No. But we both have to get up early tomorrow. Maybe we should just get it over with?"

"Hey, if you've changed your mind…" He tilted his head, waiting for a response.

"No. Definitely not."

"Fine. Then we'll do it my way. Do you need to call your grandma? Because you're going to be late."

Her chin tucked against her chest. "How late are we talking?"

"Well, that depends on how many times you want to lose your virginity tonight."

The corner of her mouth tugged into a half grin. "Technically, I can only lose it once."

"Then we better make it last a very long time." He bent down to grab the hem of her dress.

She hopped off the counter as he lifted the garment up and over her head. Standing before him in nothing but a sturdy white bra and a netted underskirt, her skin flushed. Her fingers reached for the top button on his shirt. As she pushed the button through the hole, she ran her tongue over that full bottom lip. By the time she'd undone his shirtfront, his dick strained against the zipper of his jeans.

What was it about this woman that turned him on so much? With anyone else, he would have figured the hesitance and tentativeness as an act. With Dixie, it was just who she was. He slid his arms out of his shirt, letting it drop to the floor. With one fluid motion, he whipped his undershirt over his head.

Dixie's eyes widened as she took in the expanse of bare chest. He liked her reaction. Liked it so much he undid his belt buckle and his jeans and tossed them on top of the pile.

"Your turn." Standing in front of her in nothing but his boxer briefs, he waited to see if she really would take the next step.

She slid her underskirt down her thighs. He followed it with his eyes, taking in the curve of her hip, the long expanse of leg. Then she reached behind her to unclasp her bra.

"Damn, you're beautiful." How had he not noticed it before? All of these years—she'd been right in front of him.

"I don't feel very beautiful." Her gaze met his for a moment, then she looked to the floor.

Presley spun her around to face the mirror. "Do you see what I see?"

She kept her eyes cast down. "Stop."

He finished unhooking her bra and let it fall forward. As he nestled his lips against the curve of her neck, he urged her to look up. "Beautiful."

Her gaze met his in the mirror. He traced his fingertips up her arms, over her shoulders, down her collarbone. His lips didn't break contact with her skin. Not when her breath hitched. Not when she pressed her backside against him. Not when her eyes glazed over as he finally cupped her breasts in his hands.

"So fucking beautiful," he whispered against her neck.

As she slowly twirled around, she brought her hands up between them. He twined his fingers with hers while he moved closer to capture that lower lip with his teeth. Slowly, he lowered their hands. The exquisite torture of her breasts on his chest made him crazed with want. She was so tentative, yet so trusting. He didn't deserve her trust, her faith. But he wanted it.

He rimmed the waistband of her panties with a finger. A shiver coursed through her. Ticklish. That could be fun. Later though. Now he needed to show her how good it could be. Show her what she'd been missing out on all of these years.

Her fingers went to the front of his briefs, tugging downward, just enough to create a tiny bit of friction. His eyes rolled back in his head. She was so unsure of herself, so unaware of how turned on he was.

Keeping her mouth occupied with deep kisses, his fingers dropped lower, then lower still, until he brushed the sweet spot he'd been searching for. Her knees buckled, and she gripped his shoulders with both hands and buried her nose into his chest.

"Oh. That's...oh my gosh..."

He swept her up in his arms, cradling her against him. Forget the shower. Forget the fact that his siblings would tar and feather him. Her butt hit his bed, and she bounced. Before she had a chance to get situated at the head of the bed, he dropped to his knees to hover over her.

Kisses rained down on her hair, her lips, her cheek. With nothing left between them, bare skin slid on bare skin, the pleasure at having her spread before him almost too much to bear.

Her finger slid over his ribs. He didn't even wince he was so focused on how her skin felt under his touch. With a hand propping up his head, the other was free to taunt her and tease her, dipping into those fire-red curls then back out again. Her body responded to his demand for control. For once in her life, she didn't fight him, just gave in and let him touch her the way he wanted—the way she deserved.

He wanted to take his time, savor her the way she was meant to be. But hell, her hips started making small circles against his fingers. With her eyes closed, she'd fisted two handfuls of his quilt in her hands. Her brow furrowed in concentration. She looked so serious, he almost wanted to laugh.

"You don't have to work so hard."

"Huh?" She didn't open her eyes, just continued to make small, controlled circles with her hips.

"Dixie." As her name rolled off his tongue, she cracked an eye open.

"What?"

"Just relax. I'm going to make you feel good. Trust me."

She nodded, dropping her hips back down to the bed. He leaned over her, licking the salty taste of sweat off her skin. His lips trailed from her neck to her breast. He circled her nipple with his tongue then took it into his mouth, sucking, nibbling.

Her hands fumbled against his hips. A finger ventured lower, dancing across his dick. He pulled her nipple deeper into his mouth, lightly scraping it with his teeth. A moan started in the back of her throat, and she loosely wrapped her hand around his cock. He guided her hand, showing her how to stroke it. He didn't expect her to be such an enthusiastic learner. As he transferred the attention of his mouth to her other breast, she nudged his hand away, sliding her hand over him, up and down, like she'd been fisting his dick in her capable hands forever.

He lay there, enjoying her touch as long as he could bear it. If it were up to him, he'd have his way with her right here, right now. Drive into her, over and over again until they both found their release. But this night wasn't about him, it was about her. So he rolled over her and lowered himself until his lips lined up with her belly.

"Your whiskers." She squirmed under him.

"Hold still. It's about to get better."

She lifted her head. "Better? How could it get any better?"

He dipped his head in between her legs and finally let himself get his first taste of her. Her entire body tensed, her hips lifting off the bed.

"Told you it was going to get better," he joked. Then he put his mouth on her again.

As Presley coaxed her to sensations she'd only imagined, Dixie finally shredded the last remnants of resolve and gave in. Wave after wave of exquisite pleasure washed over her. His tongue and his fingers and, good God, what was he doing with his other hand down there that felt so incredibly good?

Unashamed, she sprawled in front of him. Naked as the day she was born while he had his way with her. She couldn't even bear to get changed in a community dressing room, and yet here she was, sharing parts of herself not even she had explored.

While he focused his tongue and his lips on her quivering core, his fingers played across her breasts. She wanted to feel him everywhere at once. Suddenly, his mouth, his fingers, his tongue weren't enough. A part of her ached for him, somewhere deep inside.

"Presley, I need…" Her voice faded as his tongue swept over her. "Oh."

"Go with it, Fireball." His whiskers rubbed her inner thighs.

She didn't have a choice. The sensation started as a low hum and grew as it sawed along every nerve ending she had. Presley didn't let up, continuing to guide her, never breaking contact with her skin. Her hands grappled for his shoulders. She needed an anchor, something to keep her secured to earth, or she feared she might float away.

Finally, after what seemed like both forever and not nearly long enough, she crested, suspended in some sort of zero-gravity zone while uncontrollable pulses racketed through her body. Fully sated, she clung to him. As she gently drifted back to an awareness of her surroundings, Presley's arms encircled her. He held her close to his chest as they both struggled to catch their breath.

"You okay?" His whiskers tickled her ear.

"No." She shook her head.

He pulled back to look at her. "Really? Tell me. What's wrong?"

"Nothing." She held his head against her chest, not quite able to make eye contact with the man yet. "Nothing's wrong. I just don't think I'll ever be okay again. That was so not okay."

"Not okay? Oh shit. Are you sorry?"

"No. I'm just sorry I didn't do that years ago." Her body was already so hot, she couldn't tell if she was blushing or just flushed from overexerting herself.

"Oh, Dix. You've got a lot to catch up on."

"Yes, I think I do." She finally dropped her gaze to his.

Smiling, he propped himself up on his elbows. "Ready to get started then?"

"Wasn't that enough for one night? Look"—she lifted her arm and let it drop back to the bed—"I can't even lift my arms."

He reached into the drawer of the nightstand and grabbed something. "Don't worry, your arms don't need to be involved."

She scooted up the bed until she could lean against the headboard.

He unrolled a condom into place. "We haven't even got to the best part yet."

"I don't know if I'll survive the best part." She eyed him with a lazy smile. How could he have so much energy left when her legs felt like she'd run a marathon? "You've worn me out."

"Do you mean that?" Concern creased his brow.

"Nah. Just need to catch my breath."

"You'll survive, Fireball." He pulled her down the bed until she was flat on her back again. "Not only that, but I bet you'll be begging for more."

She barked out a laugh. "So you're ready to lose another bet? Didn't you learn your lesson the first time?"

He nudged her legs apart and leaned over her. His mouth pressed down on hers. "I'm learning that sometimes the only way to win is by losing."

She wrapped her arms around his neck, pulling his mouth down to hers again. How could something she'd been told was so wrong be so amazing? Presley kissed along her cheek, pressing his nose into her hair.

"You smell incredible. Drives me crazy."

Tingles raced up her side as his tongue rimmed her ear. His hand trailed over her ribs. The need she'd felt earlier returned. Her body ached for him. She didn't think she had the ability to feel anything else—hadn't she already felt enough for tonight? Heck, for a lifetime?

Presley's mouth continued to pay homage to her earlobe. She shifted her hips underneath him, restless, needing more. He settled between her legs. His fingers slipped down her stomach, edging past her navel and tickling her inner thigh.

"Stop." She giggled, the mixture of sensations making it difficult to hold still.

"Stop what? This?" He took her earlobe into his mouth. Warmth shot through her.

"No, not that. That's nice."

"Then what? Stop this?" He slipped a finger just inside her.

Her legs tensed. She should be embarrassed at the way her body automatically responded to his touch. But she wasn't. The only thing she felt was the desire for more. She wanted everything Presley had for her—everything he was willing to teach her. "Oh, no, definitely don't stop that."

Making small circles over her most sensitive bundle of nerves with one hand, he slid his other finger in and out. Her hips matched his rhythm, small movements at first. But as he kept stroking and kissing and circling, her body ignited from within. Some primal need she was unprepared for took over. A frantic desire to wrap herself around him, surround him, enveloped her.

Presley brushed her hair off her cheek. "This may hurt a little bit. Are you sure this is what you want?"

She met his gaze and nodded. He hovered over her like he didn't want to smush her. Then he slowly lowered himself onto her, his gaze never leaving hers. She felt pressure as he pushed into her. At the resistance, he paused.

"Ready?"

She bit her lower lip. What she was about to do with Presley couldn't be undone. Her hands gripped his back, and she pulled him closer, urging him to continue. The pressure shifted to a sting. Then suddenly, it was gone, replaced by the same slight buzz she'd felt before.

Presley coaxed the tingle to a crescendo. His mouth took hers, searing her skin with his kisses. His hips moved in a rhythmic dance her body seemed to already know. His eyes never left hers.

"You feel amazing." He smiled between kisses, reaching a hand down between their legs to touch her like he had before.

"You feel pretty good to me too," she admitted, still not quite comfortable acknowledging how incredible he made her feel.

As he focused his attention on her sex, sensation took over. Her nails dug into his back, drawing him closer, needing him to finish what he'd started. His hips circled, and he pulled out slowly. She ached at the emptiness until he thrust forward, filling her again. Finally, when she couldn't take it anymore, her nerve endings exploded. Presley pushed into her one more time, holding himself still while a range of emotion swept over his face.

He'd always been the most gorgeous man she'd

ever seen. But like this—in a moment of complete release—the release she'd caused—he glowed.

He held himself over her, stretching out the moment, every muscle in his body taut. Her fingers ran over his arms, enjoying the tightness, the strength he held in check. Then he grinned. But instead of the smug, trademarked Presley Walker smirk she'd grown so accustomed to, he wore a tentative smile.

"What do you think?"

Spent, she gazed up at him. Her muscles were like Jell-O. "I think I should have done this a long time ago."

He rolled to the side and gathered her against him. "I'm glad you didn't."

"Really?" She searched his face. "Why?"

His hand brushed her cheek. "Because then you wouldn't have waited for me."

Dixie nestled into him, burrowing her face into his chest. She should get up, go. Insist Presley take her home. This was just a box she needed checked. Lose virginity. Done. It was natural to have a little bit of a hangover after the earth-moving experience she'd just shared with Presley. But that was it. They'd go on being the same antagonizing force in each other's lives. The fact that they'd just had sex—hot, mind-bending sex—shouldn't change a thing between them.

But it had. She could feel it in the way he held her close. In the way he cradled her. In the way she clung to him.

In that moment, Dixie knew there was no going back when it came to Presley Walker. What she hadn't quite figured out was how they would be able to move forward.

chapter
TWENTY

PRESLEY LAY STILL, HOLDING DIXIE CLOSE. HE'D HAD MORE than his fair share of dalliances. More than several men's fair share—and yet he'd never done what he'd done tonight. He'd never taken a woman's virginity. God, he hoped she didn't regret it.

Her head rested on his chest. He played with an errant curl, twisting it around his finger then letting it spring back into place. He had to keep his hands busy, or he'd run them all over her again. The curves, the skin as soft as a perfectly ripe peach. He couldn't get enough of her. Too bad this was a once-in-a-lifetime, one-night deal. Maybe that's why it seemed so bittersweet. By tomorrow at this time, they'd probably be flinging zingers at each other again.

"Dixie?"

"Mm-hmm?" Her breath floated across his chest.

"You okay?" With a little bit of encouragement from her, he'd be ready to go again. But that wasn't part of the bet.

From the light filtering in from the open bathroom door, he could make out the outline of her cheek. He ran a finger over it, wanting to say something to perfect the moment. But everything that popped into his head sounded way too cheesy.

"Yeah." She made a move to get up.

"Hey, wait a sec." He wasn't sure why, but he didn't

quite want the magic to end just yet. Not without acknowledging what had changed between them.

"What?" As she waited for him to speak, she caught her
bottom lip with her teeth.

He wanted to nudge into her, to capture that swollen
bottom lip with his mouth. He shook the feeling off, trying
to shed it like a jacket that didn't quite fit. That's the way
the two of them were—they didn't fit together. No matter
how much he'd enjoyed the evening, they wouldn't ever
be a match.

"I guess I wanted to say thanks."

She propped herself up on her elbows, the hint of a
smile lighting up those gorgeous green eyes. "Shouldn't I
be the one thanking you?"

His cheeks heated. When was the last time a woman
had made him blush? "I meant thanks for trusting me."

"Why, Presley Walker"—she gave his chest a playful
swat—"I do believe you're being sincere."

"Is that so hard to believe?" He captured her hand in his
and brought it to his lips.

She pulled away. "No. You surprised me. I think there's
a lot more to you than you let on."

"Oh yeah?" He rolled off the bed and felt around on
the floor for where he'd left his jeans.

"Yeah." The bed creaked as she sat up on the other
edge, the quilt wrapped around her.

He rounded the bed as he slid his jeans over his hips.
"What if I told you you might be right?"

"Ha. I might faint from the shock of you admitting it."
She lifted a brow. "Wait, are you serious?"

He held her gaze for a long moment. A glimmer of
something akin to hope sparked in the depths of her eyes.

He wanted to tell her everything. About the desire to turn his back on his job and strike out on his own for a change. About maybe wanting to settle down and try to make a relationship work for once in his life. But that glint of hope scared him more than anything. What if she took a chance on him and he blew it? He wouldn't be able to live with himself if Dixie put her trust in him and he let her down.

"Aw, I don't know. I get ideas every once in a while."

"Like what?" She patted the bed next to her.

He sat down. "Did you know my granddad used to make fiddles?"

She nestled her head into his shoulder. "I've heard people talk."

"His equipment is still out in one of the shops. Makes me think about firing it up someday and trying my hand at it. See if any of his talent got passed down through the generations." He ran his hand down her hair. "Does that sound crazy?"

"What, you making fiddles?"

He nodded, letting his chin rest on the top of her head. "I haven't really talked to anyone about it before."

Her finger traced circles on his chest. "I think it's admirable to follow your dreams. If that's something you want to try, what's stopping you?"

What was stopping him? Fear. Fear of failure. Fear of being a laughingstock. Fear of pretty much everything. He sighed. "Everything. What if I suck at it?"

A soft breath on his abs sent a shiver racing down his side. "You couldn't suck at it. Seems like everything you try works out. You've got to be the luckiest person I know."

If only that were true. Sure, he'd been fortunate and had ample opportunities handed to him based on his family, his looks, and his name. But the things that really mattered in life, he'd learned those were things he couldn't win with charm. Those were things he'd have to work at, to give his all and still have no guarantee of success. Like making fiddles. Or trying to build some kind of future with Dixie.

Would he be better off to leave things as they were? No expectations meant no disappointments.

But he'd lived that life already. He was ready to put himself out there—to fight for what he wanted.

"You really think I could do it?" he asked. Her faith in him meant more to him than he'd thought possible. If she believed in him, he could probably do just about anything.

Before she could answer, a knock sounded at the front door. He glanced at his watch. After midnight on a Sunday night? He wasn't expecting anyone.

He pulled his shirt on over his head. Before he could reach the door, it flew open. Statler barged into the room.

"Presley, you've got to come quick."

"Hey"—Presley glanced at the doorway to the bedroom—"what's going on?"

Statler grabbed his hand, pulling him toward the door. "I'll explain on the way."

"Wait. Tell me what's happening."

"It's Kermit. Somebody took all of his toads. Bins and bins of them. Doc and I were playing poker with some guys who've been performing over at the Rose when we heard. Why the hell didn't you answer your phone? We're wasting time, come on!"

Dixie bustled out of the bedroom. "Let's go."

"Dixie?" Statler's grip on Presley's arm loosened.

"Nice to see you too, Statler." Presley had to hand it to her. She didn't break her stride, not until she paused in front of him and whispered. "Can you please finish zipping up my dress? I can't reach the back."

He resisted the almost-uncontrollable urge to nip at her neck as he pushed her hair out of the way and pulled her zipper to the top of her back. The cat was out of the bag now. So much for keeping their one-night bet a secret.

If it bothered Dixie, it didn't show.

"Where's Kermit now?" Dixie asked.

Statler stood, mouth open, hanging halfway to his chest. "On the roof."

"Which roof?" Dixie and Presley asked in unison.

"The roof of the Rose. Says he won't come down until whoever took his toads brings them back."

"Well, what are we waiting for? Let's go." Dixie grabbed hold of Presley's hand and jerked them both toward the door.

Statler followed, a quizzical look on his face. "You want to tell me—"

Dixie and Presley interrupted that request before he had a chance to finish. "Don't ask."

By the time they reached the edge of town, Dixie had gotten all the info she needed. Poor Kermit. Who would have taken his toads like that?

Presley made it clear whom he suspected. He'd

quizzed Statler about who was at poker, who'd still been at the Rose, and who might have a vendetta about horned toads until Statler couldn't even speak. Then he'd summarized his suspicions in one word: SoCal.

"Who else could it be, Dixie? Who else has a reason to want Kermit to give up his land?" Presley twisted in his seat to glance back at her.

"He'll never give up his land, not while the horned toads live there."

"Exactly!" Presley gave her a wink. "What better way to get him to leave than take his toads?"

Dixie couldn't help but agree. "I'll admit, there's reason for suspicion, but you can't just assume."

"I'm not assuming anything. Statler said SoCal wasn't at poker. He's the only one who has a good reason to shut Kermit down."

"Yes and no," Statler finally got a couple words in.

"What do you mean?" Presley turned on his brother.

Dixie sighed. At least she'd been able to get out of the hot seat for a brief reprieve.

"Buster was running his mouth at poker. Seems Mayor Mayfield has been in talks with a certain company about bringing in some more tourists to Holiday."

Presley slapped his hand against the dash. "You've got to be kidding me. Why would she do that?"

"You'll have to ask Buster when you see him. I hope we're not too late." Statler pressed on the gas, and the truck increased its speed.

As they approached the Rose, an ambulance sped by, lights flashing and siren blaring.

"That's not a good sign," Statler observed.

Dixie didn't wait for the truck to come to a complete

stop in the parking lot. She hopped out while it was still moving. Presley followed.

"Hey, slow down. I'm sure the police have everything under control." He reached for her arm, but Dixie brushed him away.

"I've got to see if I can help." Her thoughts were on Gram. It would crush her grandmother to lose another friend. As she made her way to the barrier the police had constructed at the edge of the sidewalk, her eye caught on a platinum curly bob in the middle of the roof.

"Oh my gosh, Presley, that's my gram." Dixie pointed to where her grandmother sat huddled next to Kermit. "What's she doing?"

Presley grabbed her hand. "Looks like she's talking to him."

"I need to get up there." She ducked under the caution tape, towing Presley behind her.

Cash, Presley's brother and the local sheriff's deputy, put a hand on her arm. "Where do you think you're going, Dixie?"

"Cash, that's her grandmother up there. You've got to let her go," Presley argued with his older brother.

Dixie took the opportunity while the men sized each other up to scoot past the barrier. Nothing could keep her from her grandmother. Not a line of sheriff's deputies, not an army of tanks, not a—

"Forgetting someone?" Presley snagged her hand, matching her stride for stride. "I'm not letting you go up there by yourself."

Grateful for his show of support, she didn't bother to send him away. They jogged, hand in hand, to the front of the Rose. The fire department had set up a flood-light that lit up Gram and Kermit like they were some celebrity couple on the red carpet, not two senior citizens who had no business being forty-some feet off the ground.

"Gram!" Dixie wheezed, trying to catch her breath. "What's going on?"

"Oh, Dixie, what are you doing here?" Gram took in the sight of the clasped hands. Her eyebrow lifted.

Dixie slid her hand from Presley's. "What's happening? Is Kermit threatening to jump?"

"Heaven's no." Gram waved off her concern like she was batting at a pesky horsefly. "Although he's just sick about the loss of his toads."

"Then what are you doing up there?" Dixie put a hand to her forehead to shield her eyes. It looked like high noon with the lights trained on the couple on the roof.

"He's protesting. Says he won't come down until whoever stole his toads comes clean."

"For fuck's sake," Presley muttered.

"Hey"—Dixie whacked him in the stomach—"language."

Presley slung an arm around her shoulders. "Mrs. Holbein, I'm sure the authorities are doing everything they can to locate the, uh, missing specimens."

Cash joined them and shouted toward the roof. "Yes, we are. If Mr. Klaussen would like to come down, we can take an official statement. I'm sure that would help."

"I told you to call me Eugenia." Gram bent her head and conferred with Kermit. "And Kermit says he already gave Tippy a statement. Dixie, are you canoodling with Presley Walker?"

Dixie stepped away from Presley's side and faced Cash. "What did Kermit tell Tippy?"

Cash shook his head. "Nothing. Just said some guys came around and made him an offer on his land. He threatened to pull out his twelve-gauge and told them to get the hell off his property. Came to the Rose for poker, and when he got home, the toads were gone."

"I told you SoCal's behind this." Presley hitched his thumbs in his belt loops.

"Who's SoCal?" Cash tilted his chin toward Presley.

"A real estate investor from California who's been trying to romance Dixie. You should go talk to him. He's staying at the B and B."

Dixie wanted to tell Cash not to bother. "Presley, if you're right and he's got something to do with this, having Cash go pounding down his door is only going to scare him away. Let me try to get the info out of him."

Presley shook his head. "No. I changed my mind about that."

"Since when?" Last time they'd talked about it, he was still gung ho for her trying to get some intel on Chandler's intentions.

"Since...dammit...since about an hour ago, okay?"

"What happened an hour ago?" Cash asked, glancing back and forth from her to Presley.

The realization hit her like a shovel over the head. An hour ago she and Presley had been sweaty and naked and...her face flamed like she'd just stepped into the floodlight herself. "Oh my gosh."

"Wait, not you two?" Cash pointed to Presley then her and then back at Presley. "No. Please don't tell me you—"

"Played mini-golf," Dixie chimed in. "Yep, we sure did."

"Mini-golf?" Cash raised a doubtful brow.

"Yeah, it was a beautiful thing," Presley added. "Right up until she beat me and then—"

"We left." Dixie shrugged. "Now, let's talk about something important like how we're going to get my grandmother off the roof."

"Mini-golf?" Cash asked again, his dark eyes narrowed.

"Yep." Presley clapped a hand on Cash's shoulder. "Seems SoCal has invited Dixie to play a round of mini-golf with him too. But we played so well together, I just can't imagine her playing mini-golf with someone else."

Dixie clamped her hands to her hips. "That's not fair. He said nothing about mini-golf. Just dinner. You're the one who wanted me to go out with him in the first place."

"I'm telling you, that man has more than dinner on his mind." Presley shook his head. "First he'll take you to the Farley Inn, and before you know it, he'll be inviting you to grip his putter all night long."

"Wait." Cash pinched the bridge of his nose. "I don't get what this has to do with Kermit's missing toads. Can we focus on the details here?"

"Drop it, Presley. Just because I played golf with you doesn't mean I can't hit the ball around with anyone else for the rest of my life."

"I'm not asking you to."

"Then what are you asking me?"

Cash squinted, casting a glance back and forth between them. "Yeah, what are you asking her, Pres?"

"Hell, I don't know. I just really enjoyed"—he glanced to Cash then back at Dixie—"playing mini-golf with you. A lot more than I expected. Maybe, if you're up for it, we could play another round sometime. Maybe follow it up with dinner, make it a regular thing."

Dixie shook her head. "Presley Walker, you confound me."

Cash raised a hand. "Yeah, I'm pretty confused too. I didn't even know Presley liked mini-golf."

Dixie and Presley both looked at Cash like they just realized he'd been standing there all along. Then Dixie turned back to Presley and grabbed his arm. "We'll talk about this later. Right now we need to get my grandmother and her beau off the roof. They had to have used a ladder to get up there. Can you go find it?"

Presley's jaw ticked. Then he wheeled around and took off to the back of the building.

Cash glanced up at where Gram and Kermit huddled on the metal roof. "I have a feeling you weren't really talking about mini-golf, were you?"

Dixie groaned. "Can we tackle one crisis at a time?"

"Yep. Let me go see if I can help Pres find the ladder." Cash traced Presley's steps and rounded the back of the Rose.

Dixie shielded the glare from her eyes and glanced toward the roof again. She should be thinking about her grandmother and what she could do to help find Kermit's toads. But she couldn't seem to get past Presley's invitation. Did she want to see him again? Her heart tap-danced through her chest at the idea of her and Presley on a real date. She didn't know. There were too many unanswered questions. But one thing she did know for sure. She'd never think about mini-golf in quite the same way ever again.

PRESLEY SPENT TEN MINUTES SEARCHING FOR A LADDER UNTIL he realized Kermit had pulled it up onto the roof behind him. Dixie was going to blow her top when she found out her grandma had stranded herself on the roof. That was, if she hadn't already lost it after his impromptu invitation. He'd had no intention of extending their romantic involvement beyond making good on his end of the bet. But the thought of her on a date with SoCal made his blood heat up hotter than the oil Angelo used to deep-fry his chicken-fried steaks. If he could keep his trap shut until tomorrow, he could sleep on it and see how things seemed in the morning.

Refocused on the task on hand, he wondered how long it would take to run over to Waylon's to get the tall extension ladder from the back of the barn. Cash had a tall ladder at his place too. While Presley contemplated which relative would have the best ladder option, Tippy's pickup crunched across the gravel, coming to a stop at the edge of the police tape.

"Good news!" Tippy climbed out of the truck, holding a bucket close to his chest.

"What kind of good news?" Mrs. Holbein called down from the roof.

"We found one." Tippy held the bucket up, as if

Kermit and Dixie's grandma could see what was in the bucket from forty feet away.

"One what?" Kermit shouted.

"One of your toads. Poor little sucker was in a bin all by himself. They must have missed him." Tippy lowered the bucket.

"Is it Fernando?" Mrs. Holbein inched down the metal roof. "Dixie, see if it's Fernando."

Presley and Dixie reached Tippy at the same time. Both peered into the bucket.

"Is it Fernando?" Presley muttered.

"How am I supposed to tell?" Dixie squinted at the creature in the bucket. "Looks to be about the same size."

"If it is, do you think that will get them off the roof?" Tippy asked.

Dixie glanced from the bucket to Presley. He nodded. What was the difference between one toad to the next? His immediate goal was to get the folks off the roof and put some distance between him and Dixie. He needed to think. All he'd been able to do since the whole bet started was react. He needed to take some space, figure out what the hell had happened between him and Fireball earlier and what he needed to do about it. The sooner the better too.

Being around her hadn't been a problem before. But now, every time she swished her hair, he caught the scent of her irresistible shampoo. Every time she stuck her lower lip out in a pout, he wanted to capture it in his mouth and do naughty, naughty things to her with his tongue.

Dammit.

"Sure looks like Fernando to me. What do you think, Dixie?" Her claim that she'd never tell a lie was about to be put to the test.

She waffled. "Well, this one is about the right size to be Fernando."

"See?" Presley yelled up to the roof. "Even Dixie thinks it's the little guy you saved yesterday."

That must have been good enough for her gram. She and Kermit conferred for a long moment then she called out. "I'm coming down to double-check."

The ladder screeched as Kermit lowered it to the ground. Dixie ran around behind the building. Presley followed, hot on her trail.

"Be careful, Gram!" Dixie held the bottom of the ladder while her grandmother slowly climbed down.

"Don't you worry about me. I've done a fair amount of climbing down ladders in my lifetime. How else do you think I snuck out to go joyriding with your grandfather back in the day?"

Dixie shot Presley a look that seemed to beg for intervention.

"Kermit sure is upset over this, isn't he?" Presley asked. He had one hand on the ladder while the other reached out to steady Mrs. Holbein as her feet finally touched solid ground.

She turned to face him. "Of course he is. Those horned toads are his life's work. We've just got to find out who did this."

"We will, Gram," Dixie promised.

"I know you will." Her grandmother hugged Dixie for a long moment before she gestured to Presley. "Now get on in here and give me some sugar, young man. We're going to need all the help we can get."

Presley wrapped his arms around the women, torn
between wanting to feel Dixie tight against him again
and needing the chance to get as far away as possible.

Before he could really start to enjoy the moment,
Dixie broke the hug. "Come around front and you
can make sure we've got Fernando, okay?"

Mrs. Holbein nodded and allowed Dixie to lead
her back to the front of the Rose, where Tippy held
the bucket at arm's length. After taking a good
long look, Dixie's gram declared the tiny toad to be
Fernando, and a cheer went up from the small group
that had gathered in the parking lot.

"Come on down, Kermit. You need to take care
of this toad." Cash tapped his boot while he waited
for a response.

"I ain't coming down until I get all of my toads
back," Kermit called down from the roof.

"I'm not surprised," Mrs. Holbein said. "He's a
man of principle. It's one of the traits I most admire
about him."

Principle. Presley wondered for a split second what
his most admirable trait might be. He could make
most people laugh. He made a mean margarita. But
when it came down to the real stuff, the stuff that
made a man a real man, what would someone he
admired say about him?

He wanted to be the kind of man a woman would
talk about the way Mrs. Holbein talked about Kermit.
His mind flashed back to earlier, when Dixie had said
she trusted him. If he was capable of earning the trust
of a woman like Dixie, maybe he wasn't in as bad a
shape as he thought.

"Well, you're not going back up there." Dixie's warning to her gram brought him back to the present. "I'm never going to hear the end of it from Mom and Dad as it is."

"Don't worry." Her gram patted Dixie's hand. "I was starting to get the vertigo." She stage-whispered to Presley, "I'm afraid of heights."

He chuckled. "I wouldn't have known it if you hadn't said something." Dixie and her gram had that in common— the ability to tackle any situation without apparent fear, no matter how they might be feeling on the inside.

"So we're just going to leave Kermit on the roof?" Dixie asked. "What if he falls off? What if he gets cold? What if—"

"Why don't you take your gram home and I'll come back with some supplies for Kermit?" Presley offered. Surely he could find a sleeping bag and a pillow at home. And maybe he'd even be able to talk the old coot out of his crazy roof protest if he brought back a fifth of something good.

"That sounds like a good idea." Mrs. Holbein leaned close and gave Presley a smacking kiss on the cheek. "Make sure you give him that when you see him, okay?"

Presley stepped back. "Yes, ma'am."

"Gram, what exactly is going on between you and Kermit?" Dixie clamped her hands to her waist, drawing Presley's attention to those hips he'd had the luxury of grasping such a short time before.

"Well, sweetheart, I'd say a true lady doesn't kiss and tell."

"Gram…" Dixie warned.

"But seeing as how we both seem to have a lot of telling to do, maybe we can make an exception this time." Mrs. Holbein linked her arm through Dixie's and tugged her toward the parking lot. "Come on, we can take Kermit's truck home and bring it back in the morning. Sounds like we have a lot to catch up on."

"Just a sec, Gram. I'll meet you over there okay?" Dixie disentangled herself from her grandmother and turned to face Presley.

Cash had wandered off to confer with Tippy, so that left Presley alone with the siren formerly known as just Dixie. Presley cleared his throat. "So, uh, I guess I'll make sure Kermit gets settled and see you back here in the morning?"

Her gaze darted left, then right, finally settling on a spot on the ground between her toes. "About earlier…" Her voice held a quiver.

Presley put a finger under her chin, nudging her eyes up until she met his gaze. "You play a thrilling game of mini-golf, Ms. King." She tried to look away, but he cupped her chin and tilted her face toward his. "I mean it."

So many emotions flickered through her gaze: fear, hope, warmth, affection. "We should probably talk about what happened tonight."

"Yeah, we probably should. But not now. Let's sleep on it."

Relief course through her eyes. "Okay. Tomorrow then?"

"You bet." He opened his arms, offering a hug.

She nestled against his chest, wrapping her arms around him. "No more betting, okay?"

He chuckled into her hair. "You got it. No more betting."

With Dixie clasped against him, a lightness filled

his chest. He wanted more—more of the feeling he got when he was with her, more of the hope she instilled in him of a possibility of a future between them. But he'd wait to tell her. He didn't want to scare her off. Tomorrow would be soon enough.

~#~

Dixie kept to herself most of the ride home. Driving Kermit's truck took all of her concentration. The old Ford bounced over the gravel drive, sending rocks scattering in its wake. Gram kept up enough conversation for both of them by filling Dixie in on what had transpired between herself and Kermit.

"Do you think it's possible to find true love three times in a lifetime?" Gram asked.

"Hmm?" Dixie glanced toward the passenger seat.

Gram hugged her arms around her chest. "The other ladies' guild members think Kermit's a lost cause. But we've got a spark. It's just too bad about him having to give up his land."

"What do you mean? He said he told those investors to take a hike."

"Well, he did, sugar. But the Christmas tree farm isn't doing as well as it once was, what with all those new fake trees they have out now. People just don't want the real ones anymore. What with the needles and the sap and trying to keep them watered…" Her voice drifted off.

"So who's he selling to?" Dixie gripped the wheel tighter.

"He doesn't know yet." Gram looked at her lap. "Sorry, he asked me not to say anything, but you know how I am about keeping secrets."

Yes, she knew. Gram couldn't hide the truth if her life depended on it. Her best tactic was to talk around a subject so many times a person forgot their original question. Usually worked like a charm, but not with Dixie.

"You're saying Kermit has to sell his land but he doesn't want to sell to the people who made him the offer?" Dixie asked.

Gram nodded. "That's right. Those toads are all he has. He won't sell to someone unless they vow to keep up the conservation effort."

So Presley hadn't been right about everything, but he was right about part of what was happening. She hadn't had a chance to sort through her feelings about what had happened between them yet. Here Gram was talking about finding true love three times in a lifetime. Dixie would be happy to settle for just once. The closest she'd come was the eternal torch she'd carried for Presley Walker ever since she could remember. But Presley wasn't love material, and she'd be downright foolish to think that what had transpired between them was anything more than him making good on a bet.

Still, she and Presley were knee-deep into trying to figure out what was going on with the land around the Rose. She'd have to pretend all was well, at least until Charlie returned and she could go back to her normal shifts. That meant continuing the cockeyed plan of pressing Chandler for info.

"So is Kermit planning on putting his property on the market soon?" They were almost home. She'd have to talk fast if she wanted to wrangle any more info out of her gram.

"He'd rather sell it to someone he knows. I was thinking about that money I have set aside. Maybe I could buy it and then rent it back to him."

"I doubt Mom and Dad would go along with that plan."

Gram smacked her hands together. "It's my money. I don't know why your mother thinks she has any right to decide what I do with it."

Dixie was at a loss on that one. She hadn't been privy to the conversations involving her parents and her grandmother's lifelong savings. But she did know that her parents thought Gram was losing her marbles and had taken steps to protect her assets.

"Sorry, Gram. I don't know anything about that."

"I know, sweetheart." She patted Dixie's shoulder as the truck creaked into the driveway. "We'll figure it out though. That's what us Holbein women do."

Dixie hoped her gram was right. Because in that moment she felt like she had a world of fixing to do and not one iota of the wherewithal it would take to figure out how to do it all on her own.

She waited in the truck while her grandmother climbed out and made her way to the front door. There was one thing she did have some say in—one little thing she could take control of and see if it made a difference. As she followed her gram across the porch, avoiding the soft board Presley had pointed out the day before, she pulled her phone out of her purse. Chandler's last text glared up at her from her phone screen.

We still on for dinner tomorrow night? The Farley Inn?

Dixie hadn't responded to confirm his invitation. Now, with everything that had happened to Kermit's place, she owed it to her gram, to Kermit, to Charlie, even to Presley to find out once and for all what part, if any, Chandler had in the events of the past few days.

She made a mental note to text him in the morning. If all went well, that meant that in less than twenty-four hours she'd be going on her second date in two days. And no matter what happened, she could almost guarantee she wouldn't be as confused as she was after her night out with Presley.

She entered the house and set down the keys. Finally, alone with her thoughts, Dixie replayed the early events of the evening in her mind. What had possessed her to make that crazy bet with Presley? She didn't regret a thing. Being with Presley was everything she'd hoped it would be plus more. She closed her eyes, willing herself to feel his fingertips on her skin again. Instead she heard the buzz of a june bug as it hit the light fixture on the ceiling and bounced off and into her hair. She swatted it away, the sensation of Presley's hands on her already fading into just a memory.

She sighed and got herself ready for bed, listening to her gram humming down the hall. Could Gram and Kermit have actually found true love? If they had, Dixie was happy for them. Her gram deserved a little bit of sunshine in her life. And poor Kermit, the whole town had mourned with him when he'd lost his wife. It was high time he found someone to love again.

Maybe some people were just destined for happiness. Gram had once said if a person wanted to be happy, all they had to do was think happy thoughts and happiness would find them. What did she call it? The law of attraction or something like that. Well, Dixie was ready to attract some sunshine and roses of her own. She'd had a little taste of heaven in Presley Walker's arms, and she was ready to wish her own happily ever after into existence.

She turned off the bedside lamp and pulled the sheet up to her chest. The moon peeked out from behind a cloud, sending a silvery ray of light through her bedroom window. As she peered up at the dark night sky, the twinkle of a star caught her eye.

"Wish I may, wish I might…" Dixie tried to remember the words to the rhyme she'd said so many times as a child. "Have this wish I wish tonight?" That sounded familiar. She closed her eyes, took in a deep breath, and wished with all her might that her own Prince Charming would show up in the morning.

PRESLEY SHOULD HAVE BEEN MEETING LEONI AT THE ROSE for her to finally take a look at his fiddle. But after all that had happened the night before, he needed to see Dixie. Even though he was dying to find out what Leoni thought about his creation, he had to see where things stood with Fireball before he could focus on much else. So he'd canceled his coffee plans with Leoni and driven to Dixie's grandma's place instead. When he arrived, he tucked a few planks under his arm, grabbed his toolkit from the back of his Jeep, and then headed up the sidewalk to Mrs. Holbein's porch, ready to use wood rot as an excuse for his early arrival.

"Good morning, Mr. Walker." Mrs. Holbein met him in the side yard wearing waders up past her hips.

"Good morning. Figured I may as well fix those couple of boards for you before I head in this morning." He held the door open for her, and they entered the screened-in porch.

"How's Kermit doing?" she asked.

"Up with the roosters." And unfortunately still up on the damn roof. Presley had tried talking some sense into the man the night before when he'd returned with a sleeping bag and a pillow. Kermit wouldn't even lower the ladder, just waited while Presley attempted to toss the items onto the roof.

"Any word on his toads?" Mrs. Holbein's eyebrows rose, probably hoping for good news.

"Not yet." Presley knelt down to pry the bad board away. "How's Fernando doing?"

"Good. I've got him in a bin with a heat lamp in the shed out back. I was just trying to find him a few friends down in the tall grass." She pointed to her waders. "Dixie doesn't like it when I tramp around in the mud."

Presley smiled up at the older woman. "Well, what Dixie doesn't know won't hurt her, right?"

"What Dixie doesn't know about what?" Fireball herself glared down at him from the cracked front doorway.

Presley slid his gaze up her legs to the hem of her night-shirt. Two screen-printed kittens frolicked across her chest with a ball of yarn strung between them. Damn lucky cats. "Well, good morning."

"What's going on out here?" Dixie hugged her arms to her chest.

"Just making good on a promise to fix that board." Presley held a nail in place then raised the hammer.

"And you had to do it right now? This day is going to do me in, and I haven't even had a chance to make coffee yet."

"Thought you'd never ask. I take mine black." Presley grinned before he brought the hammer down to strike the nail on the head. By the time the nail sat flat against the board, Dixie had shut the door and gone inside.

"What's eating her today?" he asked.

Mrs. Holbein shrugged. "You help yourself to some coffee when you're done out here, okay? I'm going to head back to the pond. You can tell Dixie I'm over at Maybelle's."

Presley raised a brow. "You want me to lie for you?"

"Heaven's no." Mrs. Holbein put a hand to her heart. "I'm going to walk past Maybelle's on my way."

"Be careful out there." Presley shook his head. Poor Dixie was in over her head with her grandmother.

Ten minutes later, he knocked on the front door. When she didn't answer right away, he crack the door. "Dixie? You in there?"

"You're still here?" Her voice came from the general direction of the kitchen.

He opted to take that as an invitation and entered the house. "Is that offer for coffee still good?"

"I don't recall ever offering you a cup of coffee in the first place." She leaned against the counter, a cup of steaming coffee in her hands.

He stopped when they stood toe to toe. "Do you want to talk about last night?"

Her gaze lingered on the dark liquid in her cup. "What's there to talk about?"

His hands wrapped around hers. "A hell of a lot if you ask me."

"I don't really see the point in having a conversation. You lost a bet, you fulfilled your part of the deal, and now you're free to go on about your business and pretend like it never happened."

She tried to fake indifference, but the quiver in her bottom lip gave her away, and she caught it with her teeth. If they'd been playing poker, he'd have called it her "tell."

"Is that what you want me to do?" he asked.

"Doesn't matter." She shrugged, her eyes still locked on the mug of coffee.

Presley worked the mug free and set it on the

counter next to her hip. "So it wouldn't matter to you if I said I wanted to start seeing somebody?"

A flash of spitfire blazed in her eyes before she shut it down. One shoulder shrugged up, and the other went down. "It's a free country, right?"

He caught her hands in his and held them against his chest. "I thought you said you'd never told a lie."

Her gaze met his for a fraction of a second. "I haven't."

He laughed, a deep belly laugh that had her yanking her hands from his. "Dixie, the person I want to start seeing is you."

"Me?"

"Yes, you." He bumped her hip with his. "I think we need to start over though. Maybe go out for dinner a few times before we jump into another round of mini-golf."

"But we're all wrong for each other."

"Says who?"

"Everyone. You and I want different things out of life. I want kids someday, and—"

"I love kids."

She tilted her head like she was trying to get a read on him. "Sure you do, but I want kids of my own. The kind I won't be able to pass back to someone else as soon as they start crying."

"I'm great with crying kids. What else?"

"A dog. I want a big, slobbery dog with huge paws."

Presley crossed his arms over his chest and leaned against the counter. "I ever tell you about the mutt we had growing up? Two hundred pounds of wagging, wet, crazy beast."

"It's not just about kids and a dog. I want it all. A man I can count on through the good and the bad. Someone who won't hightail it out of town when the going gets tough."

"That settles it."

"What?"

He held his arms out wide. "I'm your guy."

"Presley, stop joking."

"I'm not joking. I've been thinking about things for a long time. I want the same things you want."

She rolled her eyes.

"Hey, is it so hard to believe that I want to settle down?"

"Yes."

"Why?"

"Because...because you're Presley Walker. You don't have a serious bone in your body."

"Aw, come on. Did you know the human body has two hundred six bones? There's got to be at least one serious one in there."

"See?"

"What about this one?" He held up his pinky finger. "Think this one can be serious?"

She shook her head. Her breasts jiggled.

"Damn, you keep that up, and I guarantee you there's going to be a serious boner going on."

"Oh my gosh. You're horrible. My gram could walk in at any moment."

"Nah, she went over to Maybelle's." He nestled her bare feet between his boots.

"You liar. I heard her say she was going back to the pond."

254 DYLANN CRUSH
254ual

Presley circled his arms around her waist. "Let your gram have her little bit of fun, and maybe she'll stay away long enough for us to have ours."

Her arms went around his neck. "I can't believe I'm actually considering this."

He pulled back, meeting her gaze. "Give me a chance, Dixie. I want to try this."

"I don't want to be a test case, some experiment you want to try out then get tired of and—"

His lips pressed to hers, silencing her concerns. "You're not. And you don't have to believe me right now. But you will. Because I'm going to show you I'm serious. You're going to get so sick of me being serious you're going to beg me to crack a joke."

She smiled at that. "Okay."

"Okay? Really?" His hands played up and down her rib cage. The damn-thin-cotton nightshirt clung to her curves, making him wish they didn't have a full day of work ahead of them.

"But what about my date with Chandler tonight?"

Presley's gut wrenched into a knot. He'd temporarily forgotten about that. "Can you cancel?"

"I just confirmed this morning. If it's our best shot at getting any information we can, then I want to move forward."

"I'm not sure that's such a good idea. Maybe we could send someone else instead."

Dixie shook her head. "I want to go. For Charlie, for the Rose, for you."

"Yeah"—he nodded—"you're right. It's our best shot. But I'm not going to be happy knowing you're out with SoCal while I'm sitting at home."

"Oh, you won't be. Remember, you said you'd take Gram and Mrs. Mitchell to bingo tonight."

"It was a weak moment," Presley protested.

"They're looking forward to it. It's the highlight of their week."

"All right. Starts at seven?"

"That's right. But they like to get there a little early so they can set out all of their lucky charms. I'd leave around six fifteen."

"Done deal. Now, back to the idea of giving us a shot. You in?"

"I hope I don't regret this." She rested her forehead on his chest.

He ran a hand over her hair, trying to convey the levity of the moment through his touch. He hadn't seen this thing with Dixie coming—it had knocked him over like a stampede of cattle, leaving his head rattling and his brain spinning. But he knew she was the one. He'd never fallen so fast, so furious, so fearlessly for someone before. She made him want to be all the things she needed. All the things she wanted. All the things he wasn't.

"I promise you, Fireball. You won't regret this."

Then he leaned down and cemented his promise with a kiss.

chapter
TWENTY-THREE

D<small>IXIE ADJUSTED HER SKIRT THEN CROSSED AND RECROSSED</small> her ankles. She'd just started examining a strand of hair for split ends when Gram sat down on the settee next to her.

"What's going on, Dixie Mae?" Gram set a hand on Dixie's arm. "You're about as jumpy as a cat in a room full of rocking chairs."

"I know. It's this date with Chandler."

"Chandler? I thought you and Presley finally got your heads out of your butts and decided to start dating."

"It's complicated. Presley thinks Chandler has some connection to the people trying to buy Kermit's land. We're hoping that if I can get him talking he might spill the beans so we can figure out what's going on."

Gram's brow knit together. "And how do you expect to do that?"

Dixie laughed. "That's the best part. Presley expects me to use my feminine wiles."

"No offense, sugar, but do you have a plan B?"

Groaning, Dixie got to her feet to peer out the giant front window. "Plan B is to get Chandler drunk and hope he starts talking."

Gram came up behind her and put a hand on her shoulder. "I think plan B is your best shot."

"Thanks, Gram." Dixie shook her head. The evening

was doomed before it had begun. Even Gram knew Dixie didn't have what it would take to sweet-talk Chandler into divulging any info.

"Is there anything I can do to help?"

"No. Just keep Presley out of my way. The last thing I need is for him to get a wild hair and show up during my date."

"Maybelle and I will do our best. Why, I can't wait to walk in for bingo on Presley Walker's arm. The women in the guild will turn green with envy."

"Go easy on him, okay, Gram? I don't think he's ever been to bingo before in his life. You'd better go get ready. He's supposed to be picking you up at six fifteen."

Gram turned away from the window and moved into the kitchen. It would take her at least fifteen minutes to gather all of her supplies. Dixie had watched her go through the routine countless times. First she'd test all of the bingo daubers she kept in the kitchen drawer. Then she'd pick the three with the best stamp. Next she'd move on to her lucky charms, which, depending on the night, might consist of a rabbit's foot, a pressed flower from the garden, even a stuffed animal. Dixie smiled as she imagined Presley among Gram's bingo ladies.

Speaking of Presley, why was he pulling up in front of the house? He wasn't supposed to be picking up Gram and Maybelle for another twenty minutes. She'd hoped she and Chandler would be long gone by the time he rolled in.

She met him on the screened-in porch. "What are you doing here?"

He pulled her into his arms and crushed his mouth to hers. Her knees buckled as his tongue swirled around hers, making her wish she was spending the evening doing exactly this instead of heading out on a fake date.

Once he'd kissed her breathless, he set her back on her feet. "Just wanted to stop by and wish you good luck on your date."

She put a hand to his chest and pushed him away. "And how am I supposed to go out on a date now that you've got my brain scrambled like a pan of eggs?"

"I didn't want you to forget about me while you're out with SoCal."

Forget about him? The idea that she'd ever let herself forget about the way he made her feel went beyond ludicrous.

"I could never forget about you." To prove her point she rose to her tiptoes and pressed a sweet kiss to his lips. "But now I've got to go fix my lipstick since you got me all smeared."

He followed her to the guest bathroom and leaned against the doorframe while she wiped her remaining lipstick off with a tissue.

"You want to come over tonight after your date? I wouldn't mind smearing your lipstick some more. Plus that would give us a chance to talk about what you find out while it's still fresh in your head."

She lined her lips the way Liza had shown her. Peering into the mirror and applying her makeup while Presley watched seemed intimate in a way. She liked it.

"I'm pretty sure my date will be over long before you get home with Gram and Maybelle. We're only going to dinner. Bingo lasts all night, especially if they talk you into staying for the final blackout session."

Presley's eyes narrowed. "What exactly did I sign up for?"

"Don't worry. You're going to have a good time. I can't believe I'm saying it, but I'd rather go play bingo with you tonight than have dinner with Chandler, even if he is taking me to the Farley Inn."

"Make sure you order the most expensive thing on the menu. Whatever it is, get two of them. And lots of drinks. Keep the drinks coming for him. They'll loosen his tongue." He nodded. "I don't suppose you want to wear a wire?"

She laughed. "A wire? Don't you think you're taking this a little too far? Besides, do you even have a wire?"

"No." His head dipped. "But you could keep me on speakerphone all night so I could keep tabs on what's going on."

She finished with her lipstick and tucked the tube back in her purse. He made a move to kiss her again, but she turned her head and gave him a peck on the cheek instead. "Don't you dare mess up my lipstick again. Stop worrying—I've got this."

The doorbell rang.

"You stay here. I'll get him out of here as quick as I can, okay?"

Presley nodded, looking like a dejected puppy.

"Oh stop it." Dixie tapped on his chest. "You know I'll be thinking about you all night."

His face lit up. "You sure I can't give you one more kiss? One more thing for you to be thinking about?"

"Behave. Now stay here in the bathroom until I'm gone, okay?"

Presley nuzzled her neck with his mouth. "You drive a hard bargain, Ms. King."

Her body revved like it always did when Presley made contact with her skin. The doorbell rang again, and she reluctantly pushed him away.

"Stay here." She put her palm up, the universal sign for "wait and don't screw things up." Then she rushed to the door where Gram stood, already inviting Chandler into the living room.

"I'm sure y'all have time for a glass of sweet tea before you go." Gram gestured to the settee.

"Actually, Gram, we don't. I think Chandler made a reservation at the Farley Inn, and we don't want to miss it." Dixie adjusted the strap of her purse on her shoulder.

"I'm sure I can move it back a little. They probably don't have a huge crowd on a Monday night. You look lovely tonight." Chandler leaned forward, and Dixie realized he was about to attempt a quick kiss. She made sure he caught her cheek.

"Thank you, so do you." She gave him a quick once-over. The flat-front khakis, loafers, and white polo shirt gave him that all-American vibe. "Gram, you don't have time for a glass of tea anyway. Don't you have to finish getting ready for bingo?"

"That's right. Is Presley here? I thought I heard his voice a few minutes ago." Gram looked around, missing Dixie's desperate silent signals to drop it.

"That obnoxious Jeep is parked on the street." Chandler gestured to the door.

"Maybe he's next door at Mrs. Mitchell's," Dixie said. "Why don't you walk over and see if she's ready to go?"

She glared at Gram, trying to give a subtle nod in the direction of the bathroom.

"Oh, all right." Gram bustled back to the kitchen, hopefully to grab her things.

"Ready?" Dixie asked, eager to get Chandler out of the house. She wasn't sure she'd be able to go through with the evening if she had to deal with the two men in the same room.

"Let's." Chandler moved to the front door and pulled it open.

Gram's voice came from down the hallway. "Well, Presley! There you are. Where have you been hiding?"

Dixie groaned inside. She'd have to set Gram down sometime and have a conversation about reading body language. Before she could shove Chandler through the door, Gram came down the hall, toting Presley behind her by the arm.

"Look who I found." Gram beamed like she'd just discovered buried treasure.

Chandler turned from the door. "Walker."

Presley gave a tight-lipped smile. "Bristol."

Dixie's gaze bounced between them. Chandler's head tilted a smidge. Her stomach churned as she noticed what probably brought on the confused look on his face. It had to be the perfect set of pink lip prints pasted onto Presley's scruffy cheek. She gaped at Presley.

"What?" He shifted his weight from foot to foot, aware something was off but not aware enough to play it off on his own.

"Gram, did you leave lipstick on poor Presley's cheek?" Dixie searched her purse for a tissue. Finding none, she settled for a wet wipe they handed out to customers who ordered the ribs at the Rose. She handed it to him.

He reached for it and plastered on a smile. "Eugenia, honey, I told you if you keep that up I won't be able to find my next girlfriend. If y'all will excuse me for a minute?"

Gram stood there, her expression a mix of resignation and surprise. "Well, I just can't help myself. Call me a cougar, I guess."

A bubble of hysterical laughter threatened to spill through Dixie's clenched lips. She needed to get Chandler out of there, and the sooner the better. "We'd better get going."

"Y'all have a nice time tonight." Gram waved as Dixie led Chandler through the door.

Not sure how she was going to survive the evening, Dixie linked her arm with his. She could pretend he was Presley and this was their first date. Maybe that would make things go a little smoother. But a side glance to Chandler's baby-soft cheeks confirmed pretending would be impossible. Chandler was too clean-cut, too West Coast charm. Presley was rough and tumble and wildly inappropriate…all the things she'd never thought she'd be attracted to in a man.

The best she could do was get the information they needed and get through dinner as quickly as possible. Then she and Presley could come up with a plan to save the Rose and hopefully start something of their own.

"Bingo!" Mrs. Mitchell's hand flew into the air, clutching the flimsy sheet of bingo cards.

Presley was still searching for O-71 on his one sheet of cards, and the caller had announced that one two numbers ago.

One of the bingo helpers came to the table to check Mrs. Mitchell's card. He ran his finger down each row. "That's a good bingo. Congratulations."

"You're on a roll, Maybelle." Genie gathered the cards from the last game and slid them into the middle of the table where a huge stack of newsprint bingo cards were piled up. "How are you doing, Presley?"

He rubbed a hand over his chin while he shook his head. "I don't know how y'all do it. I've got one sheet to keep track of, and you're both playing three."

Mrs. Mitchell snickered. "Don't worry, you'll get it. By the time we leave tonight, you'll be a pro."

"I don't think so. I'm going to sit this game out." He pushed back from the table, his metal chair making a screeching sound on the linoleum floor. "I'll be back in a few."

He wound his way through the packed hall to the front door. How was Dixie doing tonight? Had she managed to get SoCal to talk? He slid his phone out of his back pocket to send her a text.

How's it going?

While he waited for a response, he took a turn around the building. It was the kind of night that promised rain. The clouds swirled overhead, and thunder rumbled off to the west. His thoughts immediately went to Kermit. Surely the old fool would be smart enough to realize he couldn't stay up on a metal roof during a thunderstorm.

Presley's phone vibrated.

Not well. He's had one drink and isn't talking.

Damn. He should have invited Chandler out for a poker night with the guys instead of sending him off with Dixie.

Keep trying.

The response came much faster this time.

I AM trying.

Presley's shoulders sagged. If it were up to him, they had all the info they needed that SoCal was up to no good. But without physical proof, it would be hard to rally the residents of Holiday against him. Dixie had to get confirmation from Chandler. Otherwise there would always be that little bit of doubt in her mind.

Just keep him at dinner and I'll come up with something.

He wondered if Mrs. Mitchell and Eugenia were up for a little investigative outing. It might be his only hope of proving to Dixie and everyone else that their little town was under attack.

What are you going to do?

He could almost hear her frustration through the text message.

Not sure yet. But keep him away from the B&B.

I've got to stop texting before he thinks something is up. Whatever you're thinking about,
DON'T DO IT.

Presley laughed to himself. Heroes weren't made by
playing it safe. Hell, heroes weren't made by doing
something as stupid as what he was considering either.
But somebody had to get to the bottom of SoCal's
intentions. Dixie wasn't cut out for espionage. It
didn't suit her. That's part of what attracted him to the
woman in the first place: her trusting nature, her ability
to believe the best about people, including himself. It
wasn't fair to put her in the situation in the first place.

Presley?

His phone vibrated again. He glanced at the screen
then shoved it in his pocket. He'd have to figure out a
way to get the two bingo mavens home safe and sound
before he paid a visit to the B and B. Dixie would
never forgive him if he pulled her grandma and Mrs.
Mitchell into the illicit activities he was considering.

He reentered the bingo hall. Eugenia stood and
waved her arms in the air. "Get on over here, Presley."

As he slid into his seat, Dixie's gram rubbed her
hand over his arm. "You must be our lucky charm
tonight. My numbers have been popping up all
night, but as soon as you stepped out, my luck went
downhill."

Mrs. Mitchell was a little subtler in her efforts to
rub the luck out of him. "Mind if I just touch you
for luck?"

Presley spread his arms out. "Be my guest. Looks like you two are the only ones who will be getting lucky tonight."

Eugenia's mouth opened in mock shock. "I hope you're not referring to my granddaughter with that last remark."

Heat prickled across his cheeks. He must be getting rusty. The reference to him getting lucky with Dixie hadn't crossed his mind. "No, ma'am. Just trying to figure out how to get the intel we need to put a stop to that California investor. Doesn't seem like luck is on my side tonight."

Eugenia dotted her card with hot-pink ink as the caller continued to shout out bingo numbers. "Well, your luck is about to turn around. Just let us get through the jackpot round, and Maybelle and I will help you come up with a plan."

Maybelle nodded. "Genie can be quite the sleuth when she needs to be."

Presley grinned. "I have no doubt she can. But what I'm considering would be on the, let's just say, dark-gray side of the law."

Eugenia dismissed his concern with a wave. "Oh, pshaw. Maybelle and I have been waiting for years for a little excitement to enter our lives. Whatever cockeyed plan you come up with, count us in."

"With all due respect, ma'am, Dixie would skin me alive if I got the two of you involved in—"

"Excuse me." A little old lady with a grizzled gray bun tapped on his shoulder.

"Yes?" Presley turned toward her.

"I couldn't help but notice you seem to be a lucky visitor tonight. Do you mind if I just give you a quick rub? For luck?" she asked.

Presley glanced to Mrs. Mitchell and Eugenia. "Is this typical?"

The two women twittered. "You might not have noticed, but you're the only good-looking, able-bodied male in the whole joint. Nellie here probably thinks your good luck will rub off on her too."

"Um, sure." He held out his arm.

The woman ran her hand over it then touched her bingo cards. "The next game is mine, I can just feel it."

Nobody was more surprised than Presley when Nellie ended up the only winner of the five hundred–dollar prize.

"Are you ladies about ready to go?" He'd had about all he could take of bingo night. Eager to get started on his plans for exposing SoCal, he handed his remaining bingo cards to the woman next to him.

"Okay, okay." Eugenia tucked her bingo markers into her bag. "You've already jinxed us."

"How? I thought I was some special good luck charm."

"You were." Mrs. Mitchell pointed to a group of older women who were arranging themselves into a line behind him. "But now everyone wants to rub our lucky charm."

"Oh no." Presley pushed back from the table and stood. "I'm sorry, ladies, but there's no more rubbing happening here tonight."

A chorus of disappointment rose around him as he scooted away from the table with Mrs. Mitchell and Genie behind him. If he was going to spend the night being rubbed by somebody, he'd damn sure get to have a say in who it was. And right now the only woman whose hands he wanted all over him was on a date with someone else. Granted, he'd asked her to do it, but it wasn't sitting well with him.

He'd get Mrs. Mitchell and Eugenia settled at home and then figure out how to get into SoCal's room at the B and B. With a glance at the brooding sky, he figured he'd better hurry. There was only one thing worse than breaking and entering: breaking and entering in the middle of a summer thunderstorm.

TWENTY-FOUR

DIXIE SWIRLED HER STRAW AROUND IN HER FROZEN PIÑA colada. Dining at the Farley Inn was definitely an experience. An experience that seemed like it would take all night, based on how slow the service had been. First they'd had drinks. Then Chandler ordered an appetizer she could barely force down. They'd moved on to their salads a few minutes ago, and her nerves were rattling like a set of maracas.

"So college at UCLA and then I went straight to work for my great-uncle's business." Chandler cut his romaine into bite-sized pieces. "How about you? Where did you go to college?"

Dixie gulped down a bite of bread that got stuck in her throat. "I'd rather talk about you. What kind of work do you do for your uncle?" The more she could get him to talk about himself, the more likely he might be to let something slip.

"He's got his hands into just about everything…real estate, retail developments, even a chain of gourmet coffee shops out East." Chandler dabbed at his mouth with the cloth napkin from his lap. "I never really know what kind of project he'll have me working on from one day to the next."

"What are you working on now?" She positioned the straw between her lips, hoping the soft candlelight from the votive on the table between them would make her look curiously sexy. The straw slipped from her lips, and a few drops of piña colada dribbled onto her salad.

Chandler didn't appear to notice. He took a sip of his second drink and appeared to contemplate her question. "I'm not sure I should talk about it."

"Oh?" Dixie tried to keep the interest from leaping into her voice. "Is it a secret project? You're planning on taking over the Farley Inn?"

He let out what she considered a bit of a nervous laugh. "No, nothing like that. My uncle would like to reestablish some roots in Texas though. I haven't been completely honest with you about my intentions."

She'd just taken an awkward, too-big bite of salad, so she nodded, encouraging him to go on.

He covered her hand with his across the table. "I probably shouldn't say anything, but I feel like I can trust you." His gaze met hers. "Can I trust you, Dixie?"

Forcing the salad down, she pulled her hand away to reach for her water. She took a sip, considering her response. Lying wasn't an option. "I don't see why you shouldn't."

He let out a sigh. "It's been killing me, trying to keep this from you, what with our history and all."

Dixie nodded as she crossed her fingers under the table. "Go on."

"My uncle has been carrying a grudge against the Rose. Bad blood from decades ago. I've tried to reason with him and get him to move on, but he can't."

"What happened?" Desperate for information, she ignored the ringtone Presley had set on her phone for his calls. Toby Keith belted out lyrics about a girl born in

Dixie who fell in love with a bad boy while Dixie
tried to lower the volume under the tablecloth.

"Do you need to get that?" Chandler asked.

"No, I'm sure it's just a telemarketer. Tell me
about your uncle. Why does he have something
against the Rose?" Her phone stopped ringing, and
she let out a sigh of relief.

"It's complicated. He's a big-time fiddle player.
Used to play with a band that traveled the world. I
guess something happened one night at the Rose.
My uncle got into it with a friend who accused him
of cheating at poker. The owner tossed him out and
banned him for life."

Dixie sucked in a breath. She'd heard rumors of
a story like that before but always assumed it was
another tall tale.

"It gets worse." Chandler took another sip of his
drink. Dixie sent silent vibes of encouragement across
the table for him to down it. He must have subcon-
sciously heard her because he drained the last bit of
amber liquid. "When his band was finally invited to
play the Rose, a huge rite of passage back in the day,
my uncle wasn't allowed to go onstage with them. He
couldn't even be on the premises."

"Oh my gosh." Dixie covered her mouth with her
hands, not wanting to distract him from finishing his
story.

"So…Uncle Leroy has spent his entire life trying
to get even. Now he's got me—"

Dixie's phone rang again.

"Why don't you go ahead and answer that?
I'm going to excuse myself for a minute anyway."

Chandler pushed back from the table and made his way toward the men's room.

Dixie whipped her phone out from under the table. "What?"

"Nice to talk to you too." Presley's voice came from far away. Something loud sounded in the background.

"Where are you?"

"You're not going to like it." A woman said something she couldn't quite make out.

"Are you still at bingo?" She put a hand over her other ear, trying to shut out any other noise.

"No. I got tired of older women rubbing me."

"What?" She pulled the phone away from her ear to look at it. Did he say "rubbing"?

"Never mind. I'm on my way to the B and B to check SoCal's room. Can you keep him there for another hour?"

"Where's Gram?" If he'd left her gram at bingo, he'd be sorry.

"She's right here."

A loud scuffle came through the phone, then Gram's voice blared into Dixie's ear. "How's your date going, sugar?"

"Gram, what are you doing? Why aren't you at bingo?" She should have known better than to trust Presley with her grandmother.

"Bingo was a bust. Maybelle won a game, but then everyone wanted to rub on Presley for luck. We decided helping him out on his investigation would be more fun." She giggled into the phone. "Besides, once he can prove SoCal took Kermit's toads, we can get them back, and I can get my own horny toad back on level ground."

She didn't. Her grandmother absolutely did not refer

to Kermit Klaussen as her own horny toad. What was the world coming to? Her parents were definitely going to remove her from Gram duty as soon as word of this made its way back to them.

"Gram, listen to me. Tell Presley to take you home and wait for me there. I've almost got what we need to prove Chandler is trying to take down the Rose." She kept her voice low, casting covert glances around her as if someone might be keeping tabs on her conversation.

"Sorry, hon, you're breaking up. What did you say?"

Dixie looked around then raised her voice a notch. "I said go home. Do not go to the B and B. I forbid it."

"And ruin the most fun I've had in decades? I will not." Gram sounded like a petulant toddler as opposed to a grown woman who had a family and a reputation and, holy moly, her son-in-law's capital campaign at stake.

"Gram, that's breaking and entering. Do you want to go to jail? We'll get the info some other way."

"See you at home later, sweetheart." The line went dead.

Dixie held the phone in front of her, checking the screen. Her gram did not just hang up on her. Impossible. She'd been so close to getting the information from Chandler. Why did Presley think he had to swoop in and mess everything up? As she lifted her gaze, she realized things were worse than she'd feared. Chandler stood across the table from her, his usually even-toned complexion turning into a mottled mess of red and pink.

Her chest squeezed as her lungs failed her.

Coughing, she reached for her water. "How long have you been standing there?" she finally managed to spit out.

"Long enough to know that our dinner date was made under false pretenses." He pulled a few bills out of his wallet and tossed them on the table. "Now if you'll excuse me, I trust you can find your own way home?"

It didn't take but a moment for Dixie to realize she was about to be abandoned in the middle of the Farley Inn. As Chandler stomped toward the door, she raced after him. "Wait."

He spun around as he reached the door. "You, Dixie Mae King, are not the same sweet girl I fell for in sixth grade."

"I'm sorry." She put her hand out, intent on touching his arm, but he jerked it away. "My loyalties lie here. With the Rose, with Holiday, with the people I love." The people she loved. Like Gram and her family, Charlie and her coworkers at the Rose, Maybelle, kooky Kermit, and all the others. And maybe even Presley. Was it too soon to admit her lifelong infatuation may have somehow turned to deeper feelings over the past several days?

Chandler's icy glare froze any warm feelings she'd had growing inside. "Well, my loyalties lie with my family. So may the best one win."

With one last sneer, he ducked out into the rain. Dixie had been so preoccupied with fishing for information she hadn't noticed the sky had darkened and a true summer thunderstorm now raged outside. Now what was she supposed to do?

She returned to the table. No sense in letting the rest of her piña colada go to waste. As she took a sip of the giant frozen beverage, she pulled up Presley's number.

He'd have to abandon his crazy mission and come get her. They could figure out their next step as a team. If Gram and Mrs. Mitchell wanted to pitch in, that would be fine too. In fact, getting the whole town of Holiday to rally against the outside threat and put up a united front wasn't a bad idea at all.

The only problem was she didn't know exactly what kind of threat they were fighting. Obviously Chandler and his uncle wanted Kermit's land. She'd have to start there. Convinced she was on the right track, she waited for Presley to pick up his phone.

chapter
TWENTY-FIVE

"SO WE'RE ALL CLEAR ON WHO'S DOING WHAT?" PRESLEY asked.

Mrs. Mitchell and Genie nodded.

"Do you want to run through it one more time, just to be sure?" he asked.

Genie rolled her eyes. "Don't be such a worrywart. We've got this."

"It's just like being on one of those shows on TV." Mrs. Mitchell's hands fluttered under her chin. "Do you think Angela Lansbury felt like this when she was filming episodes of *Murder, She Wrote*?"

Presley twisted in the driver's seat and pointed a finger at Mrs. Mitchell. "This is nothing like *Murder, She Wrote*, okay? I need you to understand, if we get caught, there could be serious consequences. Y'all can wait in the car if you want. If it looks like things are going bad, then take off in the Jeep, and I'll catch up to you later."

"Neither one of us is supposed to drive." Mrs. Mitchell shrugged.

"Would you relax?" Genie reached into her purse and pulled out a black knit beanie. "I grew up in the sixties. I'm not afraid to go to jail or stage a protest." She handed the beanie to Presley. "You might need this."

"Neither one of you is going to jail." Presley humphed.

He'd gotten more help than he'd bargained for when he'd agreed to let the two women take part in his espionage. "And why do you have a black cap in your purse?"

Genie shrugged. "You never know when you might need it."

"Genie's always prepared." Mrs. Mitchell nodded.

"Thanks—this might actually come in handy. Okay, you ready to go?" He cracked his door.

Dixie's gram reached into her purse and pulled out an umbrella. "Come on, Maybelle. I've got us covered."

The two women climbed out of the Jeep and walked to the front door of the B and B while Presley pulled his Jeep around the corner and killed the engine. While they were inside distracting Mr. and Mrs. Knotts, he planned on scaling the side of the stone building and trying to find a way in through the window.

He waited, making sure the women received an invitation to come in, then ran across the lawn and pressed himself against the building. Peering through a dining room window, he watched as Mrs. Knotts took their coats and hung them on the coatrack in the entry. The light flickered on in the dining room, and he crouched down, duck-waddling to a stretch of stone wall that didn't have windows.

Muted laughter reached him through the driving rain. Good. With the owners occupied, he'd have a few minutes to see if he could figure out a way inside. His fingers scraped along the stone blocks, trying to find a place to grab. No luck. He should have tossed a ladder onto his Jeep. Or a grappling hook. Or even a fishing pole.

He circled the property for the next fifteen minutes while the pouring rain soaked through his shirt, his pants, and his boots. With no way to climb up, his plan seemed doomed. Then the front door opened, and Eugenia called out. "Presley? Where are you?"

Dammit. She was going to ruin everything. He ignored her, moving farther down the wall.

"Presley? Come inside. Beverly says she'll open the room for you. There's no reason to sneak around in the dark out there."

He pushed away from the wall and stalked toward the door. "The idea of a covert operation is that it's covert. You do understand that, don't you?"

"Of course I do. But we started talking to Beverly and Jim, and before we knew it, we'd filled them in on your concerns. Beverly's daughter Darby is married to Waylon Walker, you know."

"Yes, of course I know that. She's my sister-in-law." Presley stepped into the vaulted foyer. He'd only been inside the historic home a few times.

"Well, that makes us family too." Mrs. Knotts held out a towel. "If one of my guests is threatening my family, he's not welcome here."

Relief flooded Presley's system. Why hadn't he thought to just ask for access? Because evidently running around in the rain and scraping his fingernails against unyielding stone seemed like so much more fun.

As he rubbed the towel over his hair, he tried to find out how many of the beans Dixie's gram and Mrs. Mitchell had spilled. "So you understand why it's important to take a look around Mr. Bristol's room?"

"Absolutely." Mrs. Knotts held out a key.

"I don't want you to get in trouble for this."
Presley hesitated to take the key.

Genie knocked the key out of Mrs. Knotts's hand.
"Oh look, Presley. There's a key on the ground. I
wonder what it goes to."

He huffed out a laugh. "You think it's that easy?"

She winked at him. "No, but who knows what will
happen when we go back to the kitchen for a piece
of that huckleberry cobbler Beverly's been talking
about? It's a big house. We probably won't be able to
hear a thing. Would you say that's right, Bev?"

"I'm having a hard time hearing you now, Eugenia.
Didn't you say you wanted to listen to that new polka
CD Jim ordered online?" Mrs. Knotts gestured to the
swinging door leading through the dining room and,
Presley assumed, on into the kitchen.

He glanced at his feet while the women and Mr.
Knotts filed through the doorway. Alone on the entry-
way rug, he tugged off his boots and soaked socks.
Then he carefully crept up the stairs, hoping none of
the other guests happened to come out of their rooms.
He'd just shut the door behind him and entered
SoCal's room when the front door slammed, shaking
the solid walls of the mansion down to the foundation.

Presley didn't have much time. He locked the
door behind him and swept his gaze over the room.
Everything was in its place. The king-sized bed had
been turned down for the night, and the bedside lamp
cast a warm glow over the peach walls. He flipped on
the overhead light and headed toward the window.
An antique rolltop desk sat to the left. Papers stacked
in a tidy pile rested on top.

There had to be something here. Something that implicated SoCal and his uncle in stealing Kermit's toads and trying to bully him into selling his land. Presley skimmed through the stacks. Voices argued downstairs. He couldn't tell what they were saying, but he knew his time was limited. Under a pile of newspapers, he found something. Finally. A blown-up black-and-white picture of the inside of Kermit's barn. Someone had circled the bins with a black marker and drawn an arrow that bled off the side of the page.

The doorknob jiggled. Although Presley had flipped the lock, it wouldn't last. Not with an angry guy the size of SoCal on the other side. A fist pounded on the door. Presley dropped the paper. Dammit. He squatted down to retrieve it as it hit the ground and slipped under the bed. Reaching for it, his hand brushed against something hard. Presley knelt down to peer under the antique bed. A briefcase had been tucked against the wall. He snagged the handle and dragged it out.

With his heart thudding in his chest, he glanced at the window. He had to get out of there with the briefcase. It was his only chance of figuring out how far SoCal would go to ruin the Rose. The voices reached a crescendo directly outside the bedroom door. Any moment SoCal would be barging through the door and Presley would be out of time.

He flung the window open. Rain pelted the sill. Papers lifted from the desk and floated around the room. Presley looked out into the darkness, trying to gauge the distance to the ground. With the storm raging, he couldn't see a thing. He said a quick prayer. Something along the lines of "Dear God, please don't let me get too fucked up."

Then he held tight to the handle of the briefcase and jumped.

Dixie handed the cab driver a few bills as she exited the vehicle. He waited for her to close the door then sped off down the road. The rain had stopped, and the imposing B and B blazed against the dark night sky. Every light in the house must be on. Dixie shuddered at the thought of how much that electric bill must cost each month.

She didn't know what she might find when she arrived on the scene, but she'd expected some evidence of a brawl. Presley's Jeep was nowhere to be found, and Chandler either hadn't made it back yet or had already come and gone.

With no other choice but to rap on the front door, Dixie made her way up the sidewalk. As she raised her hand to knock, the door flew open.

Gram stood on the other side. "Where in the world have you been, child?"

"Me?" Dixie didn't care for the accusatory tone in her gram's voice. "Where have *you* been? And where's Presley? His shenanigans landed me at the Farley Inn without a ride home."

"Come inside. You missed everything." Gram ushered her in and closed the door behind her.

"What happened? Did you break into Chandler's room?" Dixie didn't know where to start with the questions. "Where are Mr. and Mrs. Knotts?"

"They're at the sheriff's office talking to Deputy Walker. He figured this might somehow be related to the disappearance of Kermit's toads and I think they're trying to put the pieces together. I wanted to get over to the Rose to check on Kermit, but nobody knew where you were, so they thought it was best I wait here in case you showed up." Gram led the way into a sitting room. "I tried your phone, but it went straight to voicemail."

"My battery died." Dixie slumped into a chair. "Where's Presley?"

Gram shrugged. "No one knows. He jumped out the window and took off in his Jeep."

"Jumped out the window? What window? Is he okay?" Dixie stood, but Gram's hand on her arm guided her back to her seat.

"He must be. Landed in a clump of Texas sage. Flattened poor Beverly's bushes, but he was lucky they broke his fall."

"I've got to find him." Dixie fumbled with her phone. "My battery's dead. Do you have your phone on you, Gram?"

"Nope. You know I don't like carrying that thing around with me everywhere."

"But that's why we got it for you. For emergencies. So you could call if you needed help."

Gram pointed to the dead phone on Dixie's lap. "Doesn't look like your emergency phone is doing you much good."

"That's not the point." She stood, brushing Gram's hand away. "What happened to Chandler? Did he show up here?"

"Sure did." Gram twisted her lips into a frown. "Came crashing in, madder than a wet hen. He wasn't here but for a minute. Argued with Jim something fierce. Then Presley jumped and Chandler chased after him. Haven't seen hide nor hair of either one of them since."

Dixie needed to think. If she were Presley, God help her, where would she go? A vision of his workshop seeped into her mind. That's where he was; she knew it. "I think I know where Presley is, but I need a car."

"Keys to the Chevy are on the hook at home." Gram clamped a hand to her hip. "You love him, don't you?"

"Who?" Dixie was already heading toward the door.

"Your parents may treat me like a child, but I wasn't born yesterday." Gram stepped close. "You know who I'm talking about. Presley Walker, that's who."

Dixie bit back the hysterical laughter that threatened to escape. "Don't be silly, Gram. I barely know him."

"I gather you know him a lot better than some. Probably in ways his own mama and daddy don't." Gram lifted a brow.

"That's ridiculous. Presley and I are all wrong for each other." Perfectly, stupidly, incredibly wrong. That's probably why being with him felt so good.

"Lovebug, you listen to me." Gram hadn't called her that since she was a kid. Dixie's heart warmed at the nickname. The overwhelming need to laugh subsided. "I may not know much about the newest gadgets you want me to carry around, but I do know about matters of the heart. I've buried two husbands, God rest their souls, and managed to find another good man to love in my prime."

Dixie's eyes watered. Her gram was the strongest person she knew.

"We don't always get to choose who we love, but we can choose how we love them." She nodded. "You get what I'm saying?"

"But Daddy—"

"Stop right there. I know you love your daddy with all your heart. But your parents have been putting too much pressure on you since you were a little girl. We all knew Liza wasn't going to be able to toe the line, so your daddy heaped all of his expectations on you. He had no right to do that, sugar. Your life is your own. Now get on out there and live it."

Dixie nodded. Gram's words rang true. She and Presley weren't a perfect fit, but that didn't mean they had to be a mismatch. "I'm going to go find him, okay?"

Gram pulled her close and kissed her cheek. "You find him, and if he's a good man, the kind of man who will treat you well and love you the way you deserve to be loved, then you hold on tight and never let him go, okay?"

"I love you, Gram."

"Love you too."

Dixie was almost out the door when she remembered something Chandler had said during dinner. "Hey, do you remember somebody name Leroy Bristol, who used to live around here?"

Gram put a hand to her chest. "Now there's a name I haven't heard in a long time."

"So you do?"

"Oh, Leroy Bristol. Honey, we don't have enough time tonight. He used to live out on the edge of town. Was a real troublemaker back in the day." Realization dawned, transforming her features. "Oh my word. Leroy Bristol is SoCal's uncle, isn't he?"

"Great-uncle." Dixie put her hand on Gram's shoulder. "Do you need to sit down?"

"No. I just can't believe I didn't put two and two together on my own. It all makes sense now."

"What?" It might make sense to her, but Dixie was growing more confused by the second, and she didn't have time to spare to figure it all out.

"Leroy Bristol and Duke Walker. That's Presley's granddad, you know. The two of them got into it one night at the Rose. By that time Leroy had left Holiday to play fiddle for some big-time country star. He came back, all full of himself too."

"What happened?" And what did that have to do with Chandler and his great-uncle trying to take over massive amounts of land in Holiday?

"You know how those boys like their poker games. Duke caught Leroy cheating. Leroy denied it and started a huge fight. Knocked over one of the lanterns outside, and the front porch of the Rose burned down. The Holiday family banned Leroy from ever entering the Rose again, and he left town right after."

"So that's why he wants to build a huge honky-tonk right next door. To put the Rose out of business once and for all." Dixie's shoulders slumped. She needed to find Presley. "I've got to go. Do you want me to go get the car and come back for you to take you home?"

"Are you kidding? I'll make Jim run me home after he and Beverly get back. I can't wait to hear what kind of questions they get asked at the sheriff's station."

"Okay. I'll meet you back at home later." Dixie

pulled open the door, ready to make the fifteen minute walk back to Gram's in half the time.

"Take your time, hon. I'm not planning on waiting up."

How could her grandmother have produced a child like her mother? Some days Dixie spent more time pondering that thought than others. But not tonight. Tonight was for finding Presley. She had to know he was okay. Once she held him in her arms, she'd be able to focus on what to do next. Whatever it was, they'd do it together.

IT WAS ALL THERE IN BLACK AND WHITE. CORRESPONDENCE between SoCal and his great-uncle filled the briefcase. Memos. Who sent memos anymore? Hadn't the old man ever heard of email? By the time Presley had skimmed the majority of the documents, he'd pretty much figured out their plan. Buy up the land surrounding the Rose and build a country and western theme park with a brand-new technotronic honky-tonk right smack-dab in the middle of it all.

But why? That's the part that still had him stymied. He tried Dixie's phone again. Straight to voicemail. At least Cash had called a little bit ago and reported that Chandler had blazed out of town in the powder-blue Caddy. One of the deputies had stopped him on the highway doing ninety-eight in a seventy. Presley figured a speeding ticket was an appropriate parting gift.

The paperwork even left a trail Presley assumed would lead to the missing toads. If he could just get a hold of Dixie, he'd swing by to pick her up so they could head out and take a look for themselves.

He was about to get in the Jeep and start searching for her himself when the sound of a vehicle coming down the gravel road to his granddad's old shop startled him. A classic red-and-white Chevy stopped in the drive. Dixie got out, caught sight of Presley, and ran around the car to fling herself into his arms. He caught her, lifting her butt as she clasped her legs around him.

It took a few minutes of kissing to make sure she was really there in his arms. "Where have you been?" he asked, finally managing to pull back far enough to speak.

"I got stranded at the Farley Inn. Dinner was awful. He heard my end of our conversation and went flying out of there."

"Yeah, I figured. How did you know where to find me?"

"You told me about this place the other night after we——" Her gaze shifted to her feet.

"After we made love." He tipped her chin up so she'd meet his gaze.

"Is that what it was?" she whispered.

"Not what it was, Fireball. What it is. What it's going to be. You all in on this with me?" He had to know.

"Gram gave me some good advice tonight."

"Oh yeah? I've gotten to know your gram over the past several days, and that doesn't surprise me. She doesn't seem to be shy about sharing her hard-earned experience with anyone. What did she say?" He pulled her close, taking the moment to nudge his nose into her hair. If he lived to be a thousand years old, he'd never tire of the scent of her shampoo.

"She said you can't always choose who you fall in love with, but you can choose how to love them."

"That right there is million-dollar advice."

"You think so?"

"I know so. It's true then, isn't it?"

Dixie peered up at him through long lashes. "What's true?"

"You must love me." He shrugged, enjoying the shock on her face. "Don't laugh now. I know you want to."

She bit her bottom lip. "I never want to laugh in moments like this. It just happens."

"Then kiss me. You can't laugh if you're kissing me."

She did, telling him with her mouth what she wasn't ready to say yet with words. And he told her right back. Dixie was right. Nonverbal communication could be downright satisfying.

"I hate to end our private party, but"—Presley lined his nose up with hers—"I think I know where the toads are."

"You do?" Dixie jerked backward and took him by the hand, dragging him toward the car. "Why didn't you say so? Let's go. We need to get Kermit off the roof."

"Okay. But give me the keys. I've got to get behind the wheel of this baby."

Dixie tossed him the keys and waited while he opened the door for her.

"This is going to be a good night, Dixie King." With her by his side, SoCal out of the picture, and a souped-up V8 rumbling underneath him, how could it be anything but?

The Chevy eased to a stop in front of the remains of a dilapidated old farmhouse.

"Are you sure this is the place?" Dixie asked.

Presley pointed to the side of the road where a

dented mailbox perched on a tilted post with "Bristol" scrawled across the side in faded white letters. "I think this is it."

"You didn't happen to bring a flashlight, did you?" She climbed out of the passenger side into some tall grass. Who knew what might be slithering around by her feet?

"Just my phone." A thin beam sliced through the darkness. "You want to come back when it's light out?"

Why hadn't he suggested that twenty minutes ago? "As long as we're here, we may as well make sure this is where the toads are. I don't think they'll all fit in the trunk, so we'll have to come back later anyway, right?"

"Yeah. Watch your step." Presley took her by the elbow, guiding her past some rusty farming implements.

"Do you think this is where Chandler grew up?" She didn't pay that much attention back then to where her classmates lived. Unless they were on her bus route, folks were too spread out for a kid her age to care.

"I think his family lived closer to town. But maybe this is his uncle's old place."

Dixie picked her way through the grass, being sure to stick close to Presley. She couldn't help but wonder how the house had fallen into such disrepair. It was a shame too. From what she could tell, it looked like it had been a nice place at one point in time.

"I'm going in." Presley reached the front porch first.

Thankful for the promise of solid footing, Dixie skipped up the steps. "I'll wait here."

Presley paused. "Chicken?"

She shook her head. "It's not chicken I'm worried about. It's what you're going to find on the other side of that door."

"Chicken," Presley muttered, more to himself than to her.

The door squealed on rusty hinges, and then he was gone, swallowed up by the darkness inside.

Dixie tapped her foot, hummed a little tune, and hugged herself tightly while she waited for him to return. It had to be almost midnight. The storm had moved on, but clouds still hung overhead, blocking out any light from the moon. Her eyes hadn't adjusted to the darkness yet, and as she peered out from the porch, she could have sworn she saw all kinds of creatures lurking in the darkness.

Tired of waiting, she moved toward the door. "Presley?" She pushed the heavy door open with her foot. "Are you in there?"

"Boo!" He jumped out from behind the door, holding his phone under his chin and looking like a ghoul.

"Don't do that to me!" Her heart thundered through her chest. "You could have scared me into last week."

He wrapped his arms around her waist. "Hell, if I did, none of this would have happened yet."

She didn't relax into him right away. A scare like that required a few minutes' grudge.

His hand pressed over her heart. "Your heart's pounding away in there."

"I know."

"I'm sorry. I didn't mean to give you a fright. Good news though. As far as I can tell, all of Kermit's toads are in there."

"Are you sure?" She leaned on him a little.

"Well, I didn't count them all. But there are a lot of bins."

"Good. Let's go tell Kermit. Gram's going to be so happy." Dixie swayed in his arms. Things were working out. Kermit's toads were safe, and Gram would get her own happily ever after. Presley was all in one piece and wanted to give a real relationship a shot. Everything was coming up roses.

Then why did she have the sinking feeling the worst was yet to come?

TWENTY-SEVEN

DIXIE BEGAN THE NEXT MORNING WITH RENEWED PURPOSE. Kermit had managed to avoid being struck by lightning during last night's storm and had finally come down from the roof. With the second weekend of the chili cook-off almost upon them, she was grateful to not have to figure out how to explain to visitors why they had a man living on the roof of the Rose.

"You ready to go?" She paused in the doorway of her grandmother's bedroom. Gram had gone all out for their visit to the bank. She wore a bright-purple suit jacket over a formfitting black skirt. A silky white blouse with miles of ruffles at the neck completed the ensemble. Dark-brown nylons peeked out under the hem of her skirt and disappeared into a pair of white patent heels with a peekaboo toe.

"Just about. Can you help me fasten this bracelet?" Gram held out her wrist. Dixie took the silver chain.

"Where did you get this?" She fingered the tiny frog charm.

Gram blushed. "A gift from Kermit."

"How did he get you a bracelet? He's been sitting on the roof of the Rose for days." Dixie clasped the chain around Gram's wrist.

"I think Presley helped him out a bit." Gram shook her wrist, letting the charm dangle.

Presley Walker was just full of surprises. He'd been the one to arrange the meeting with the banker today. Gram had her heart set on buying Kermit's land. She and Dixie had stayed up half the night talking about it. Kermit would get to keep his horned toad conservation. Dixie would be able to realize her dream of having her own studio and retail space, and Gram would become a landlord.

Presley had assured them the deal was as good as done. It had taken every ounce of willpower Dixie possessed not to spill the beans to her mom and dad. But Gram was right—it was her money, and she could spend it how she saw fit. Dixie knew the fallout from this particular decision would probably haunt her for quite a while, especially when her dad had been counting on Gram's contribution to his capital campaign.

"Speak of the devil…" Dixie peered out the front window in time to see Presley's Jeep pull into the drive.

"I'm so glad the two of you got out of your own way." Gram winked at Dixie's reflection in the mirror as she clipped on an earring.

"What's that supposed to mean?" Dixie asked.

"Nothing." Gram gave her a look full of mock innocence then bustled down the stairs.

Dixie followed, eager to get her hands, and her lips, on Presley Walker.

"Don't you look pretty as a peach today." He kissed her on the cheek when she reached the bottom step. She wrapped her arms around him, still getting used to the idea that they were a thing.

"Ready?" Gram slipped her purse onto her arm. "If my hand doesn't cramp from signing my name a thousand times, you'll be looking at a real estate investor by this evening."

"Now, Mrs. Holbein, I told you it doesn't happen quite that way. Kermit defaulted on his payments. My buddy said it's a done deal, but it will probably take some time for the paperwork to go back and forth within the bank." Presley shot Dixie a smile.

"I know, I know. I'm just so excited." Gram raised onto her tiptoes and pressed a candy apple–red kiss to Presley's cheek. "I can't thank you enough for helping me through this."

Dixie used her thumb to rub the lipstick off. "We'd better get going. Being late won't make a very favorable impression on the banker."

He held the door for both of them then helped Gram into the Jeep. She kept up the chitter-chatter for the short ride into town. Her smile could have lit up a small country, she was so jazzed about being able to save Kermit's conservation charge. The smile lasted all the way through the pleasantries with the bank officer Presley introduced as one of his old buddies, Blake, past the review of her account, and up to the point where Blake received a message from his secretary informing him the bank had just accepted an offer from another party. One that offered more than the going rate on Hill Country acreage. One that happened to be from a recently formed LLC out of southern California.

"Dammit." Presley slapped a hand onto the desk in front of him. "You knew we were coming in this morning to talk about this. How could you sell it right out from under us?"

"I wish I could say it wasn't all about the money, but"—Blake shrugged—"it's all about the money."

"Can we make a higher offer?" Presley asked.

"It's done. Paperwork was signed early this morning. I just found out about it."

"I don't understand." Gram glanced from Presley to Blake. "You sold my land to someone else?"

"Technically, it was never your land…" Blake began to explain.

"It should have been. I told her it was for sure." Presley leaned over the desk. "You know you just sealed our fate, don't you?"

Blake shuffled some papers into a stack on his desk. "It's just a crappy piece of marshland."

"What are we going to do?" Dixie stood, glaring at Presley. "You promised me you had this all under control. You've got to fix it. We can't lose the Rose over this."

"What about Kermit's toads? What's he supposed to do with them now?" Gram stamped her foot. "My last chance at having sex before I die is going to have his heart broken into a million pieces. This will kill him, Dixie."

"Gram!" Dixie took her grandmother by the elbow. "Let's get you some fresh air."

Presley clenched his jaw. "I'll figure something out."

"I knew I shouldn't have listened to you. If you'd kept your cool, let me handle things with Chandler, none of this would have happened." Dixie clutched her grandmother's arm, more for her own benefit than Gram's.

"So this is all my fault." Presley blew out a breath.

"You're the one who had a plan." Dixie should have known better than to let her heart lead the way when it came to Presley Walker.

"And I'm sure if we'd done things your way everything would be fine by now." Presley wasn't backing down. He'd probably never had to admit fault before. That's what happened when he didn't stick around long enough to suffer the consequences of his actions.

"I guess we'll never know now, will we?" Dixie guided Gram across the street to the diner. There was no way she was getting back in the car with Presley now. She'd rather call her sister or even her mother for a ride than spend one more moment with the man. How could she have trusted him?

"Fine. If that's the way you want to leave things, so be it." He spun on his heel and stalked across the road. "But just remember, you're the one who's giving up, not me."

She shook her head. Giving up? The last thing she was going to do was give up. She was going to do what she always did...put her own wants and needs aside again for the goodness of the community. That's what she should have done in the first place. But she'd let Presley sweet-talk her and get her wishing and hoping for things that never would have been possible. That's what happened when she wished on silly stars. From now on, she'd put her faith in the one person she'd always been able to count on...herself.

It was the look that did him in. The look in her eyes that said she'd known he'd fail her somehow, some way. Damn, he hated that look. Not because it crushed him. Not because it slayed him. But because she was right. He should have been more careful. He'd let his need to come through like a fucking knight in shining armor drown out the voice in his head that whispered he needed to double- and triple-check the facts before he made promises he wasn't sure he could deliver on.

He hadn't given SoCal enough credit. The laid-back, surfer-style attitude belied the fact that the jerk was a shark underneath. If he wanted to play hardball, Presley was game. But he was done messing around with the front man. If he was going to come through for Dixie, for her gram and Kermit, for Charlie and Beck and the whole town of Holiday, he was going to have to go straight to the source.

As he hopped into the driver's seat of his Jeep, he pulled up his contacts on his phone. Filed under "Do Not Dial, Ever," he found the number he was looking for.

It rang once, then a gravelly voice barked on the other end. "Yeah?"

"You ready to do this?" Presley asked.

"I was born to do this, son."

"I'm not your son."

The man let out a sharp laugh. "You're right about that. My kin knows when to call it quits."

"I'm not even close to calling it quits. Hell, I'm just getting started."

"Friday night. At the Rose. You and me."

"You're on. You bring the paperwork for Kermit's land."

"And you bring your granpappy's fiddle. Sure will be nice to have another piece of the old geyser finally bend to my will."

"It'll stay where it belongs, right here with me," Presley promised.

"You sure are a cocky son of a bitch."

With that, the phone line went dead. Presley tossed his phone on the passenger seat. The only way to fight fire was with fire. He just hoped he didn't get burned in the process.

TWENTY-EIGHT

chapter

TWENTY-EIGHT

DIXIE RAN THROUGH HER LAST-RESORT OPTIONS UNTIL SHE couldn't keep her thoughts straight. She'd spent the past three days racking her brain for some option she'd overlooked. She could come clean with her dad and plead with him to step in and help. She could call Chandler, beg for forgiveness, and see if she could buy some time. She could climb into bed, pull the covers over her head, and pray she'd wake up to find the whole giant mess had just been a bad dream.

Out of those options, hiding in bed was definitely the most appealing. Also, the most unlikely to result in a positive outcome. If the Bristol family got their hands on that land, they'd move forward with their plans. The Rose would be doomed, Holiday would turn into some cheesy country and western tourist trap, and Kermit's toads would be left to fend for themselves.

It was high time she started preparing for the worst. Charlie and Beck were due back today, guaranteeing the worst was definitely upon her. If only she and Presley had been able to work together. Surely the two of them could have come up with some solution.

But he'd disappeared. Nobody had seen or heard from him in days. Dixie couldn't help but want to kick herself for taking a chance on the man.

Even Gram had lost her happy-go-lucky attitude. She'd been spending every waking moment out at Kermit's place, helping him get his toads ready for their third move in less than a week. They'd release as many as they could back into the wild, far away from Kermit's land since it would soon become a major construction zone.

Dixie shook her head, wishing reality would fade away. She'd been so concerned about everyone else losing their dreams that she hadn't yet mourned the loss of her own. With that giant theme park coming to town, Holiday wouldn't be the same. Definitely not the right place for her to start up a handcrafted artisan compound. She'd even gotten her hopes up that Presley might eventually want to join her venture. He could move all of his equipment to a studio right next to hers, and they'd be able to work side by side to make their dreams come true.

She let out a sharp laugh. That dream had lasted about ten minutes. Her relationship status hadn't fared much better.

Gram shuffled down the hall in her house shoes. "Dixie? Are you heading to the Rose today? Don't you have that chili thing still going on?"

Dixie pulled a pillow over her head and groaned into it. "Yes."

"What?" Gram paused in the doorway. "I can't hear you with a pillow over your face."

She peeked out from underneath and blew a duck feather from her lip. "I suppose I should, although I don't see the point. The Rose will be wiped off the map before next summer thanks to me."

"Now, sweetheart." Gram perched on the edge of the bed. "Maybe Charlie and Beck will know what to do. I still have faith that Presley is going to come through. You haven't given up on him, have you?"

Propping herself up on her elbows, Dixie let out an epic sigh. "He's gone, Gram. Probably ran off to Nashville to find his brother and start up his business there."

"Not Presley." Gram clutched her hand to her heart. "I can't believe he'd leave his family, his friends, and his girlfriend in a lurch like that."

"I'm not his girlfriend anymore." Dixie burrowed back under the pillow. "That dubious honor lasted about as long as Presley having a heart did."

"You want to know what I think?" Gram asked.

"No."

"Well, that's too bad because I'm going to tell you anyway." Gram stretched out beside her on the full-sized bed. "I think Presley's going to swoop in at the last moment and save the day."

Dixie peeked out again. "How? By telling a joke? That seems to be the only thing he's serious about...not being serious."

"Oh, honey." Gram smoothed back her hair, making Dixie feel about ten years old again. "I know you're hurting, but you can't let a momentary setback keep you down."

"It's not a momentary setback. Everything is ruined, and it's all my fault." Dixie tossed the covers back and crawled out of bed on the opposite side from Gram.

"We'll adapt." Gram swung her legs over the side of the bed and sat up. "That's what God's creatures do."

"Not the horned toads." Dixie pulled her shorts on

under her nightshirt. "They're not adapting, they're going extinct. Just like the Rose."

"It'll work out how it's supposed to, you'll see."

"Gram, I know you're just trying to make me feel better, but please stop. I need to be miserable for a while." She turned away, gathering her hair into a messy bun on top of her head. "Are you going to Kermit's today?"

"Yes. The poor man doesn't have much, so it won't take long to help him pack."

"When does he need to be out of there?" Dixie ducked into the closet to change her shirt. Pretty soon her stack of hot-pink Rose shirts would become collector's items.

"Oh, no one's said yet, but he'd rather get it over with and be on his way."

She stuck her head out of the closet. "Where's he going to go?"

"I wanted to talk to you about that."

"What?" Dixie heard the hesitation in her gram's voice. She peered around the doorway of the closet. Gram stood at the foot of the bed, wringing her hands together. A crease the size of the Rio Grande bisected her forehead. "What's wrong?"

"I've been wondering. What would you think about Kermit moving in here with us?" Gram grimaced, like she was bracing herself for an outburst.

"I think if it makes you happy, then it's fine with me." As Dixie closed the distance between them, the crease disappeared. Her grandmother's face took on the glow of someone very much in love. Dixie envied her her happiness. Not because she wanted it for herself instead, but because she couldn't share in it. The wound Presley had left on her heart was too new, too raw.

"Your daddy's going to shit a brick when he hears about this." Gram clucked her tongue.

"Gram!" Dixie laughed. "A brick's too small. He's going to crap a cinderblock."

"You're probably right about that."

"So are you going to make an honest man out of Kermit?"

"We'll see. At my age, you learn to take your blessings as they come and enjoy one day at a time." Gram put her hand on Dixie's arm and gave it a squeeze.

"That sounds like good advice. I think I'd better get out there and start counting my own blessings." After a final hug from Gram, Dixie made her way down the steps and out into the sun.

Presley ran a palm over the neck of his granddad's fiddle. He'd spent the better part of the last three days fully restoring the vintage instrument until the shine would be too much for even Leroy Bristol to resist. Now only one task stood between him and his final play to save the Rose. He gingerly set the fiddle in the case and snapped it shut. Grabbing the handle in one hand, he snagged his most recent creation in the other and made his way to the Jeep.

He ran a palm over his scruffy chin as he shifted into drive and pulled onto the road. He'd royally botched things with Dixie. He still hadn't let himself dwell on the circumstances surrounding their breakup long enough to try to figure out what happened. Every time he started to think about it, an image of Dixie popped into his head.

Dixie flaring those emerald eyes at him. Dixie with her hands on her hips, ready to rip him a new one. Dixie pulling that swollen lower lip into her mouth like he'd been dreaming about doing for what seemed like forever.

As he pulled into the parking lot of the obscure dark building, a memory of making this same drive with his granddad hit him. He'd been here before. He had to duck as he entered the doorway with peeling pink letters. The Fiddlin' Kitten. Yes, he'd definitely been here before, he could feel it in his bones.

The guy behind the counter eyed him as he approached the register. "What can I do for you?"

"I wanted to get an opinion on a couple of fiddles if you have a minute." Presley laid the case on the counter.

"You're the guy who called earlier?"

Presley nodded.

"Let me go get Ernie. He's the best one to take a look."

Presley tried not to sweat while he waited for the man to return. Fiddles in every color hung from the walls. They had memorabilia, pictures, and autographs from some of the greatest string players he'd ever heard of, including a glossy black-and-white of his grandfather holding one of his own creations. Presley had half a mind to take the two cases and run before he embarrassed himself. Before he could, a man came out of the back room. He held a cane in a gnarled hand. A felt fedora sat at a tilt on his head and thick bottle lens glasses perched on his nose.

"I hear you have something for me to look at?" He peered up at Presley with curious dark eyes.

"Yeah, but I don't want to waste your time."

"Looking at an instrument is never a waste of my time, son. Any chance I have to encourage the love of fiddling in the younger generation is a chance I have to take. Besides"—he winked—"you never know when you're going to come across a real gem."

Presley shifted his weight from foot to foot.

"Mind if I take a look?"

"Go ahead."

He leaned his cane against the counter and reached for the older case first with shaky hands. As he flipped the top back, he let out an audible gasp. "My word. Where did you get your hands on this?"

Presley swallowed. "It belonged to my grandfather, Duke Walker. He mainly ranched but made a couple dozen fiddles over the course of his lifetime. He left the plans and all of his equipment in one of our old barns."

"I know the name well. Your grandfather and I used to get together from time to time to lay on the strings."

"Really?" Presley leaned closer. "I was only about ten when he died. But I loved watching him coax a tune from the strings. Some of my favorite memories are sitting in the corner and watching him take a chunk of wood and turn it into a masterpiece."

"Mind if I give it a whirl?"

"Please do." Presley gestured toward the fiddle.

Ernie picked it up and nestled it under his chin. He drew the bow across the strings, eliciting a rich note. "They don't make them like this anymore."

Presley grinned.

Ernie closed his eyes and began a tune Presley knew he'd heard before. Had to be something his granddad had played a long time ago.

When Ernie finished, he reverently set the fiddle back in the case. "Thank you. I thought I'd have to go the rest of my days without getting the chance to draw my bow over a Duke Walker original. Now, what do you want to do with it? I've got collectors worldwide that would pay an arm and a leg for something of this quality."

"Really?" Presley's heart pounded in his chest.

"Honest to Betsy. Quality like this is hard to find. You can pretty much set your own price. There aren't very many left out there in the world. The last time I saw one it was in the hands of your grandfather himself. Nobody could make the strings sing like him. Nobody."

"I actually wasn't planning on selling it. Can I show you something else?"

"Absolutely. I've got nowhere pressing to be. You get to be my age, and there's only two things on your schedule each day that you can't work around. Your bedtime and your bowel movements." Ernie lifted his hat to wipe a handkerchief across his brow. "Mess with either one of those, and you'll be paying the price for days."

Too nervous to laugh, Presley unfastened the other case and braced himself for the moment of truth.

Ernie reached for the fiddle inside, a hand-carved beauty Presley had finished a few weeks ago.

"Did your grandfather make this one too?" Ernie balanced the fiddle on his shoulder. "No, it's too recent to be Duke's work."

Presley gave a slight nod.

Ernie pointed at him with a crooked pointer finger. "You've definitely got the Walker genes. You made this, did you?"

"Yes, sir." It was hard to get a read on the older man. Either he liked the fiddle and hadn't quite said so yet or he was trying to figure out a way to let Presley down easy. As Presley waited for the final verdict, Ernie picked up the bow and tested it out against the strings.

"Beautiful. Like I said, they don't make them like this anymore. Is it maple?"

"Yes, sir. Along with some spruce. And see the bridge there? Granddad's plans called for it to be a tad bit shorter, but I felt like it would give a richer sound if I raised it just slightly."

Ernie nodded. "Nicely done."

"So do you think it's worth trying?"

"Worth trying what?" Ernie reached for his cane.

"Worth trying my hand at a career making fiddles, I suppose. Do you think the one I made comes close in quality to the ones my granddad crafted?" Presley closed the case on his fiddle, eager for Ernie's verdict.

Ernie hesitated, like he wanted to choose his words carefully. "I think your granddad would be proud."

"So I should try?" Presley asked.

"Don't try, son. Do."

"Do what?" Presley got the sense his time with Ernie was running out, and he still had questions for the man.

"The greats don't try to be great. They just are. Share your talent with the world. Don't deprive musicians of the gift you've been given. And if you ever want to stop by, we've got a session every Sunday night that likes to get together over at the roadhouse just on the other side of Mustang Ridge for a few hours. I'd be mighty honored if you'd come sometime so the guys can check these out."

"I'd love to."

"Great. Here's my card." He slid his hand into his pocket and pulled out a dog-eared business card. "Come anytime."

"Thank you." Presley stuck his hand out. Ernie gripped it with a strength he didn't appear to possess.

"Now go practice. If you're going to jam with us, you're going to have to be able to keep up." Ernie winked at him again.

Presley took the cases from the counter, more fired up than ever to put plans in place to make his dreams come true. As he marched back to the Jeep, his two treasures in hand, he barely let himself think about what it might feel like if he lost his granddad's fiddle in the process.

THE HOURS DRAGGED. DIXIE PASTED ON HER MOST CHEERY smile and did her best to convince herself and everyone else that it was just another day of work at the Rose. By the time seven o'clock rolled around, she was ready to slip on her pajamas and curl up with a good book or, better yet, some of Mrs. Knotts's huckleberry cobbler she'd seen Gram tuck into the fridge before she left the house this morning. Too bad she was working solo and had at least another seven hours on the clock before she'd be able to get anywhere near her favorite nightshirt.

"How you holdin' up?" Shep called out across the bar.

"Meh." She filled her water bottle from the cooler they kept for the staff. It would be another couple of hours before the sun dipped down below the horizon, taking the worst heat of the day with it.

"Chin up, Dixie." Shep gave her a solid thumbs-up. She reciprocated with a thumbs-up of her own, although she was tempted to turn her thumb upside down.

She hadn't shared everything with the staff yet, although most of them could tell something was up. Hoping they assumed it was just a funk from Presley bailing on her, she let them think what they would. It wasn't her job to tell Charlie's employees they'd most likely be out of a job in the near future.

At least the crowd had come back for the second weekend of the festival. They must have brought their friends with them. It took Dixie much longer than expected to reach the back of the stage. A quick glance at her watch told her she was going to be a few minutes late announcing their first act of the night. That didn't set well with her.

As she prepared an apology in her head on how she'd address the tardy start time with the crowd, a voice boomed out over the loudspeaker.

Presley.

She didn't pay any attention to what he was saying—she was so mad he was speaking at all, she'd be liable to chew up nails and spit out a barbed-wire fence.

Coming from the back of the stage, she couldn't see him, but she sure could hear him. All of a sudden the crowd began to boo. Dixie slid between the gate and a set of bleachers. She knew she'd be mad when she saw him, mad as a snake who'd found its tail tied in a knot. But she didn't figure the sight of him would pull at something so deep inside that her knees would buckle and she'd lose her ability to remain upright.

Lowering herself to the edge of the bleachers, she took in the scene on the stage. Presley stood at the mic stand with the opening band behind him. A group from Little Rock was playing the first set. They appeared to be as confused as Dixie. Presley seemed to be the only one with any inkling of what was going on.

As she waited, along with several hundred other

people, to see what would happen, a hand grabbed her shoulder. She whirled around, straight into Charlie's arms.

"It's so good to see you, Dixie. The Rose looks great, the crowd is huge, and Presley seems to have it all together onstage. I don't know how you did it. I suppose I can tell you now, but I never expected you and Presley to get along. I mean, he's my brother, so I'm familiar with his faults, and my God, I wouldn't wish him on my worst enemy, much less a good friend. But you did it."

Dixie stood, gnawing on her lip, wanting so desperately to spill her guts, to lay it all out there for Charlie.

"Dixie? Are you okay? Is everything all right?"

Dixie turned her attention toward the stage. "I'm not sure. But I think based on whatever Presley's got up his sleeve, we're about to find out."

Presley wavered when Charlie gripped Dixie in a hug. There had to be over a thousand people in the crowd, and of course his gaze managed to land on the one woman he wasn't ready to face. Well, two women if he counted his sister. But the show must go on. He wasn't going to give up without a fight, so he was fighting the only way he knew how.

He turned to the poker table he'd set up at the front of the stage. "Ladies and gentlemen, I want to tell you a story. A story that started right here, at the Rambling Rose, many, many years ago."

The guitarist from the band waved to get his attention. He gestured to the acoustic guitar strapped across his chest. "Want us to play some background?"

Presley nodded. That would be nice. A little music to

set the scene. He pulled the mic from the stand. He could think better if he was moving. Since he hadn't practiced any type of script, it would be better if he didn't stand still.

"It's a story about two men, two fiddle players, in fact. Both of them well-known, at least around these parts. Maybe you've heard of them? Duke Walker and Leroy Bristol?" A smattering of applause came from the crowd.

"Well, Duke was my granddad. He grew up around here with ranching in his blood and fiddling in his heart. He loved two things almost as much as playing his fiddle." Presley held up a finger. "Taking a chance at the poker table." He held up another finger. "And, two, my grandma, Ravina."

Charlie waved her arms, trying to get his attention. He looked her way but kept talking. He couldn't lose his nerve now, not when so much depended on what would happen next.

"It so happened that one night Duke sat down to play some poker with his good buddy and fellow fiddler, Leroy. Duke got into a jam like we've all been known to do and suddenly found himself out of cash. Leroy suggested he put up his fiddle. Being the gambling man that he was, Duke agreed."

The music slowed. Presley kept talking. "There are quite a few accounts of what happened next. Some say my granddad lost that hand fair and square. Everyone knows four of a kind beats a full house."

Heads bobbed up and down, nodding. They were following him.

"But some say four of a kind doesn't count when

314 DYLANN CRUSH

a player has four threes and there are two more in the discard pile."

The drummer decided to join in.

"Needless to say, a fight broke out. Leroy and Duke spilled out onto the porch. A lantern broke; a fire started. The Rose took the side of my granddad, the right side I might add, and banned Mr. Bristol from ever darkening its doorstep again."

The steel guitar picked up on the rhythm, and Presley found himself accompanied by a full band.

"So tonight I've invited Mr. Bristol back. He's got something I want, and I've got something he's waited most of his lifetime to claim." Presley walked to the side of the stage and came back holding the fiddle over his head. People whistled and yelled. "The game's called Texas hold 'em. If you'll indulge us, we'll play it out right here, right before the eyes of all of you good people. No cheating, no fights. What do you say, Mr. Bristol, do you accept?"

Hell, he didn't even know if Leroy Bristol had made it to town. The whole thing could blow up in his face. While he waited for a response, he glanced toward Dixie and Charlie. Dixie stood, furiously whispering in his sister's ear. Charlie shook her head then covered her eyes with her hands.

Presley had a momentary flash of regret. Maybe this was a mistake. Maybe he was making things worse, not better. Maybe he should call the whole thing off, just offer the man the fiddle in exchange for the deed to Kermit's land. But he feared it wouldn't be enough. Playing to Bristol's ego, dangling something in front of him that he'd wanted for so long and then setting the stage so he could win it in front of a crowd, proving once and for all that he'd been entitled to it all along, that was the only way he'd entice the man to play.

He held the mic away from his lips, afraid his nerves would be broadcast for the whole crowd to hear.

Then, from the corner of the stage, a wiry man wearing a long, grizzly braid and a straw cowboy hat on his head walked toward Presley. With a glint in his eye that could strike fear into a man twice his size, he grabbed the mic from Presley.

And in that deep voice Presley had never been able to get out of his head, he said the only two words Presley wanted to hear in that moment. "I accept."

"WHAT THE HELL IS GOING ON?" CHARLIE LOOKED LIKE SHE hadn't slept in days, and Dixie could have sworn she had a milk stain or maybe spit-up from baby Sully across half of her T-shirt. But since she hadn't stopped cursing and waving her arms around since they'd entered the office, Dixie hadn't had a chance to point it out.

"Relax. I've got it all under control." Presley put a hand on Charlie's shoulder. If it was meant to calm her, it had an adverse effect.

She shrugged him off and went toe to toe with him, something Dixie had never seen anyone else attempt. "I left you in charge of a perfectly good bar. I've barely been gone a week. How is it that you've managed to practically run me out of business?"

"I think you're overreacting."

Dixie almost felt sorry for Presley. Almost. But she also wished she could give him a piece of her own mind. Maybe not in quite the same manner as Charlie, but something close.

"You think?" Charlie shrieked. "You thinking is what got us into trouble here in the first place."

"Dixie and I did our best while you were gone. In fact, I'm not sure you could have done much better if you'd been here." He offered a tentative smile in Dixie's direction. It almost sucked her in.

But then Charlie's arm went around her shoulder. "Don't you dare pull her into this. Dixie, I owe you an apology. I should have known better than to try to get you to work with Presley. He would have steam-rolled anyone."

Dixie waited for Presley to defend himself, but he didn't. They'd both made some bad calls over the past week. True, he'd jumped the gun and should have let her try to get the info out of Chandler at dinner before breaking into his room. But he did have everyone's best interests at heart.

"Actually"—Dixie ducked out from under Charlie's arm—"Presley's right. Things happened so fast. We did our best."

"Did you sleep with her?" Charlie put her hands on her hips. The moment strung out between them.

Presley didn't move. His eyes sought Dixie's, and he waited for her lead. A lead she was too chicken to take. Finally, he spoke. "That's not fair, Charlie."

"Gosh, you're right. I know Dixie has better sense than that. I'm sorry." Charlie put a hand on Dixie's shoulder. "Can you give us a few minutes? I'd like to skin my brother in private."

Dixie was almost to the door when she froze. Her feet refused to carry her through the threshold to safety. She slowly turned around. Presley's gaze had dropped to his feet, ready to take the tongue-lashing his sister surely had in store for him. She wouldn't let him suffer alone.

"Basically"—Dixie took a step toward Presley—"he didn't sleep with me. I slept with him."

Presley grinned. The spark in his eye was worth

the brief moment of embarrassment. He held out his arms, and she buried her face against his chest. "Welcome back, Fireball."

"What has been going on around here while I've been gone? Has the whole world lost its mind?"

A chorus of voices filtered in through the open window. "Get out of my way, Angelo. This has nothing to do with you."

Metal screeched against metal.

"I think you'd better check with Charlie on this, Waylon. She's not going to like it."

Charlie pulled the curtain to the side and shouted out the window. "Waylon, what are you doing? Why do you have a trailer backed up to Pork Chop's pen?"

"Oh shit." Presley clapped a hand to his head. "I'll be right back."

"Presley!" Charlie raced after him.

Dixie decided she'd better go along. He might need her help in standing up to Charlie. By the time she reached the pigpen, she could tell exactly what was going on. Waylon had delivered both pigs back to the Rose. Pork Chop and Ham Bone stood in the corner of the pigpen, snuffling through a bucket of slop like they'd been roommates all of their lives.

"I told you to come back by Tuesday. It's Friday now." Waylon closed the back of the trailer and brushed his hands against his jeans.

"Waylon, please. Give me one more day. That boar is a beast. You saw what he did to my side. He can't stay here—he's a hazard." Presley followed Waylon, undoing the latches on the trailer right after he'd secured them.

"What now?" Charlie tossed her hands in the air.

"Who's Ham Bone, and why is there a boar in the pen with Pork Chop? Y'all remember the last time this happened?"

Dixie held back a smile. Who could forget the sight of Charlie and Beck trying to break apart two pigs that'd been obviously intent on making bacon?

"He can't stay at the ranch anymore. Damn boar busts through everything. I can't fix the fences as fast as he breaks them."

"If he's breaking out, why not let him run away?" Presley mumbled. "Seems like that would be a win-win for everyone."

"Because he doesn't run away. He runs to her." Waylon pointed at Pork Chop. "Then he busts into her pen. You want to keep them separate, you start mending fences. I'm done." He did up the latches one more time and pointed a threatening finger at Presley. "You touch those again, and I'll break your fingers."

Presley backed off, holding his hands in the air. "In light of everything else we have going on tonight, I'm going to suggest we leave the pigs to their own devices."

"Fine. But if we end up with a litter of piglets, it's all on you." Charlie waved to her oldest brother. "See you later, Waylon. Come back when you're in a better mood."

He shook his head as he climbed into the pickup and drove away.

Dixie turned to Presley. "So what's your plan, Mr. Walker? How are you going to save the Rose?"

"Yes, Mr. Walker, do tell." Charlie slung an arm

around Dixie's shoulder and pulled her in. "Didn't I warn you about my brother? How did you get sucked in?"

"I can tell you that," Presley said. "Someone a lot wiser than me once said you can't choose the people you fall in love with, but you can choose how to love them."

"Really? Who said that?" Charlie wrapped her other arm around Presley and began walking both of them back toward the stage. "Was it Mother Teresa? Shakespeare? Am I on the right track?"

Presley leaned back and met Dixie's gaze. Her heart expanded like a helium balloon, filling her chest, as he mouthed three little words to her...*I love you.*

She reached over and slapped him on the butt. Gram would be so proud. "Then prove it to me. Get out there and win back Kermit's land."

Presley nodded, pressed a kiss to his sister's cheek, then laid a mind-numbing version on Dixie, leaving her reeling and struggling to stand up straight. By the time she regained her balance, he was halfway to the stage.

"Now what do we do?" Charlie asked.

"We keep our fingers crossed that Presley gets the right cards."

"Fantastic. Did I ever tell you that Beck's ancestors originally won the Rambling Rose in a poker game?"

"Really?" Dixie didn't like where this was going. Not at all.

"Yep. Of course, it was just a one-horse bar in a two-horse town at the time. So you understand I'm not terribly excited at the prospect of Presley hinging all of our fates on a few hands of poker."

"I can appreciate that." Dixie bit her lip, trying to offer some wisdom or some kind words that would alleviate the seriousness of the situation. "I guess there's one more thing we could do."

They'd almost reached the grassy area where people had set up chairs and blankets to watch the bands.

"Oh yeah, what's that?"

Dixie glanced up at the stage to see Chandler take a seat at the table with his uncle. "Pray."

chapter
THIRTY-ONE

PRESLEY GLANCED OUT AT THE CROWD THEN BACK AT THE cards in his hand. A queen and a one-eyed jack stared back at him. He and Leroy had been going at it on the stage for more than an hour. The pot seemed to go back and forth between them. Leroy would go up a couple stacks of chips, and then Presley would win it back. Per the house rules they'd discussed before the game began, the antes had been increasing every ten minutes. In another thirty seconds or so, it would be time to raise them again.

Leroy checked his cards. Presley wasn't a professional poker player by any stretch of the imagination, but in the last couple of hands, he'd discovered Leroy's tell. When he got a couple of cards he was excited about, his left eyebrow would wiggle a little. Like a fuzzy caterpillar trying to line dance across his forehead.

"What are you looking at?" Leroy growled.

"Nothing. Just trying to read your mind to see what cards you're holding."

"Good luck with that, Walker." The eyebrow wiggled as Leroy tossed in two hundred dollars' worth of chips.

"Too rich for my blood." Presley folded. It killed him to toss in the cards with a queen and a jack in his hand, but those one-eyed bastards seemed to have it in for him.

"Raising the ante," the dealer announced over the mic.

Presley slid his chips into the middle. While he waited for his cards, he sought out Dixie in the crowd. She looked nervous. Her hands couldn't seem to stay still. He gave her a wink, not sure if she'd be able to see it from that far away. Still, her presence offered a calming influence over him. Knowing she was out there cheering for him gave him the confidence he needed to try to pull this off.

The dealer passed out the cards. Presley took a quick peek. A pair of threes. Not his best start of the night but certainly not his worst. He tossed a handful of chips onto the stack. "Raising you four red and a blue."

"That's three hundred in chips, asshole." Chandler had been quiet most of the game, but even he must be getting bored.

Presley waited for the eyebrow wiggle. It didn't come.

"What the hell. Let's see the flop." Leroy shoved his chips onto the pile.

The dealer turned over the first card in the middle. Another three. No way. That gave Presley three of a kind. He had to continue, but he had to play it cool.

"I'll raise you another four red ones." He plucked the chips off his stack and tossed them in the center.

Leroy followed. "Sure, let's see another card."

The dealer turned over a jack. The eyebrow wiggled. Best guess was that Leroy was sitting with a pair of jacks in his hand. Still, three threes beat a pair of jacks all day long. Presley tossed in two blue chips.

"You cocky SOB." Leroy matched and raised him another two blue.

Presley checked and met the bet. The queen of

hearts came next. The eyebrow again. Presley could almost guarantee Leroy was sitting on two pair. But if he was right, his three threes would still put him ahead. He'd come too far, sucked Leroy too deep to turn back now. "In for a penny," Presley muttered as he added two more blue chips to the stack.

Leroy checked, and they both waited for the next card. When the dealer flipped a three, Presley knew he had it made.

"In for a pound. I'm all in." Presley pushed his stack of chips to the middle of the table.

The band stopped playing. Chandler scooted back from the table, knocking his chair over as he stood.

"How much have you got there?" Leroy separated his own chips into stacks while the dealer organized Presley's all-in bet.

"He's got more than you, sir. If you go all in and lose, he'll win the game." The dealer was a pro. His expression didn't convey a thing.

"What do you think you're up to?" Leroy fiddled with the end of his braid. "Fine. Let's end this. I'm all in too."

The drummer started a soft drumroll. It grew louder as the dealer's hand reached for the last card in the center of the table. He turned and flipped, and a one-eyed jack peered up at Presley. Full house. Leroy had a full house.

"Congratulations, Mr. Bristol. That's a great hand."

"Damn straight it is. Are you going to show me what you've got or just toss in?"

"I swear, this has never happened to me in all the years I've been playing poker." Presley slowly flipped his cards, enjoying the moment when Leroy Bristol realized he'd been beat. "Four of a kind. And threes. Crazy, isn't it?"

"Dammit!" Leroy's fist slammed onto the table, scattering poker chips across the stage.

That didn't matter. What mattered was the piece of paper he reluctantly held out to Presley. Title and deed to Kermit's acreage.

As SoCal and his uncle stormed off the stage, Presley was surrounded by his family and friends. The only person he wanted to see was Dixie. She slammed into him, almost knocking him off his feet.

"You did it!" Her arms went around his neck.

"We did it." He nuzzled his nose into her neck, breathing her in.

"Congratulations, you two." Kermit and Genie joined them.

"Does this mean my toads get to stay where they are?" Kermit asked.

"You'll have to ask Dixie about that," Presley said.

"Me?" Dixie pulled back to meet his gaze. "You won the land. Why would he have to ask me?"

He pressed the piece of paper into her hand. "I want you to have it. You can run your studio and shop on the front half here by the Rose, and Kermit can keep the toads on the back half."

"I can't accept this. You should give it back to Kermit." Dixie pushed his hand with the piece of paper in it toward her grandmother.

"Don't you dare give it to Kermit," Eugenia said. "If he gets to keep his land and his house, he'll never agree to move in with me."

"Your grandma's right, hon. I don't need that much space anymore. It's time I moved closer to town. As long as I have a place for my toads, I'll be happy."

"See?" Presley held the paper out to her again.

She took it. "Kermit, I promise as long as we own this land, you'll always have a place for your toads."

Presley nodded in agreement. "Wait, we? Who's we?"

She rose to her tiptoes and spoke into his ear. "There's plenty of room for my jewelry studio and space for a woodworking workshop too, don't you think?"

"What, like partners?" He searched her gaze. All he saw there was a reflection of his own happiness.

"Exactly like partners. What do you say, Presley Walker? I think we'd make a pretty good team."

He pulled her tighter against him. "I couldn't agree more. But with one change to our agreement."

"What's that?"

"More kissing, less talking."

She laughed into his shirt. "That's my kind of agreement."

"Then prove it, Fireball."

"You think anyone would mind if we slipped away for a round or two of mini-golf?"

His lips split into a wide smile. "I thought you'd never ask."

EPILOGUE

THE CROWD SAT IN WHITE FOLDING CHAIRS SHE'D RENTED especially for the occasion. Dixie peered through the back window of the house, her gaze lighting on all of the people she loved. All of the people except her parents. They hadn't come around to the notion that not everyone would bend to their will, so they'd refused to attend. As far as Dixie was concerned, that was a blessing in disguise. The afternoon would be more fun without them.

Liza poked her head through the door holding little Bea in her arms. Bea wasn't old enough to walk down the aisle by herself, but Gram thought she'd make an adorable flower girl, even if Liza carried her down the aisle flinging rose petals as she went.

"You ready?" Liza asked.

Dixie nodded.

"You look beautiful."

"Thanks. So do you."

Liza and Bea stood on the porch, the signal that the violinist should begin. Presley had suggested a fiddle, but Dixie had talked him out of it, arguing that a violin was more appropriate for a classic backyard wedding.

The first strains of "Canon in D" played across her heartstrings.

"Wait!" Dixie reached into the plastic bin on the table next to her and pulled out the tiny ring bearer. "You can't go down the aisle without Fernando."

Liza tucked the horned toad into the basket of rose

petals along with the miniature pillow holding the two rings. "I can't believe we almost forgot him."

As Liza and Bea started down the aisle, Dixie reached for her bouquet.

"Come on, Gram, they're ready for us."

Dixie's nerves flickered, causing a burst of laughter to form in her chest. Then Liza stepped out of the way, and Dixie's gaze fell on Presley. The man was a sight to contend with in denim, but in a tux he was otherworldly, not designed for her mere mortal eyes.

Her heart fluttered like the wings of the monarch butterflies she and Kermit had lovingly raised from caterpillars. If all went well, they'd be releasing them right after the "I do's."

Presley's steady gaze pulled her down the aisle. Not too fast, not too slowly. Just the way they'd practiced.

When she reached the end, she turned. Gram stood at the other end, glowing in a silver gown with thousands of seed beads hand-sewn to the bodice. She only had eyes for Kermit. The "Wedding March" began, and Dixie followed Gram's progress down the aisle, one step at a time.

To see the love Gram and Kermit had for each other filled Dixie with happiness. She glanced to Presley as Gram reached for Kermit's arm and they turned toward the preacher. After a short ceremony, the butterflies were released, and the real party began.

Dixie moved from helping with the buffet to cutting the cake to making sure the gifts were stashed inside. She made more tea, gave Bea a bottle so Liza could take a break, and helped Gram change into her travel attire. The newlyweds were going to be taking a monthlong honeymoon with a stop at the National Park in Indonesia to see Komodo dragons.

As the happy couple strolled down the aisle and climbed into the backseat of Gram's Chevy, Dixie finally sank into a chair, put up her feet, and relaxed. It didn't take Presley long to find her. He sat down next to her, pulled her feet into his lap, and began to rub.

"Oh my gosh, that feels amazing." She closed her eyes and let her head fall back against the chair. "Your hands are your greatest gift. I called that way back when we first started dating, remember?"

"That's right. You said I had nice nails." He dug his fingers into her heel, just the way she liked it.

"I meant hands. Who looks at a guy's nails?"

"That's what I said."

"Oh shut up, you love me." It gave her a thrill to be able to say that, to feel so secure in her relationship with Presley that she could count on his love and affection.

"I do, I do." As he shifted positions to show her other foot some attention, a button popped off his shirt and bounced across the floor.

Dixie cracked an eye open. "What was that?"

"Damn, I lost a button."

"Where?" She peered at the floor underneath the table, her eyes too bleary to properly focus. "You'd better find it. Whitey will charge us an arm and a leg if we bring your rented tux shirt back without a button."

"There it is." Presley leaned down to pick up the button up off the floor. "Hold on, I'll be right back."

She wanted to call out not to leave her feet unattended. Lavishing attention on one of them and not the other left her feeling unbalanced. But she was too tired to summon the energy to speak.

By the time Presley returned, she was practically asleep. He shifted her feet back into his lap.

"Rub."

"Awfully bossy tonight, aren't you?" he joked.

"Why aren't you rubbing?" She cracked open an eye. "What are you doing?"

"Hold up, I'll be done in a minute."

"Presley! What are you doing to your shirt?"

"Relax." He bent low, took something between his teeth, then sat up. "There. Good as new."

"You've got to be kidding." She glanced from his face to his shirt and back to his face again. "Did you seriously just sew on a button?"

His cheeks pinked. It had to be the cutest thing she'd ever seen. Big bad Presley, sewing a button on his shirt at her grandma's wedding.

"Do you have any idea how turned on I am right now?" She bit her lip, knowing it drove him crazy.

"Really? From a button?"

"Yes, from a button." She climbed into his lap, snuggling up against him. "After I sleep for a few days, you're going to get some great sex."

"Car sex?" he asked.

"No."

"Damn. You know, I've been thinking." He rubbed small circles on her back with one hand.

"Uh-oh. Last time you did that we ended up hand-feeding piglets 24/7."

"This is different. You know when Kermit and your gram come back, they're going to be moving into her house."

"Yeah?" Dixie had been waiting for this conversation. It was inevitable.

"What would you think about maybe moving your stuff into my place?"

She wouldn't make it easy for him. "Just my stuff?"

He brushed her hair off her cheek. "Your stuff and you."

"I could maybe do that."

"Maybe? But I learned how to sew a button on for you."

"That was a great start, honey, and I'm so proud of you. But I've been thinking too."

"Uh-oh. About what?"

"I think it's time you also learn how to cook."

Presley let out a bellow of laughter before he lowered his head to nibble on her ear.

Dixie sighed, letting herself enjoy the man's embrace. She'd learned a few things over the past several months: how to let go of her guilt, how to stop putting everyone else's needs first, and how to place her trust in someone else.

And it was all because of him.

Who knew her pig-wrangling, cursing, antagonizing childhood crush had actually been her knight in shining armor in disguise? She did know one thing though—she'd follow her gram's advice. Gram had told her once that if she found a good man, a man who'd treat her well and love her the way she deserved to be loved, she needed to hold on tight and never let him go.

Dixie pulled back and looked into Presley's eyes.

She'd found a good man.

And that's exactly what she intended to do with him.

Acknowledgements

A huge thank you to those of you who have read and enjoyed the books in the Holiday, Texas series. I love reading your reviews and hearing from you! Special thanks to the team at Sourcebooks for making me look good, especially my editor, Mary Altman. To my agent, Jessica Watterson, I owe you one…you helped me whip this baby back into shape, and I'll be forever grateful. Kudos to the other authors who are walking beside me in this crazy publishing journey—my critique groups (Jody, Joyce, Paula, Christine, Diane, Miguella & LeAnne.) And piles of hugs and kisses to my co-host of Romance Happy Hour, Dawn Luedecke, for putting up with me and to my Romance Chicks who have been there from the start… Christina Hovland, Jody Holford & Renee Ann Miller. I wouldn't be doing this without you, chicks! Finally, to my family and friends who have bought my books, suffered through impromptu plotting sessions, and always had my back, especially Mr. Crush, HoneyBee, GlitterBee, and BuzzleBee. Always.

Hungry for more?
Go back to where it all began with

All-American
COWBOY

chapter
ONE

NO THREE-HUNDRED POUND PIECE OF PRIME PORK WAS GOING to get the best of her. Charlie Walker adjusted the tilt of her cowboy hat against the glare of the Texas sun and leaned down, putting herself eye to eye with the enormous pig. "Someone's not feeling very photogenic today, huh?"

Baby Back grunted in response and made a break for the right. Charlie dove after her, trying to grab the pig's blinged-out collar. She missed by a country mile and went down, sending a cloud of dust flying as her hip hit the gravel with a crunch.

"You've got to be kidding me." Charlie scrambled to her feet with a scowl. If that's the way the hellacious hog wanted to handle things, then so be it. But she was going to play this *smart*. Her mama always said the best way to get someone to cooperate was to kill them with kindness. Forcing something close to a smile, Charlie took the giant marshmallow she'd been saving as a special treat out of her back pocket. Baby Back obviously wasn't going to earn the reward with good behavior. Might as well use it as a bribe. "*Sooey!* Here piggy, piggy."

Baby Back's ears perked.

"You want an ooey, gooey marshmallow?" Charlie tore off a tiny bit and tossed it in Baby Back's direction.

The pig snuffled it out of the dirt, squealing in appreciation.

"Come on, piggy. Want some more?" Charlie lobbed another chunk, waiting until Baby Back was snout-deep in her search before taking a tentative step forward. If she could just grab the collar... She leaned in, her fingers almost grasping the hot-pink band of leather.

Before she could so much as blink, Baby Back rushed her, snagging the marshmallow out of her hand, knocking her flat on her rear, and dashing toward the damaged stretch of fence. With a thud and a crack, the rail split. Baby Back bolted through the break in the fence and disappeared.

Again.

Add another exclamation point to the day from hell.

"Almost had her that time," Darby, Charlie's best friend since birth, called from her safe perch. "I swear, if you'd just lunged a little bit farther..." She raised a bottle of Coke in Charlie's direction and took a swig.

Charlie took her time getting to her feet. "*Almost* doesn't count—"

"Except in horseshoes and hand grenades, right?" Darby served up a wink alongside the smart-ass comment.

"Yeah. That's what Sully used to say anyway." Sully, her boss, her mentor, and the last living Holiday in Holiday, Texas. Well, the last living Holiday until he'd passed away, leaving Charlie struggling to keep everything together.

Darby's amusement faded, her eyes crinkling with concern. "How you holdin' up, sweetie?"

"Okay, I guess. I just wish I knew what was going to happen to the Rambling Rose."

Sully's lawyer had surprised everyone by keeping his

mouth shut for a change. The only tidbit of gossip anyone had been able to extract from Buddy Hill, Esquire, was that he'd been trying to contact Sully's grandson—some hoity-toity real estate tycoon from New York City—about the will. The Rambling Rose was the oldest honky-tonk in Texas and had been in the Holiday family for more than 125 years. Charlie couldn't imagine working anywhere else.

Hopefully she wouldn't have to.

"I know Buddy's trying to figure that out," Darby said. "Hard to believe this will be the first time in history we don't have a Holiday on the Rose's float for the Founder's Day parade."

A deep ache pulsed in Charlie's chest. She rubbed the spot over her heart with her palm. Sully had always loved being the grand master of the annual parade. But she couldn't think about that now—she had bigger issues. Like the fact that her maintenance man had walked out on her this morning, her bartender forgot to put in an order for the favorite local brew, and she hadn't crossed off a single item on her to-do list for the biggest concert of the year.

Or—he huffed out a sigh—the fact that a tour bus full of senior citizens had pulled up not ten minutes ago, wanting some of the Rambling Rose's famous ribs and a picture with the most celebrated pig in Conroe County.

One problem at a time.

"Damn pig. I'd better get the truck and chase her down. Last time she got out, she plowed through Mrs. Martinez's garden and ate all of her green peppers." Charlie secured the gate behind her—not that it would do much good unless she found someone to fix the fence. "I'm still getting blamed for her salsa coming in second place at the county fair."

"Remind me why y'all insist on having a pet pig as a mascot?" Darby climbed off the rail and fell into step with Charlie.

"Tradition. You know Sully. The Rambling Rose has had a pig on staff ever since it opened. They sure as heck aren't going to lose one on my watch." Not even if her watch might be coming to an abrupt end. She ducked through the back door of the honky-tonk and grabbed her keys off a hook. "You coming?"

Darby shook her head, sending her dark curls bouncing. "I'll leave the pig wrangling to you. I gotta get home and get dinner going. Waylon will skin me alive if he finds out I spent all afternoon hanging out with his baby sister."

"Now I know that's a lie." Charlie yanked open the door of the late-model dually pickup. "He's got you on such a high pedestal I'm surprised you don't get a nosebleed from the lack of oxygen."

"He does love me, doesn't he?" Darby slung her arm around Charlie's neck and pulled her in for a hug. "We'll try to stop by later, if your mama's up for watching the kids."

Darby and Waylon had been married for nine years, but it could still get weird, thinking about her BFF swapping spit with her brother. So Charlie tried not to think about it at all. As in, ever. "Has she ever not been up for watching them?"

"True. Be sure to save us some seats up front tonight, okay? That band is supposed to be real good." With a squeeze and a quick kiss on the cheek, Darby stepped away. "And don't worry about Sully's grandson. He'll probably fly down, take a look at the place, tell you what a great job you're doing, and be on a plane back to New

York City before you even have a chance to pour him a draft of Lone Star."

Charlie snorted. "Oh yeah? With my luck, he'll realize he's always wanted to manage the oldest honky-tonk in Texas, and he'll toss me out on my backside."

"He might just like your backside." Darby waggled her perfectly plucked eyebrows.

"My backside isn't up for review. Besides, if he ever does have the nerve to show up around here, he'll be the one getting tossed on his ass. Would it have killed him to pick up the phone and give Sully a call sometime? Maybe even come down for a visit?"

"Honey, I know you loved Sully like family. But not everyone loves as fierce as you. Give the guy a chance."

A chance? In the eight years she'd worked for Sully, there'd been no word from either his son or his grandson. It had broken her heart to watch the cancer eat away at him, knowing she was just about the only family he had left.

But Darby was right about one thing—Charlie did love fierce. Fierce enough to know that the most important thing to Sully was keeping the Rambling Rose in the family. So even if it killed her, she'd do whatever she could to ensure his dying wish came true. She'd try to give his grandson a chance, assuming he had the decency to show up sometime in the near future.

"Hey, will you let Angelo know I'm hog hunting? Maybe he can stall lunch so I have a chance to bring back the prodigal pig to pose for pictures."

"You bet. Good luck."

With a final nod to Darby, Charlie climbed onto the bench seat and cranked over the engine. How many times had Baby Back broken out over the past month? Two? Three? She'd lost count of how many mascots they'd had over the years, but none of them had ever been as ornery as Baby Back. That pig had a devilish streak as long and wide as the Rio Grande.

She shifted the truck into drive and wondered if anyone would believe her if she said Baby Back got taken out by a combine. Sully was the only one beyond the tourists who gave a hot damn about the pig. She gripped the steering wheel tightly, fighting back a fresh surge of emotion.

For Sully.

Then she put the pedal to the metal and fishtailed out onto the main two-lane road that would take her through the center of Holiday in pursuit of the runaway porker.

About the Author

Dylann Crush writes contemporary romance with sizzle and sass. A romantic at heart, she loves her heroines spunky and her heroes super sexy. When she's not dreaming up steamy storylines, she can be found sipping a margarita and searching for the best Tex-Mex food in Minnesota. Although she grew up in Texas, she currently lives in a suburb of Minneapolis/St. Paul with her unflappable husband, three energetic kids, two chaotic canines, and a very chill cat. She loves to connect with readers, other authors, and fans of tequila. You can find her at dylanncrush.com.

Also by Dylann Crush

HOLIDAY, TEXAS

All-American Cowboy

Cowboy Christmas Jubilee

Cowboy Charming

LAST CHANCE RODEO

Bestselling author Kari Lynn Dell marries rodeo
action with raw authenticity on her home
turf: the Blackfeet Reservation, Montana

Four years ago, one thoughtless moment cost David
Parsons everything. Now he's finally tracked his lost horse
to the Blackfeet Reservation and is ready to reclaim his
pride. But the troubled young boy who's riding Muddy
now has had more than his fair share of hard knocks, and
his fierce guardian Mary Steele will do whatever it takes to
make sure this isn't the blow that levels him. Soon David
is faced with a soul-wrenching dilemma: take his lost shot
at rodeo glory…or claim what could be his last chance to
make his shattered heart whole?

*"This talented writer knows rodeo
and sexy cowboys!"*

—B.J Daniels, *New York Times* bestselling author

For more Kari Lynn Dell, visit:
sourcebooks.com

I LOVE THIS BAR

Bestselling author Carolyn Brown invites us all to the local Honky Tonk, where the beer is cold and the cowboys are hot!

When barmaid Daisy O'Dell inherits the local Honky Tonk, she's determined to prove she has what it takes to run the bar successfully. But when Jarod McElroy walks in, looking for a moment's peace and an ice cold beer, he finds himself one red hot women behind the bar instead. The minute Jarod sees Daisy with her hot looks and smart mouth, he knows he's met his match. Now if he could only convince her to come out from behind the bar, and come on home with him...

"Funny, witty, heartfelt and sexy."
—*Book Junkie*